# "I like where you're going with this . . ."

He lifted her fingers and kissed them.

"So we're on the same page?" she asked. "One night. A good time. Then tomorrow it's back to business?"

"Definitely." His hand on her waist slipped a little lower and lust darkened his eyes. "One night only."

"Right here?" she asked.

"Right now."

She slid her hand up his sleeve and enjoyed the warm, thick muscle beneath the soft fabric. "Then shut up and kiss me, Parker."

# By Candis Terry

# CANDIS TERRY

# tangled up in tinsel

**A SUNSHINE CREEK VINEYARD NOVEL**

AVONBOOKS

*An Imprint of HarperCollinsPublishers*

HarperCollins
PUBLISHERS
Since 1817

This book is a work of fiction. References to real people, events, establishments, organizations, or locales are intended only to provide a sense of authenticity, and are used fictitiously. All other characters, and all incidents and dialogue, are drawn from the author's imagination and are not to be construed as real.

First Avon Books mass market printing: October 2017

Print Edition ISBN: 978-0-06-247186-4
Digital Edition ISBN: 978-0-06-247181-9

Cover design by Nadine Badalaty
Cover photographs: © standret / Getty Images (trees); © Ashley West / Shutterstock Offset (rafters); © Shutterstock (background)

FIRST EDITION

17 18 19 20 21   QGM   10 9 8 7 6 5 4 3 2

*For my father and the many years we've lost.*
*All is forgiven.*
Vix ea nostro voco

# Author's Note

**Dear Reader,**

If you've ever read any of my previous books you've probably gotten a sense that from the Armed Forces to animal rescue, I support a lot of causes. When the holidays roll around it always makes me think of those out there who don't always have it easy. Those who struggle. And those who are working hard to make things better. In Tangled Up in Tinsel, I wanted to honor those types by bringing in a few of my favorite causes to the story.

Life's Kitchen is mentioned in the story as the place where our hero, Parker Kincade, was able to pull his life back together. I'm happy to say that Life's Kitchen exists right here in my own community of Boise, Idaho. If you'd like to find out more about this wonderful organization dedicated to transforming the lives of young adults by building self-sufficiency and independence through food service and life skills training, please check out their website, www. lifeskitchen.org.

In this book I also mention a women's and children's shelter. I've had the privilege to be associated with the Women and Children's Alliance here in Boise for many years, and I'm always surprised at how the little things such as soap and toothpaste can make these women's and children's lives just a little easier. If you don't have a shelter in your own town, please take a look at www.wcaboise.org to find out how you can help.

Thank you so much for choosing to read Tangled Up in Tinsel. I hope it will give you all the warmth and yumminess you look for in a holiday romance.

> Wishing you the very best
> of the holiday season,
> Candis Terry

# tangled up in tinsel

tangled
up in
tinsel

# Chapter 1

"**Y**ou're going to make this happen, right?"

An early November chill hung in the air as Parker Kincade regarded his older brother Jordan—a former badass NHL hockey player who'd once slammed his opponents to the ice so hard they temporarily forgot their names—and wondered how the hell a two hundred pound, two hundred percent alpha male had turned into a such a pussy.

"I said I would, didn't I?"

"Yeah," Jordan countered. "But you also said you nailed Britney Bikini Stuffer Braxton and that was a damn lie."

"Brother? I hate to be the one to inform you that maybe you've taken too many hits to the head, but you're bringing up something that happened almost two decades ago." Parker folded his arms to match his brother's stance. "I was a kid then. Kids lie to impress their older brothers who called them a pansy ass and dared them to do something stupid."

A smirk curled Jordan's mouth. "So you're admitting you lied."

"Oh, Jesus." Parker tossed his hands up. "I don't have time for this shit. In case you can't tell by the chaos, I'm trying to open a restaurant here." The restaurant in question was currently a conglomeration of boards, screws, and construction workers using various tools of the trade yet still running weeks behind schedule. It was also Parker's one chance to help get the family business back on its feet following the deaths of their parents.

"Which brings us back to my initial question."

"Dude." Parker groaned and stuck out his hand. "Hand it over."

"Hand over what?"

"Your man card. I'm revoking it because you've officially turned into Groomzilla. And last time I looked I wasn't your freaking wedding planner."

"The wedding planner isn't standing inside a partially renovated century-old barn where Lucy and I are supposed to have our reception." Jordan narrowed his Kincade trademark blue eyes. "You promised you'd get this thing done on time."

"And I will if you'll stop coming in here every ten minutes to check on the progress. Your wedding isn't happening until the week before Christmas. The pumpkin decorations are still out from Halloween, and the turkeys and pilgrims haven't yet invaded. So just chill the fuck out."

A glare darkened Jordan's eyes and a muscle in his jaw twitched.

Parker laughed. "Sorry, bro, but you can't intimidate me with your old hockey glares."

"Yeah, but I can still kick your ass."

"You can try. But do any damage to me and your fantasy wedding reception will have to take place at the Mother Lode. And just think how disappointed your sweet fiancée will be when someone gets up onstage in that dive bar and starts singing drunk-as-shit karaoke while you're cutting the damn cake."

"Fine. But I'm keeping my eyes on you, little brother." Jordan held two fingers up to his eyes then flipped them around in Parker's direction. "Don't disappoint Lucy."

"No worries. I'm more afraid of her than I am you." Parker wondered why he got such a kick out of seeing his big brother so rattled. He also wondered how Jordan's fiancée put up with him these days when no one else could. "But if you don't get your ass out of here and keep it out, I guarantee this place won't get done on time. And then you'll be crying like a little girl."

Jordan tossed out one last badass glare then did an about-face, flipping Parker the middle finger as he—thankfully—vacated the premises.

As Jordan disappeared through the large opening in the front of the barn where the new entry was being constructed, Parker rubbed the ache in the center of his chest. The pressure was on and he was doing everything possible not to let his fears overrule his motivation. Even though the expectations were huge.

Somehow in the middle of the universe tossing a shitload of personal obstacles in his life, he'd come up with the grand idea to open a restaurant. In a barn. Where horses, cows, and sheep once ate, dwelled, and did their dirty business. Where spiders didn't bother with a single web, they built entire villages. And where his older brothers were once rumored to have fast-talked a fair maiden or two out of her Fruit of the Looms on top of the haystack. Not to mention the barn sat in the middle of their family vineyard, which resided in the small town of Sunshine Valley instead of the nearby bustling cities of Portland or Vancouver where customers might actually have had a chance to find it.

What the hell had he been thinking?

Standing smack dab in the center of four bare walls, on a plywood sub-floor, he leaned his head back and looked up at the electrical crew stringing the new wiring from atop extension ladders. It would be a damn miracle if they didn't burn the place down before the fire marshal could even do an inspection.

Sean Scott, the architect/construction project manager on the job, told him it would have been easier to construct a brand-new up-to-code building instead of trying to breathe life into something that had sat unused and unloved for at least the past twenty years. But for too many reasons to count and all of them personal, Parker insisted on retaining a Kincade legacy. Regardless of what smelly farm animal activity had once occurred beneath the rafters, he loved this place his great-grandfather had built with his own two hands.

There was a hell of a long way to go for it to become the dream he envisioned, but like the little engine that could, hopefulness surged inside him.

He could do this.

He *would* do this.

He had to.

And it wasn't just because he was sinking his entire savings into the project.

In the past he'd earned the disreputable title of *black sheep of the family.* Yes, he'd overcome the shame, but he still had something more to prove to the family he'd once wronged.

"Checking for bats?"

Parker dropped his gaze from the rafters and turned toward the source of the question. In the opening where his brother had been just minutes before stood a lusciously curvy female.

"Hello." Her red high heels tapped across the plywood floor as she came into the barn, where Parker got a better look.

Jeans, faded and painted on, hugged a shapely pair of hips and thighs. One sleeve of her thin beige sweater had slipped to reveal a bare shoulder, and long, silky brown hair draped in big loopy curls down her back. When his gaze eventually made it to her pretty face, her cherry red mouth and dark chocolate eyes were smiling.

Yeah.

She'd caught him checking her out.

As she came forward and stretched out her hand, he realized she was much shorter up close. Hell, he towered over her even with her wearing those high heels.

His hand engulfed hers as they shook.

"I'm pulling a blank." Puzzled, he tilted his head. "Have we met before?"

"Not formally. Gabriella Francesca Montani," she said in a voice that sounded like a shot of smooth whiskey. "I'm your new chef."

"My what?" He glanced around the interior of the barn looking for the camera his brothers must have planted when they'd set up this prank.

She gripped his hand tight before letting go. "Surprised?"

"Being that I'm not currently in the market to hire anyone? Yes."

"But you will be soon." Her brown eyes sparkled. "Correct?"

"Eventually. For now the walls are barely up and the restaurant won't be opening until after the holidays."

"Good." She flashed a smile that exuded confidence. "I like being the first in line."

Suspicion rattled his bones. "How did you know I was building a restaurant here? I haven't made a formal announcement yet."

"But you've talked about it to your food truck customers."

"You're a customer?"

"Yes."

"And I've discussed it with you?"

"Not directly."

"Ah. So you eavesdropped."

"Probably."

"Does that mean you're stalking me?" Not that he minded. She was beautiful and sexy as hell.

"I wouldn't say *stalking*." She chuckled and the sound rippled through his blood with images he had no business envisioning. "I just like to know everything I can about an employer before I work for them."

Though she sounded more hopeful than pushy, there was no way he could lead her on about a job. Even if, on a personal level, he wouldn't mind getting to know her a little better. It wouldn't be fair. "Well, I appreciate your interest, but I'm sorry you wasted your time, Ms. . . ."

"Montani. But please, call me Gabriella."

Everything male inside of him said he'd call her anything she wanted as long as her legs were wrapped around his waist and he was getting to know her in the most personal way possible.

"Ms. Montani." No sense doing the whole how-ya-doin' thing since she'd only be here a few minutes. Unless he could talk her into staying for a far more intimate reason. "As you can see I'm hardly in the position to hire anyone right now. I'm sorry you've come all this way for no reason but . . . well, there it is. You've come all this way for no reason."

"Believe me, Mr. Kincade, anything I do is well thought out. You're offering an amazing opportunity here and I want to be your chef. I can promise you that coming here was *not* a mistake."

The woman was tenacious, he'd give her that. Unfortunately he had nothing to offer.

"You do realize that *I'll* be the executive chef, right? I mean, this is *my* restaurant. Why would I hand over control to a perfect stranger?"

"So you have a problem handing over control?"

In work? Yes.

In bed? Never.

But he didn't tell her that.

"Depends."

"No one can do everything all alone." She smiled again and he realized she used that smile like a weapon to weaken mortal fools. "I've eaten your food. I've watched you work."

"So you *are* stalking me."

"Observing. And only enough to figure you out."

"I never knew I was so easy to read." Which was bullshit. He'd been told more than once that he was an open book. Maybe it was time he became a little more mysterious.

"Only in the way you work," she said. "Your dedication is admirable, and your attention to detail is flawless."

Good thing she didn't know how he thought or she might slap him right now. Because nothing, and he meant *nothing*, turned him on more than an assertive woman who knew what she wanted and went after it.

"Thank you."

"The way you see food is important to me," she said with enough emphasis in her tone to assure him she meant business. "I won't work for someone who just slaps something on a plate and calls it a specialty. I'm looking for someone who sees food in its truest nature. Someone who, instead of trying to change the taste by smothering or crisping it to death, knows how to enhance a flavor to awaken the senses and make it a mouthwatering experience. Like the way a perfectly ripened tomato bursts sun-warmed sweetness in your mouth."

Jesus.

If the woman waxed poetic like that about food, he couldn't imagine the way she'd sound in bed.

"Then if you aspire to work for me," he said, "I'll take that as a compliment."

"I have to admit I saw you on *Chopped* and I couldn't agree more with the judges when they applauded your creativity and artistry in making your dishes visually appealing."

The compliment felt genuine. Still . . . "Are you trying to butter me up so I'll hire you even though I don't have a job available?"

"Just being honest. I can't imagine how difficult it must be to compete on that show."

"Difficult?" He shrugged. "More of a personal challenge than anything." The Food Network show wasn't as much a cooking competition as a game show. Once he'd made that realization he adhered to the theory throughout the final rounds and miraculously came out with a win.

"Well, whatever it was you conjured up to make it happen, it worked. Congratulations."

"Again, I thank you." He smiled, hoping she wasn't just some kind of foodie groupie of the show. Better make sure she knew what she was talking about. Just in case. "So what is it you do now? What job are you so eager to leave behind?"

She caught her bottom lip between her teeth and the smallest of sighs lifted her shoulders.

Her hesitation intrigued the hell out of him.

Hell, everything about the woman intrigued him.

And that wasn't necessarily a good thing.

*G*abi heard Parker Kincade's words buzz through her ears in the same way her head hummed after she'd consumed too much wine.

Dangerous.

Intoxicating.

And oh how she'd like to strip that dirt-streaked T-shirt right off his back to see those muscles that teased her from beneath the worn cotton.

*Focus, Gabi. Focus.*

His intelligent, riveting blue eyes smiled in a face so strikingly handsome it left her stupid. Not something she ever aspired to be. But the magical combination of his eyes surrounded by thick, dark lashes, a squared, stubbled jawline, and longish nearly black, wavy hair, gave him a wild look she couldn't resist.

A distraction for sure, and bad news for her all around. Anything that detracted from her goal was a dilemma she seriously needed to consider.

"Currently I'm a personal chef," she said.

"Cushy job."

"I work for Milton Skolnick. You might have heard his name before. He won the nation's biggest lottery two years ago."

"So you're well paid too." His large hand came up to absently rub the beard stubble darkening his chin. "Now I'm really curious why you'd want to leave."

She'd seen him rub that beard stubble on the episode of *Chopped* he'd been on, and she knew it meant his brain was clicking on all cylinders. When she'd discovered that he owned a food truck in her own city of Portland, she occasionally stopped there for lunch on her days off. She'd been intrigued by the creative dishes he prepared and the obvious passion with which he created them. Almost as much as she'd been intrigued by *him*.

While he worked he shamelessly flirted with his female customers and treated the male customers like buddies. He had an easygoing way about him and all of his patrons seemed to love him. If she wanted to work for Parker Kincade, she knew she needed to be more approachable, more responsive, and above all honest. Or at least as honest as she could be without actually telling him the truth.

Because telling the truth was *not* an option.

"Sometimes being well paid isn't all it's cracked up to be," she said. "Mr. Skolnick wants the status of having a personal chef but he doesn't even know the difference between a turnip and a potato. He believes that peanut butter and potato chip sandwiches are a delicacy. And he insists that Chex Mix snacks are a better party choice than a platter of crab beignets or seared steak lettuce cups."

"So you're saying you have culinary differences with him."

"Among other things." His recent *unintentional/ swears it was an accident* groping didn't help matters either. And though she needed a job, she didn't need one bad enough to submit to that kind of bad behavior. "I'm underutilized, underappreciated, and I need more creativity from my work than throwing a frozen pizza in the oven or cooking weenie kabobs over a gas stove. Mr. Skolnick doesn't want a chef with an imagination. He wants Chef Boyardee."

A smile hovered at the corners of Parker's masculine lips. "You have no room for exploration at all?" The suggestive hint of something else darkened his eyes. Something that took her imagination on a trip altogether different than the conversation at hand.

"None."

"So you're caught between a rock and a hard place. Good pay. Few benefits."

She pulled a breath into her lungs. "You have no idea." Nor would he. While her employer and his questionable behavior paid her a decent salary, she had something to prove.

"You intrigue me, Ms. Montani." As Parker settled back on the heels of his work boots, he regarded her. "But as I said, I have no job to give you."

"All I need is a chance." She doubled her efforts and reached deep. "I'll even audition."

"Excuse me?"

"I'll audition. Cook for you. I'll prove that you need me here in your kitchen." She pulled in another breath for courage. "I'll prove that more than just needing me here, you'll *want* me here."

Curiosity brightened his eyes as he scanned her face. She could almost hear his mind click through all the possibilities.

She hoped. Prayed. Quietly begged that he'd at least give her a chance.

"When?" he finally asked and she had to control the breath that threatened to rush from her lungs.

"Friday night?"

"If I say no will you keep coming back and stalking me?"

She smiled. "You can count on it."

"Okay then." A slow nod brushed his thick, dark hair against the neck of his T-shirt. "You're on. But I expect you to bring it. Don't waste my time."

"I would never do that."

"Uh-huh."

Relief sped like buzzing bees through her stomach while he grabbed a construction pencil from a nearby sawhorse. He searched for something to write on. Finally, tearing a piece from a crumpled bag, he scribbled something and handed it to her.

An address.

On a pier.

"A houseboat?" she asked.

"That's where I live."

"You want me to come to your house?"

His broad shoulders lifted. "Where else would you suggest? Like I said, the kitchen here isn't done, the food truck isn't an option, and I don't live at the vineyard. If you want to *audition*"—he made air quotes—"you'll go where you need to go. Right?"

"Of course."

"Unless you've just been pulling my leg all this time."

Her gaze unintentionally shot to the crotch of his perfect fitting jeans. "No. I'm legit, and I want this."

"Then I'll see you Friday night." He tossed her a benign smile. "Eight o'clock. At that address. Just press the button on the gate in the parking lot and I'll let you in."

"I'll be there," she said. Because she did want this.

The bigger problem?

She might want *him* too.

And that definitely wasn't a good thing.

# Chapter 2

Parker's curiosity about Gabriella Montani skyrocketed as he took a break from the construction chaos and walked past the harvested grapevines and up the hill to the vineyard office. The gravel road was still dotted with pumpkins and hay bales left over from a wedding in the event center the previous weekend. Soon the giant scarecrow welcoming all to the vineyard would be replaced by a giant turkey. Or maybe *he* was the turkey, because apparently his reasoning lately seemed overcooked.

Exactly why he'd agreed to let Gabriella audition for a place in his kitchen when he didn't even have a kitchen yet was a wild guess. Although when it came right down to it, his reasons probably had more to do with the way those jeans hugged her luscious curves than anything she could accomplish with a frying pan or colander. Aside from trying to get the restaurant constructed, the recent deaths of his parents, the vineyard being in financial trouble, his new half sister, his angry other sister, and his brother's upcoming wedding, Parker barely had time for a sane thought that wasn't family related.

Not that he didn't love them all, and not that he wasn't determined to do right by each and every one of them, but all the turmoil barely left time for anything more than a quick moment of self-satisfaction. Aka a warm willing woman who wanted nothing more than a nice dinner and a couple hours of commitment-free pleasure.

Shrugging the emotional burden off his shoulders, he looked forward to a lull in the day and a cup of his brother Ryan's coffee. When he opened the vineyard office door, all four of his brothers were arguing loudly about the previous night's game between the Pittsburgh Steelers and the Philadelphia Eagles.

Nothing unusual.

The Kincade boys argued about everything. When it came to sports they poured on the passion and it became a shouting match until someone either grew bored or left the room. No one ever cried uncle. Though Parker had been looking for a quiet break, he didn't mind the chaos. At least, for a change, they weren't discussing the vineyard finances, their parents' deaths, or their father's infidelity.

"Why aren't you working on the restaurant?" Jordan asked him, picking up the tired conversation they'd had only a few short hours ago. "Don't you know I have a wedding coming up?"

"You do?" Parker audibly gasped. "Shit. Why didn't you guys tell me Mr. Pansy Ass was getting hitched?"

Ryan, Declan, and Ethan laughed.

"Fuck you." These days Jordy's snarl possessed a lot less punch than when he'd been earning his living on the ice.

Parker was mildly tempted to cut him some slack. But where was the fun in that?

"How about you send Lucy over to do the reception planning," Parker said. "She seems a lot more laidback about the whole thing."

"Newsflash," Ryan, the oldest, said. "Lucy's handed over all the wedding planning to our dear brother."

"All of it?" Declan asked as though someone had just performed the world's greatest magic trick.

"All the way down to the flowers and figuring out how her dog is going to carry the rings to the altar." Jordan leaned forward in his chair and dropped his head into his hands. "I am so screwed."

"Is she crazy?" Ethan, the youngest brother, asked.

"She says *he's* the crazy one," Ryan said.

"More like a control freak," Declan said.

"Is he picking out the bridesmaids' dresses too?" Ethan wanted to know. "Because I have got to see that."

"You guys do realize I'm sitting right here," Jordan said.

"Even better." Parker grinned. "Then we don't have to talk behind your back or wonder what pretty outfit you're going to wear down the aisle."

"I hate you guys." Jordan looked undoubtedly flustered.

"No, you don't. You gave up hockey just to be with us," Ryan reminded him.

"I gave up hockey to be with Lucy."

"Awww." Ethan jumped into the bullshit. "That's so sweet. Now you're going to make me cry."

Jordan flipped them his middle finger. "The truth is Lucy's really busy with school. She has some difficult students this year."

"More difficult than our sister was last year?" Declan asked.

"Apparently. And since I quit hockey and haven't really figured out what to do with the eight hours a day she's gone, I told her I'd help with the wedding if she needed me to."

"Kidding aside," Parker said, "that's a really nice gesture."

"Yeah. Except I didn't know what I was walking into. I was thinking things like planning the bachelor party or moving heavy furniture. But she handed me a list five pages long and a butt load of bridal magazines. Then she kissed me and went to work. I couldn't say no. Her first wedding and marriage were a disaster. I want ours to be special."

"You've got more money than you'll ever spend. Why don't you just hire a wedding planner?" Dec, the financial wizard brother, asked. "Brooke was more than happy to hire one to plan our wedding."

"Yeah, but *your* fiancée is not only busy constructing a family fun center here while she's still commuting back and forth to Southern California, *her* fiancé is busy with his own business too," Jordan pointed out. "Lucy knows I've got nothing but time on my hands."

"Why don't you ask Lili to help?" Ethan suggested.

Not only had they recently discovered they had a new half sister, they'd also discovered she was a twenty-three-year-old woman and an event planner—a position the vineyard was in dire need of. Despite their failed efforts to be hospitable when she'd come to Sunshine Valley a few months ago to meet their father—only to discover he'd died—she'd graciously decided to give them all another chance and accepted the job.

Parker hoped the opportunity for all of them to get to know each other worked out, even as at least one of them—namely their teenage sister, Nicole—was still on the fence. No one could really blame her for her hesitancy. She'd been the one to suffer the most as a result of their father's indiscretion and emotional abandonment.

Everything in their family seemed to be balanced on a bed of lies and secrets on which only their aunt Pippy could shed some light. And so far getting the truth from her had been like trying to wrangle cats.

"I'm not sure adding another opinion to the mix is a good idea at this point," Jordan said of hiring Lili.

Dec, ever the straightforward businessman, pointed at Jordan. "So what I hear you saying is that you *like* being the wedding planner."

"I *like* making Lucy happy," Jordan retorted. "If

that means picking out flowers and decorations, then so be it."

"Damn." Parker shook his head. "I never thought I'd see the day my brothers were more worried about wedding details than winning an argument about a football game."

"Oh yeah?" Jordan jerked his chin at Parker. "You just wait until you find the right one. We'll see who's laughing then."

Parker had no plans, desire, or time to join the engaged brothers' society.

In fact, the only female oriented thing on his mind right now was wondering what the delectable Ms. Gabriella Montani planned to bring to the table on Friday night.

*B*efore Gabriella left Sunshine Creek Vineyard, she drove through the property to get a better idea of what a man like Parker Kincade might be made of. Or what he might appreciate. Dressed in his dirt-streaked T-shirt, jeans, and work boots, one would assume he'd prefer natural flavors or maybe comfort foods. Then again, sans the gold hoop earring and pirate sash, the untamed look he had going on suggested his tastes might lean more toward the exotic.

The menu for his food truck wasn't much help in deciphering either. It varied from a complex and scrumptious seafood paella to a more humble and unassuming meatball panini and all points in between.

Each delicious dish was always prepared with love and care, and was guaranteed to keep his customers coming back for more.

The mouthwatering selections he created, however, made her wonder if the very handsome Mr. Kincade's tastes in other things might be just as eclectic.

Before she let her mind wander too far in that direction, the real question she should have asked when she'd had his full attention was what type of cuisine he planned to feature at his new brick-and-mortar restaurant. Normally she'd have been on her toes, prepared for whatever obstacle was thrown in her way. Unfortunately, she'd been completely unprepared to go one-on-one with a man who simply made everything in her feminine DNA drool.

When Parker Kincade had flashed his wicked grin and his blue eyes had sparked with interest, her racing heart and hormones had gotten in the way of normal thinking. Now that she had a little space between them, her mind kicked back into gear. She needed to stay grounded. Focused. She needed to ignore the extreme hotness he brought to the game and come up with a culinary plan of attack.

In need of a little advice, she called on the one person she trusted most. The person who'd taught her everything she knew about creating meals that would appeal to anyone who had taste buds. A requirement that excluded her current employer.

When the call to Northern Italy connected on her cell phone, her heart leapt with happiness.

"Nonni!"

"*Ciao, cara!*"

Just hearing her grandmother's voice could calm any storm. When Gabi's entire world had crumbled, her grandmother had held her close and reassured her that though there may be some bumps along the way, everything would work out fine. Even though Gabi was still waiting for the end result of that journey, she was ever grateful for her paternal grandmother's love and support. Sadly, it was all she really had.

Pleasantries were exchanged, then, "I found an amazing opportunity, Nonni. But I need to know what you think."

"What's this *opportunity*?"

Gabi heard the skepticism in her grandmother's tone and wanted to offer reassurance. Even if she wasn't so sure herself. "I'm going to audition for a chef's position at a new restaurant opening as part of a family-owned vineyard. The executive chef there is the man I told you about. The one who owns the food truck near my apartment."

"The chef who won the episode of *Chopped* we watched together?"

"Yes. Parker Kincade." Gabi told her grandmother about their meeting. Of course she omitted the minor detail that she was attracted to him in a major way.

"What does this mean, you're going to *audition*?" her grandmother asked.

"There's no way I'll get a referral from my current employer, and I don't have any references except yours, so I'm going to cook for Mr. Kincade to show him my capabilities. Basically I have to prove myself and then keep my fingers crossed that he'll love what I do so much he won't ask for my credentials."

She left out the part that the audition would be at Parker's home. Her *nonni* only needed to know so much.

"But you said Mr. Kincade told you he has no job opening now."

"But he will, Nonni. Soon. And I want to be first in line. I have to get out of the dead-end job I have now. This is a wonderful opportunity for me."

"Is it really an opportunity for *you*? Or is it to prove to your father that you can build a career all on your own without any help from him?"

Gabi sighed. Her *nonni* knew her too well. She wanted this job. Needed it. More than to prove something to her father. She needed this opportunity to prove to herself that she had what it took to be a success. She needed to make a name for herself.

And she would stop at nothing to make that happen.

"I need it for me, Nonni. If I have to make peanut butter and jelly on Ritz Crackers much longer I'm going to go crazy. I need to be able to create. To use all those wonderful skills you've taught me over the years."

"I never wanted you to use them to compete with your father. Please don't put yourself in that position."

*She* hadn't put herself in that position. Her father had.

"Nonni, I promise you, I only want a chance to use my imagination and my skills. Besides, nothing I could ever do would matter to him," Gabi admitted.

"He's stubborn, *la mia bambina*. But he loves you."

Gabi doubted that. Her father had willingly walked away. No matter how hard she'd worked or what achievements she'd made, it had never been enough to earn his love. No amount of tears or, God help her, begging had ever been enough to even crack the unbreakable shell he'd constructed around his ice cold heart.

They'd not spoken in years. But to this day Gabriella could recall in vivid detail how he'd squashed her self-confidence and walked away without a backward glance, shattering every hope she'd had in her foolish heart.

She'd been only seventeen years old.

Because she knew her grandmother meant well, Gabi sidestepped the comment about her father's love. "This audition means the world to me, Nonni. You know I'll never find this opportunity at an established restaurant. What do you think I should cook?"

"Hmmm." Silence lingered as her grandmother gave the question some thought. "This Parker Kincade is very good looking, *sì*?"

"Exceptionally." No sense lying.

"Then you make something that also speaks to his heart and not just his stomach. Maybe a fresh pappardelle with a cream sauce. Or that delicious carbonara you made the last time you were here. Of course, you can't go wrong with a nice pomodoro. And for dessert, well, you know which one is my favorite. I'm sure it will become his too."

Ideas swirled inside Gabi's head. "You're a genius, Nonni! I love you so much."

"*Ti amo troppo.* Call me after and let me know how it went." Her grandmother chuckled. "Even though I know you'll do very well and you'll make me proud."

Her grandmother's encouragement warmed her from the inside out and gave her the confidence she needed to succeed. Gabi ended the call feeling even more enthusiastic than she had earlier. Now all she had to do was maintain her professionalism, keep her mind on the meal, and not fall all over the gorgeous man like some kind of Chef Parker groupie.

*B*usy filling lunch orders the following day, Parker glanced over the shoulder of his window attendant at the crowd gathered outside his food truck while his assistant chef continued to process their orders. Desperate for a mental break from the rush, he scanned the nearby trees where the fall colors were in full bloom.

At the back of the crowd, with an angel wings ball cap pulled low over her eyes, Gabriella Montani was trying hard not to be noticed.

Like she thought he wouldn't recognize her?

More like, how could he forget her?

She'd made a fast and appealing impression on

him. One he hadn't seen coming, and one he wasn't even sure how to handle.

He loved women, especially those who exuded confidence. He just wasn't always sure what to do with them. There were times when all he could do was stand in awe of their willingness to do whatever the hell needed to be done to make things work. The women he knew, most often, gave without asking for anything in return. And much like his future sisters-in-law, Gabriella Montani appeared to be far from a sit-back-and-let-it-happen type of woman.

Though a damp autumn chill hung in the air, she wore lightweight exercise clothes. Bright pink running shoes instead of drop-dead-red high heels. A body hugging racer-back tank top instead of the next-to-nothing sweater. And black athletic leggings instead of painted-on jeans.

Yeah.

He'd have to be dead not to notice her.

And last time he'd checked, his equipment was in perfect working condition.

Regretfully, he had to pull his attention away from the luscious Ms. Montani to deliver an order. He swept up a newly plated dish, leaned across the stainless steel counter, and winked at the elderly woman in sparkly sneakers at the front of the line. "I hope this pleases your palate, sweetheart."

Surrounded by her cronies—a self-proclaimed group of mall walkers without an actual mall—the woman stuck her fork in the center of the pancetta and saffron rice. She took a bite, hummed her pleasure, then gave him a big thumbs-up to let him know he'd scored gold.

Before he returned to the next item up on the order wheel, Parker slid his gaze back in Gabriella's direction. As if he'd called her name, she looked up. He crooked his finger. She glanced around as if he might be motioning to someone else. When she looked back at him, he crooked his finger again. She pointed at herself.

*Yes, you*, he mouthed. Chin tucked like she'd been caught with her hand in the cookie jar, she eased her way through the crowd toward the truck.

"Stalking me again, Ms. Montani?" He folded his arms across his apron.

"No!" Her dark eyes widened. "I was just . . . waiting. You know, for the lunch crowd to thin out before I placed my order."

"Really." The hesitation in her explanation gave away more than she'd probably hoped. For him, the revelation was enough to keep her there just a little longer. If only to break up the monotony of his busy day.

At least that's what he told himself.

"Really." She nodded.

When she criss-crossed two fingers across the front of that skintight tank top his gaze couldn't help but follow. And linger.

"I swear," she promised. "I wasn't stalking. No need to call in law enforcement."

"Furthest thing from my mind." And only because he wasn't into the whole handcuffs scene. In bed or out. "So what did you plan to order? I can get that up for you." Among other things.

"Oh no." She glanced at the others in line who were now giving her the death glare. "I'm not going to cut in and unleash an angry mob."

"Not sure that's possible. But just in case, come around to the door." He turned to his team, who were working away on orders. "Can you guys handle this for a couple of minutes?"

"Got it covered, boss."

"Thanks." He opened the door and stepped down to where Gabriella waited a few feet away, arms crossed, attempting to look like she couldn't be less interested or impressed.

A chuckle rumbled in his chest.

"So what would you like to order?" he asked.

The bling on her ball cap sparkled in the sunlight as their eyes met and the truth was revealed. She hadn't planned on ordering a damned thing.

"Ummm."

"Did you even look at today's menu?" he asked.

"Of course." A tiny furrow sprung up between her eyes as she nodded, then changed the nod to a slow shake. "Actually? No."

"So . . . stalking again?" Keeping a smile from his face became impossible, because whatever she was doing was kind of cute. And he was sure it was harmless.

Hopefully.

"*Not* stalking," she insisted. "Preparing. For my audition."

"By . . . ?"

"By studying your customers. Seeing what they order and their reactions to the taste. I'm trying to decide what to make for you and I'm having a hard time choosing between three of my specialties."

"I'd suggest making all three, but that would probably be a lot of work."

"I don't mind hard work, Mr. Kincade." Her lips pressed together. "I prefer to work hard. It's the way to success."

"Success isn't everything." It was a lot. But not everything. At least not in his book. "Some things are far more important."

Her dark eyes flashed and her chin lifted as though she didn't like having such things pointed out to her. And that made him curious as hell. "Such as?"

"Family. Honor. Loyalty. Commitment."

"But those aren't things you have to work for."

"Aren't they?" He'd had to work his ass off to earn every single item on that list.

"Maybe." Perplexed, she sighed. "Can we get back to talking about food? I can carry on a better conversation with that topic."

"So you're saying you're not good with family, honor, loyalty, and commitment. Yet you expect me to hire you as my chef?"

Obviously frustrated, she pressed her lips together again and shifted her weight to one curvy hip. "You're twisting my words."

He was actually just having a little fun, but apparently he'd hit on a touchy subject.

"Consider it part of the interview," he said. "And I apologize. I always mean what I say, but I don't always say what I mean. In tough working conditions sometimes my crew needs to bail me out."

"I'll try to keep that in mind." She glanced inside the truck where his team was working their little hearts out. "So you'll still let me audition even though I didn't really plan to order anything today?"

Let her?

Hell. At the moment, it was the only thing he was looking forward to.

"How about we start the audition right now. If you pass the first round then . . ." He shrugged. "Sure. We can go ahead with round two on Friday night."

She glanced down at her exercise clothes then back up at him. "I didn't come prepared to cook."

"Not everything about cooking is cooking."

"You're confusing me again."

"Sorry." He reached out and lightly touched her arm, simply because he had to. All that soft-looking skin had been calling out to him from the moment he'd seen her in the crowd. "Close your eyes."

"Excuse me?"

"Round one, Ms. Montani."

"Oh. Right." She squeezed her eyes shut.

With her lip snagged between her teeth, she looked so damned sweet it was all he could do not to wrap his arms around her. "Tell me what you smell."

"Ah. A sensory exercise." She smiled then tilted her head back and inhaled deeply.

With her eyes closed Parker let his gaze roam her face. She was incredibly beautiful. And, he thought, equally as complicated.

"Sumac," she whispered as though she'd discovered a secret. "Allspice, ginger, and"—she inhaled again—"saffron."

"Very good, Ms. Montani. I expected you to name the obvious."

Her eyes popped open and there were sparks of challenge within the dark brown depths.

"Naming the meats or certain vegetables would be too easy. And as you said, this is an audition." She smiled as though she'd already won. "Would you like me to continue?"

"One second." Another crazy idea sprang into his head as he reached inside the truck and pulled out the list of ingredient supplies they had on hand. He gave her the list and her eyes immediately scanned the contents.

"Choose five ingredients from that list," he said. "Then tell me what you'd make with them."

"Off the top of my head?"

"In this case, off the top of your angel wings." He gave a nod to her ball cap.

"Clever." One sleek brow arched as if to say, *game on*.

While she scanned the list, Parker became anxious to hear what she'd come up with. Much like when he'd been on *Chopped* and they'd handed him a basket of unknown ingredients, he'd had to think on his feet.

Not only to actually make something, but to make something that would please the judges. In this case, her creativity needed to appeal to him. Although he could admit right now she didn't need to do much to accomplish the deed.

"Keeping in mind that this is an audition . . ." She tapped a finger against the soft cushion of her bottom lip. "I'd never go for the mundane."

"Of course not."

"Or . . ." She gave him a sideways glance with those mesmerizing chocolate brown eyes. "Not knowing your heat tolerance—choose something too spicy."

At that moment his heat factor was topping the meter.

"And because I'd want to create something memorable, I'd have to make . . ."

Anticipation curled in his belly like a live wire. The moment she snagged her bottom lip between her teeth again, he wanted to forget the whole damn cooking audition, send everyone away, and haul her inside his truck where he could give her a piece of something memorable.

"A brioche French toast with a brown sugar and cranberry sauce."

"Breakfast?" His head went back.

"Dessert."

"Interesting. I expected you to opt for an entrée of some type."

"And there you go." A suggestive grin lit up her face, making her even more beautiful. If that was

possible. "You *expected* me to make an entré[...]
the exercise was aimed at getting an insight to [...]
creativity. Yes?"

Among other things. "Yes."

"Well then, don't you agree that an unexpected dessert can be more extraordinary, more memorable than an entrée? And a woman—especially if she's a chef—wants to be deliciously remembered at the end of the night."

While Parker stood there momentarily stunned and so turned on he needed to readjust himself, she flashed him a smile and a wink as she handed him back the list.

"I'll see you Friday night, Mr. Kincade."

# Chapter 3

"Distracted?"

Parker stopped daydreaming long enough to turn and find Lili, his new half sister, behind him inside the barn. "Hey, you made it."

A slight tilt of her head sent her pale blonde hair cascading over her shoulder. "Did you think I'd back out?"

"Given the circumstances, there was a good chance," he replied honestly.

In order to get Lili to agree to move from Philadelphia to Sunshine so they could begin the task of becoming a united family, he and his siblings had needed to sit down and have a little heart-to-heart. Getting everyone on board hadn't been an easy task. Eventually the majority of them agreed that Lili had all the credentials they needed as their event planner. Their only holdout had been Nicole, who'd eventually caved enough on the matter to give them an I-don't-give-a-shit-what-you-do shrug. Instead of putting the blame where it belonged, Nicki held Lili responsible for all her problems. And that was an issue that needed to be handled. Even if their father wasn't around anymore to defend himself, the facts were there; proven by a DNA test that Lili was indeed their father's illegitimate daughter.

In general Nicki had a good heart and a somewhat level head for an eighteen-year-old. Parker hoped eventually she'd come around.

"Can I be honest with you?" Lili pressed her lips together and looked like the slightest sound would send her running.

Wishing they knew each other well enough for him to offer a hug to put her at ease, he gave her a smile. "I hope you always will."

"For the second time in my life I'm so scared to death I can barely breathe," she admitted.

"About making the move?"

She shook her head. "About getting to know all of you. Especially Nicole."

"We're not as bad as we seem."

"I don't think you're bad. Just intimidating. After all, I'm the outsider. The 'bastard,' so to speak."

"That's not how we see you."

"Maybe not all. And maybe not anymore."

"You're right. Not anymore."

Her blue eyes widened slightly in an I-knew-it kind of way.

"Those days are behind us now, Lili. And pretty soon, we hope you'll feel like we're your family."

"I hope so too." She took a shaky breath. "Because I have given up everything—including my pride—to come here."

"I know you did." He reached out then, grasped her hand, and gave it a squeeze because he thought she needed the reassurance. Hell, *he* needed the reassurance.

"It wasn't an easy decision."

"I don't imagine it was."

"When I left here before I thought I never wanted to see any of you again."

She tried to slip her hand from his but he held on. His past had taught him many things; one of them had been that you can't always conquer things alone.

"I apologize for that. Everyone around here has pretty much been on an emotional roller coaster since our parents died. Getting hit with a multitude of other issues didn't help. But that's no excuse." He gave her a wry smile. "We were assholes."

"Yeah you were." Even though the anguish in her expressive eyes was clear, she chuckled to take away the sting of her words.

"I promise we'll do better in the future."

"No pressure to become the perfect, most amazing big brother on earth though." She withdrew her hand from his and gave him a poke in the chest. "However, I can be bribed should you want to become my favorite."

"With that sense of humor you're going to fit right in."

"Who says I was kidding?" A smile caught the corners of her lips, and besides her blue eyes, Parker definitely recognized the family genes.

He laughed. "Just so you know, I *am* the most amazing big brother on earth. Two out of three younger siblings agree. I just have to get you on board."

She let go an exaggerated sigh. "Time will tell."

"True that. So what do you think?" He waved his hand at the interior of the building. "Is it starting to come together?"

She made a slow circle and gave the surroundings her complete focus before she responded. "I think it's going to be wonderful. And what a great idea to use this old barn. It has so much character. Although . . ."

"Uh-oh."

"As an event planner, can I make a suggestion?" She scrunched her nose.

"If it doesn't require tearing down walls and starting from scratch, sure."

"Keep an open mind."

"I'll do my best." Lately with everything going on, his mind felt like umpteen thousand thoughts had been stuffed inside. Maybe it was time to open the door and let a few of them out.

"Not everyone will have a large enough party or reception to fill the event center," Lili said. "You could always replicate the barn doors on the back wall and have them open up onto a patio that would face the creek. From there you'd also have a peaceful view of the vineyard. It would be great for photo ops and would also enhance the atmosphere. You know, like when the barn doors open up at the end of that movie *White Christmas*? Plus, a lot of people just really like to dine outdoors when the weather's nice. And extra seating brings in extra dollars."

"And having another exit would probably make the fire marshal happy."

She nodded. "Definitely someone you want to keep on your side."

"It's a great suggestion, Lili. I'll talk to the project manager and see if we can make it happen."

"Make what happen?" a brother's voice asked from just inside the doorway.

Lili's shoulders stiffened when she realized Jordan had joined them. Parker sensed a huge spike in her anxiety. The last time Lili had been at the vineyard Jordan had still been running on alpha male hockey mode and hadn't been the friendliest. This was the first time they'd seen each other since Lili had come back to Sunshine.

"Lili. You remember our brother Jordan. Formerly known as Mr. Intimidation. Now not-so-fondly known as Groomzilla."

"Fu—" Jordan bit back the curse that would have been aimed at Parker. Then he plastered a smile on his face and tried to present himself as Mr. Pleasant. "Glad you decided to give us another chance, Lili."

"I think we all have to give each other a chance," she said. "We deserve that at least, don't you think?"

"I couldn't agree more."

Parker's heart warmed even as his gut twisted. Between the tragedy and the lies, the surprises and the devastation, they'd all been through enough. Now was the time to heal.

If only it was that easy.

"So what do you think of this place?" Jordan asked Lili. "Think our brother will have everything ready in time for my wedding reception?"

"*You're* getting married?" Lili asked in the same manner one might ask a husky bulldog if it had been neutered.

Parker laughed his ass off and received the flash of his brother's middle finger for his efforts.

"Yeah. Me. Go figure." Jordan grinned to put her at ease. "Want to help? These jerks we call our brothers said I should look into getting a wedding planner because my fiancée is too busy to handle everything by herself."

"A bride who's too busy to plan her own wedding? That's new."

"Long story. Not the first go-round for her. The first one was—" The bitter face Jordan made pretty much explained it all.

"Ugly?"

Jordan nodded. "I want this one to erase the other one from her memory."

"Awww." Lili patted Jordan's arm. "That was so sweet it almost made me forget you're intimidating as heck."

"Don't let him fool you," Parker said. "Groomzilla. I'm telling you."

A smile popped up on Lili's face. "If you'd like I could come up with a few ideas to help you out."

"That would be awesome." Jordan looked relieved. "How about I take you to breakfast tomorrow at Sugarbuns. We can talk about it over coffee and cinnamon rolls."

"Sounds good."

Though Parker was glad to see Jordan making an effort with Lili, he couldn't help baiting him. "Was there something else you needed, bigger and uglier brother?"

"Yeah." Jordan suddenly looked uncomfortable. "I came to tell you Aunt Pippy's back from Seattle. And you know what that means."

They both looked at Lili, who seemed to wither at the name of the only person who knew the whole story behind their father's affair with Lili's mother and the money he'd stolen from the family business.

Parker's stomach tightened. "Time for the truth."

Other than reruns of *Gilmore Girls* or her current guilty pleasure, *Game of Thrones*—because who didn't love Jon Snow—Gabriella didn't watch television often. It was even more unusual for her to watch TV in the middle of the day. Unless she was forced. Game shows and reality TV just weren't her thing. She didn't much care what was up with the

Kardashians, and spinning the Wheel of Fortune seemed about as likely as winning the lottery. Unless you happened to be Milton Skolnick.

At the moment, her current employer was home with some kind of nose sniffing, lung hacking ailment he'd contracted while playing *Plants vs. Zombies: Garden Warfare* on his Xbox. Once again he was deposited on the sofa, which had begun to show wear and tear where he sat an exceedingly large amount of the time. Now, however, he was wrapped up in a fuzzy blanket with a cowbell he clanged when he expected Gabriella to cater to his sweet tooth with another chocolate Snack Pack pudding.

In the past six hours, her job description had also encompassed nursemaid and psychotherapist. Because *God only knew why someone as wonderful as him would contract such a disease.* His words, not hers. So far she'd failed to make him understand that the common cold did not fall into the category of a life-threatening disease.

Even worse than putting up with all the sniffling, complaining, and garbage snacking, Mr. Skolnick was currently tuned in to the Food Network with the volume full blast because, of course, he couldn't hear through his stuffy ears.

Not that Gabi didn't love to watch an episode of *Chopped*, *Beat Bobby Flay*, or even a rousing battle of *Cupcake Wars*. She did. Unfortunately, the network also broadcast a particular show that gave her an acute case of heartburn—*Easy Italian with Giovanni*.

Starring none other than her very own father.

If anyone had paid attention to the tabloids years ago they'd know there was nothing easy about Chef Giovanni Altobelli. Or maybe they could ask her mother, the woman who'd been publicly humiliated by his scandalous affair with a woman barely old enough to buy alcohol.

While Gabriella slapped crunchy peanut butter on a cracker for her employer, her father's smug face instructed his viewers how to make a simple *porchetta*. The eighty-five-inch flat screen showed every pore and wrinkle on the man's face, but it didn't reveal the heartlessness hiding behind his eyes.

"Make sure you put enough grape jelly on those crackers, Gabi. You know how I hate it when the peanut butter gets stuck in my throat," Mr. Skolnick instructed.

Oh, how she'd love something to stick in his throat.

"If you're looking for comfort food, I could make you some homemade mac and cheese," Gabriella said, sickly sweet, as her father looked directly into the camera and smiled. "Maybe I could even add a little Dungeness crab for some extra flavor."

"Comfort food sounds great," her employer called back.

Finally!

Before he could change his mind, Gabi pushed aside the saltines and reached into the cupboard for a mixing bowl.

"Maybe there's still some leftover pizza in the fridge. That's the best comfort food on the planet.

And when you get done with that, why don't you come on over here and plant that nice ass beside me." He patted the sofa cushion.

Gabi's formerly dancing heart crashed and burned through the grape jelly dripping off the butter knife she'd set on the counter. Her stomach tightened with a reality check. As long as she was in Mr. Skolnick's employ she'd never have an ounce of respect. She didn't even know why she bothered to show up every day with the hopes that he'd at least allow her to make a freaking meatloaf. But now this?

He'd gone too damn far.

While she gripped the counter with both hands and tried to reclaim a small speck of dignity, from the TV her father rolled a seasoned loin of pork around a variety of stuffing ingredients. A moment later he looked up into the camera and declared, "If you're going to spend any time in a kitchen, you might as well make the best meal your imagination can create. Otherwise, why bother?"

Common sense told her the man could not see through the TV. Still, it was like he was speaking directly to her. And somehow the words he actually spoke transformed into *"You'll never be good enough, Gabriella. You'll never be as good as your brother. You'll never come close to being as good as me. You'll never live up to my name. You just don't have what it takes. Find something else to do."*

Gabi had no desire to be a superstar chef like him. She just had the desire to prove her father wrong. But that would never happen as long as she was slapping peanut butter on saltines for someone who couldn't care less about good food, style, or taste. Someone who'd gone from annoyingly creepy to outright sleazy.

She looked back up to the television where her father's smirk seemed to be aimed directly at her.

With only a passing thought to her shrinking bank account, she threw her shoulders back and grabbed the plate of peanut butter and jelly drenched crackers off the counter. She carried them into the den where Milton Skolnick sat amid countless and needless items bought with his lottery winnings. She ignored the smirking chef on the television who had zero belief she could achieve her dream, and she turned her attention to the overweight leech sprawled out on the sofa in a stained T-shirt and frayed sweatpants.

"Mr. Skolnick, I quit." She shoved the plate at him.

He narrowed his eyes as he snapped up a cracker and stuffed it into his mouth. "You can't quit."

"I just did. You don't need a personal chef, you need a caretaker. And possibly some psychiatric help. Just be glad I'm not reporting you for sexual harassment." Without losing her cool, without panicking over how she'd pay her bills, she grabbed her purse and stormed out.

She had a chance to prove herself.

To turn her passion and her dream into a reality.

Only one man could provide her the opportunity to make that happen.

Now all she had to do was not mess it up.

# Chapter 4

**E**xhaustion wrapped around every muscle in Parker's body as he leaned his head forward and let the spray from the shower pound the back of his neck. When the tension began to ease he turned, grabbed the glass of whiskey from the built-in tile shelf, and downed a good amount. The smooth essence of caramel and vanilla rolled across his tongue and he swallowed with a weary sigh.

Before he'd headed home the night before, he'd gone up to the main house to check on his baby sister and they'd ended up in a complicated conversation about the options for her future. As a big brother who loved her and wanted her to make the right decisions instead of those based on emotion, he'd taken the time to listen and advise the best he could.

On his way home, he'd driven past the restaurant just to make sure everything was locked down for the night. But when his SUV had rolled by, he noticed a light coming through the new windows. He'd been positive he'd turned everything off after the construction crew had left for the day. Still, he figured he'd better stop and check it out. Inside the barn he found Jordan on his knees, installing the hardwood flooring.

Surprised, Parker had stood back and watched his brother in action. At first glance, it seemed Jordan had decided to help move production along by lending a hand. Parker would have been touched by the generosity, but he knew better. Only one reason would keep his big brother from cozying up in bed next to the woman he would marry the following month. And it wasn't to take the pressure off Parker. Groomzilla had shown up and tried to take control of a situation where he had no business taking control.

In the end, Parker hadn't been able to convince Jordan to go home to his lovely fiancée, so he'd grabbed his own tool belt. Together they'd worked side by side until the wee hours of the morning, which left him little time to get back to Portland and get his food truck up and running for the day. Once he'd made it to his houseboat he'd taken a quick shower and run out the door.

Business had been brisk all day. Even better than usual. Parker didn't know if there was some kind of event going on downtown that brought in the new customers or whether word had spread about his food. Whatever the reason, he was grateful. The extra income would be nice. The holidays were approaching fast and the added business would provide him the ability to give out some decent Christmas bonuses for his team.

As he swallowed another shot of whiskey, he closed his eyes and wished he could grab a nap before Gabriella showed up for her cooking audition. He'd planned to be more prepared, to give her a real opportunity to show him what she could do. For whatever reason it seemed very important to her.

And Parker believed in chances.

During his troubled years, he'd been granted many. Not only by his parents, but also by his brothers. At the time he'd been pretty fucking unbrotherly. He hadn't known they'd all been battling their own demons. He'd just thought they didn't give a shit about him. So he'd returned the unfortunate favor. Lucky for him they'd proven him wrong and given him another chance. Even so, he knew there was so much he still needed to make up for.

When the parking lot security gate buzzed on the intercom near his front door, his hopes for a nap or even finishing his shower disintegrated.

She was early.

A good sign for a potential employee, not such a good sign when the potential boss was dead on his feet.

Not to mention naked.

Allowing himself to get sucked into this when he didn't have the time or even a position available didn't make sense. But when the gate buzzer blasted through his house again, anticipation skipped through his veins and he had to call bullshit on himself.

He knew *exactly* why he'd gotten sucked in.

Gabriella Montani.

The woman was sexy and mysterious.

Not that he had trouble finding female company. Lately he just didn't have the opportunity. Before now, he'd been able to dedicate more of his evening hours toward wining and dining a pretty woman. Even without the added stress of opening the restaurant, he had a busy schedule. Which meant he preferred women who had their own careers, lives, and activities. He shied away from women with visions of a wedding ring or even sharing a bed for more than a night. Getting tied down in a relationship was not in his game plan. Not now. Hell, it wasn't even on his long-distance radar. That alone prompted him to meet up with women who were . . . uncomplicated. Gabriella did not strike him as a woman who would fall into that category. In fact, she seemed like the kind of woman who could turn a man's world upside down and inside out.

Not that she was offering anything other than to cook for him. A reminder that tonight he needed to focus. To pay close attention to her cooking skills and qualifications for employment instead of what he'd like to be doing to her body with his hands and mouth.

Shutting off the shower, he downed another shot of whiskey and threw a towel over his shoulders. Dripping water across the hardwood floor, he pushed the button on the intercom and said, "Last dock. On the end."

Before he had time to take his hand off the switch, someone knocked on his door.

Couldn't be her.

Unless she was riding a motorized skateboard or was a witch with twitchy-nose magic like Samantha in *Bewitched*, she wouldn't have had time to get from the parking lot to his door that fast. He shifted the towel from around his shoulders to around his waist and opened the door.

Maybe she was magic after all, because there she stood with two huge baskets by her feet and one slung by the handle over her forearm.

"You're early," he grumbled, unsure of what to think of her mad roadrunner skills.

"And you're . . ." Her dark chocolate eyes took a lazy ride down his body before she looked back up and smiled. "Naked."

$O$f course, the appropriate response to Parker's statement should have been an apology for her early arrival. Or an explanation of how she'd quickly sweet-talked another houseboat owner to let her in the security gate when they'd arrived at the same time.

But Gabi was *not* sorry.

Not in the least.

In fact, in her opinion, she'd arrived at the perfect moment.

Just in time to watch droplets of water slide slowly

down his muscular chest, lightly dusted with short, silky hair. Just in time to see the towel he held onto with one hand slip enough to reveal the thin line of fine dark hair that trailed from below his belly button to unseen sexy parts beneath the towel. And just in time to realize that her nearly naked future employer was everything and more than she'd ever imagined.

And she had a very vivid imagination.

"Job Hunting Skills 101," she said, picking up basket number two, edging past his deliciously clean smelling body, and stepping into his houseboat without waiting for an official invitation. "Always arrive early to make a good impression."

"I was in the shower."

And didn't that create quite the little scenario in her overactive and dirty mind.

"I see that." And she should thank him for it too.

Setting the baskets down on the polished granite countertop, she took a quick scan of the interior of the houseboat. The inside proved to be more modern than she'd imagined from the Cape Cod exterior. Then again, Parker Kincade was hardly a lace curtain kind of guy.

When she went back to where he held the door open with one hand and the towel around his waist with the other, she bent down to grab the basket sitting on the doorstep, and smiled.

He had big feet.

On her way back up she realized he also had big hands.

Did she believe in the old saying?

In this case, she really didn't have to wonder.

The way a man wore jeans and a T-shirt could define him in a matter of seconds. Sloppy fit meant sloppy man with little reason to boast. Well-fit denim over narrow hips and muscled thighs hinted at what the fabric might conceal. However, a plush white towel hid nothing except the main ingredient. And judging from the healthy protrusion behind the towel, Chef Parker Kincade had a whole lot going on to boast about.

Gabi carried the last basket inside, placed it next to the others on the counter, and tried to get a grip on her racing heart and her long-denied hormones. "You can shut the door now."

Busy removing items from the baskets, a few seconds passed before she looked up again. The door remained wide open. And what do you know, the man was checking her out too.

"Chef?"

He blinked.

Twice.

When he slowly closed the door, Gabi swore she heard him mutter something beneath his breath.

"I'm sorry?" She pulled a large zucchini from the basket, grasped it with both hands, and held it between her breasts. "I didn't quite hear you."

"I said . . ." His gaze darted from the zucchini to her face. "I'll go get dressed."

With that, he disappeared into the other room,

leaving behind his clean, male scent and the squeak of wet bare feet on the hardwood floor.

Gabi imagined her traditional-minded mother would be appalled at her behavior. But her modern-thinking *nonni* would give her a wink, a nod, and a nudge. Flirting with the boss might be a bad idea, but Gabi currently lived in the world of unemployment. At the moment she might not be desperate for a job, but she also wasn't stupid. The dishes she'd designed for tonight were meant to be sensual. She'd dressed the part. Felt the part. But even though the way to a man's heart might be through his stomach, Gabi had made a promise that she'd never stoop to using her sexuality to get a job. Not even one she wanted more than she could describe.

Yes, she was insanely attracted to the mostly naked man who'd opened the door. But business came first. Which meant she was going to have to tell the good time girls in her lingerie department they couldn't come out and play.

At least not until after dessert was served.

*P*arker tossed the towel on his bed and pulled on a pair of black boxer briefs. He took the last sip of whiskey and set the empty glass on the dresser. From the other room came the sounds of drawers opening and cupboards closing. For a moment he stood there, hands on hips, shaking his head.

It didn't bother him that Gabriella had obviously

made herself at home in his kitchen. What rattled him to the core was that she'd walked past him to get to that kitchen in a pair of spiked-heel black boots and a short red floral dress that accented her generous curves. After she stepped into the house he realized the fabric of that dress was partially transparent. Behind the swirls in the pattern, he caught a glimpse of black lingerie. After that, his towel had been unable to conceal the fact that the lower half of him had looked hard at her too.

Very hard.

He'd barely managed to get out of the room without it being glaringly obvious that she completely turned him on.

Jesus.

She'd come here for a job interview. Or at least the opportunity to work her way into one. Not to be greeted by some naked guy who couldn't keep his hard-on for her under control.

Business first.

Without indulging in any further illicit thoughts, he pulled on a shirt and a pair of jeans, and ran his fingers through his wet hair. Gabriella had been bold enough to offer to cook for him. She deserved his professionalism. He could give her that. All he had to do was keep his eyes on the food—not the delicious woman preparing it.

Yep.

That's all he had to do.

And if he were a betting man he'd say the chances

of that actually happening were 100–1 not in his
favor.

When he entered the kitchen, Gabriella looked up
from dicing onions on the cutting board. "Not quite
as interesting an ensemble." She pointed at him with
the knife. "But probably more suitable. You know,
just in case you decide to lend a hand. We wouldn't
want anything vital to get maimed."

He chuckled, even though the notion of a knife
slipping on his private parts made him cringe.

Unfortunately—or maybe fortunately in this
situation—her knockout dress was now covered with
a black tailored chef's coat. He couldn't decide which
was sexier—actually seeing the see-through dress,
or imagining it beneath the coat. In any case, those
spike-heeled boots added a very nice touch.

Not that his imagination needed any help.

As a reminder to keep his mind on business, he
crossed his arms as he looked over her shoulder.
"Nice knife skills, Ms. Montani."

"I was taught by the best. She never allowed for
excuses or poor preparation."

"Oh?" Finally, a personal tidbit. "Where were you
trained? The ICE or the CIA?"

"Actually, I learned everything I know at a place
in Italy."

"Really." He hadn't expected that response. "The
ICI?"

"No. It was a very small establishment. More . . . personalized, hands-on training."

"That's the best kind," he said, wondering why she didn't give him the name of the place.

"I agree." With the knife edge, she swept the onion across the cutting board.

While they had no problem having a conversation, this wasn't the first time he'd noticed her reluctance to be forthcoming with information.

And that aroused his curiosity.

Leaning a hip against the counter brought him a little closer to where she stood. She smelled like flowers. Not roses or lilacs. The kind one used in cooking. Calendula, citrus, and allium. For him, the fragrance was far more sensual than any store-bought perfume.

"So what are the selections you've chosen for your *audition*?" he asked.

"Before I tell you the menu, I'd like you to select either the merlot or pinot noir from the basket. Or, if you have it available, a sangiovese. And if you wouldn't mind, pour us both a glass. I subscribe to the Julia Child philosophy of enjoying cooking with wine and sometimes even putting it in the food."

He chuckled. "I always loved her quote 'In cooking you've got to have a what-the-hell attitude.'"

"So you were a fan?"

"Wasn't everyone?"

"I think she was a groundbreaker," she said. "But I don't think everyone adored her."

"Hard to live up to all those expectations," he said.

"Your wine choices still don't give me much of a clue of what's to come tonight."

She turned toward him and he was immediately drawn into the depths of her rich, dark eyes. "You don't like surprises?"

"Depends."

Her mouth slowly curved into a smile. "I promise not to disappoint."

He didn't see how she could.

He might have sworn to keep his hands to himself, but at that moment he wanted nothing more than to pull her into his arms and see if those ruby lips tasted as good as they looked.

"You said you were a purist when it comes to food. I'm going to guess you might feel the same about wine," he said, going to his own wine selections instead of her basket. "So let's go with a pinot noir."

"That will work well with the meal."

"Good to know. Because anyone who works in my restaurant will need to be familiar with and recommend our family wines. Of course I'll carry other brands, but my goal is to bring attention to our own." He removed a bottle of vintage pinot noir from the wine rack and looked at the label affectionately. It was the single year his father had tremendous success with the difficult-to-grow grape.

"I've tasted your wines," she said. "I'd have no trouble recommending them."

"Then we're off to a good start. Let's try this bottle of Velvet Rhapsody."

"Sounds delicious."

"It is. My father worked hard to perfect it. The structure is delicate. The tannins are soft. And the aromatics are . . ." He pulled the cork, poured a small amount into a glass, and handed it to her.

She swirled, sniffed, and smiled. "Cherry." She sniffed again. "With notes of damp earth and"—she sniffed again—"leather."

"You know your wine." She gained extra points for the added knowledge.

"My *nonni* says it's a sin for an Italian not to know good wine from bad. Especially if he or she makes a living behind a stove."

"Nonni? Your grandmother?"

She nodded.

"She sounds like a very smart woman."

"Oh, she is." A look of deep affection brightened her face. "Which is why she's the first person I seek for advice on everything."

"Everything?"

"Yes." The hint of a smile played on her lips. "And she'd approve of you."

He wasn't sure in what way she meant. Whether it was in reference to his culinary skills or . . . something a lot more basic.

Not that it mattered. Tonight was all business.

Even if it killed him.

He tilted the bottle of wine in her direction. "Taste."

As her slender manicured fingers lifted the glass, Parker was mesmerized by the way her plump, cushiony lip pressed against the edge of the crystal. He couldn't help wondering what those lips might feel like pressed against his own.

Or other parts of his body.

Or . . . business.

Back to business.

"Very fresh," she said. Then her tongue swept out and caught the drop of burgundy liquid that clung to her bottom lip.

No doubt about it.

This business *audition* might very well kill him.

Or at least cause him to run for an ice cold shower.

"I guess if I'm going to feed you before midnight, I should get focused." She set the wine glass down on the counter. "If you'd like to pull up a stool, you can watch. You know, to make sure I know what I'm doing."

The way his body reacted to every little move she made told him she knew exactly what she was doing.

Keeping in mind she was auditioning for a place in his restaurant as a chef and not for a place in his bed, he pulled out a barstool and settled in.

Her fingers were fast and careful with the knife as she chopped pancetta, chives, garlic, and gruyère. He had to admit he was impressed with her skills. Now it came down to taste.

While he sat back and enjoyed his wine, he noticed that she'd started to hum.

"What's that tune?" he asked.

"'Che gelida manina' from *La Bohème*." She

glanced up at him from beneath her thick dark lashes. "Do you listen to opera?"

"Not really."

"Aficionados say you're either raised on it or you develop a taste for it. Most non-enthusiasts are most familiar with the aria 'Quando m'en vo'' from *La Bohème*. When I'd visit my grandmother, she thought I should have an appreciation for the classics. My tastes never seemed to follow the crowd."

"My favorite classics lean more toward . . ." He picked up the remote and turned on the sound system. Marvin Gaye's "What's Going On" played at the perfect volume.

"Ah. Sexy songs." She nodded, turning the heat up on the pot of water on the stove.

"Sexy?" *Don't even go there, jackass. Tonight is all about business.*

"Oh, come on." She flashed him a playful grin. "'Sexual Healing,' 'Let's Get It On.' What's sexier than that?"

She was.

He gave himself a mental poke. Business. Business. Business.

She sprinkled some olive oil in a pan. "You know what song turns me on the most?"

Business. Business. Business.

"Tell me." Shit.

"'Damn I Wish I Was Your Lover.'"

Now she was talking his language.

"Sophie B. Hawkins," he said.

She gave him a sideways glance as she pushed the vegetables from the cutting board into the pan. "So you know the song?"

"Yep." He knew the feeling too.

She cut off a piece of gruyère cheese, leaned into the counter, and held it up like a bribe. "Tell me your favorite sexy song and I'll let you have a bite."

Jesus. Seriously?

Business. Business. Business.

Nope. Didn't work. Beneath his jeans, his dick was thinking of a completely different kind of business.

"And do not say 'Pour Some Sugar on Me.'" She winked.

"You said sexy, not stripper."

"Right."

Although he could definitely fantasize her working a pole.

"'I'll Make Love to You.'"

Her dark eyes glittered. "Is that a song or a promise?"

Both. "Boyz II Men."

"Too obvious." She wiggled the cheese chunk like *come and get it*, and right now he was totally game. "Pick another one."

"'Need You Tonight.'"

"Oooh." When she closed her eyes and hummed, he damn near came. "INXS. Good choice. Looks like we have a lot in common."

He wondered how many more things they could add to that list. He was definitely willing to find out.

"So do I get my reward?" He eyed the cheese caught between her thumb and finger.

She smiled. "You do."

Instead of handing him the bite, she fed it to him. Then she licked her fingertips.

At that moment there wasn't a business mantra on the planet that could save him from needing to grab his hard cock to quell the ache.

"If you'd like to have a seat at the table, I'll bring you the appetizer," she said, sweet as a summer peach.

Hell. He couldn't even move.

Because right now, every on-fire muscle, cell, and ounce of testosterone in his body said *she* was the appetizer and he was a starving man.

*G*abi took a breath.

It was no secret that women in general were turned on by their senses and their imaginations. Right now, when her mind should be focused on preparing the meal, she had porn—starring Parker Kincade— playing in her head. Which was why she'd asked if he preferred to sit at the table. She needed a little distance between them before she climbed up on his lap and made a fantasy into a reality.

"If I sit at the table I can't watch you work," Parker said in that deep voice that rushed over her skin like a warm breeze.

"True." She went around to his side of the counter, took him by the arm, and led him to the dining table near the wall of windows that overlooked the Columbia River and the breathtaking peak of Mount Hood. "But I'd like you to sit back, relax, and let your taste buds do the rest. You've already seen me in action."

"Are you sure about that?" His long, dark lashes were sinfully thick as he studied her face. "I have a feeling there's a lot more to you than the way you wield a paring knife."

"Oh, believe me, there is."

The heat turned up a notch as they studied each other, and Gabi was ready to yank off her chef's coat to show him exactly how much more. But the job had to come first.

She went back to the counter, refilled his wine glass, and carried it to him. He maintained eye contact the whole time. As she set the glass down, he gently caught her hand. A wicked tremble skated through her heart and straight into her panties as he turned her hand over and lightly drew the tip of his index finger across the center of her palm. She pressed her lips together to keep from moaning.

"No scars. No blisters. Looks like you're very careful in the kitchen," he murmured in a deep, sexy voice that mingled with the sounds of Marvin Gaye singing "Mercy Mercy Me" in the background. "What about in the dining room?"

"That may be an entirely different story." She eased her hand away before she lost what remaining control she had.

Back at the stove, she prepared the shrimp in a small pan. "So tell me more about what it was like being on *Chopped*."

"Nerve-wracking." He chuckled. "Harried. Inspiring. Frustrating. Unbelievable."

"I imagine it would be very exciting."

"Do you have aspirations to be a TV chef, Gabriella?"

Her head snapped around and she checked to see if there was anything more behind his question than simple curiosity. What she saw in his eyes allowed her heart to stop racing.

He didn't know.

Thank God.

"None whatsoever," she said. "Anything I have to prove is only to myself."

"You sound a lot like me. I only went on the show to challenge myself."

"One more thing we have in common." She smiled. "That's a good thing, right?"

He raised an eyebrow.

"I meant, if we're going to be working together," she hurried to explain. "Although I admit that while I do like to be in control most of the time, I am willing to be submissive on occasion."

What the hell was she saying?

And why did everything that came out of her mouth sound like a sexual innuendo?

"I'll keep that in mind."

She closed her eyes briefly to regain her composure before she plated the appetizer. When she felt it was visually appealing, she carried it to him and set it down on the table.

"Shrimp bruschetta with Limoncello and extra-virgin olive oil. *Goditi*."

When he looked at her with a questioning tilt to his head, she translated. "Enjoy."

Parker eagerly pulled the appetizer in front of him and eyed the display she'd created. Visually, it was a gorgeous plate, but he suspected not the most extravagant she could create.

"I decided not to show off," she explained. "It would be easy to come in here and make something that would take hours to create and would completely blow your mind. But since I don't know what type of menu you have planned for your restaurant, I wanted to give you samples of what I'd boasted about when I came to see you at the barn. Food in its truest nature. Flavors to awaken your senses and give you a mouth-watering experience."

His mouth was watering all right. And not just because of the food.

"You do have a way with words."

"I have a way with other things too."

He didn't doubt that for a second.

She waved her hand toward the plate. "Taste."

He lifted a slice of bruschetta for inspection, then sank his teeth into it. Flavor burst through his mouth and he hummed his approval. "Crisp. Fresh. Light. Delicious."

She smiled like he'd given her a gift.

"This style of appetizer pairs nicely with any type of meat or pasta dish," she said. "Also, compared to a ceviche, shrimp wellington, or even something like an asparagus rolantina, it's a much lower cost to make. Which adds more to your profit. I know a large part of a restaurant's success is not only to consistently give the patrons the best food and atmosphere, but to keep the operating costs at a minimum."

"So you've studied bookkeeping too?" He was impressed. Most restaurants went out of business in the first year because they weren't managed properly.

"Some. Although I'm probably not as good as I should be. Still, it makes sense to pay less for supplies so you can ask for a more than fair price for the meals."

"I'm sure whatever skills you lack," he said, "you make up for elsewhere."

"I'll let you be the judge of that."

She tossed him a smoldering smile over her shoulder as she walked back into the kitchen.

By the time she'd served him escarole with sunchokes, shredded caciotta, and lemon vinaigrette for the salad, a sweet onion carbonara for the entrée, and pan-roasted asparagus with a crispy fried egg as the side dish, he was sold on her cooking skills. She completely dropped the mike with dessert—a smooth and creamy mascarpone sorbetto with rosemary honey. After only one bite, he thought he might be in love.

"Have you tasted this?" He held up a spoonful of the dessert.

"Is it bad?" Concern pulled her sleek dark brows together.

"Gabriella? There is nothing wrong with the dishes you prepared tonight. I'd be honored to serve any of them in my restaurant. But this . . ." He held up the spoon that nearly overflowed with the light and fluffy treat and shook his head. "Taste it."

She clutched her hands together as she came toward him. Her spiked heels tapped on the wood floor, and her sheer dress swished sensuously against her legs.

All evening the conversation and wine had flowed as easily as the food. In just a few hours he'd become so responsive to her that any gesture, expression, or movement she made felt like the snap of a rubber band.

She'd definitely awakened more than his taste buds.

When she stood beside his chair, she looked at the spoonful he held up for her to taste. Then she looked at him with a raised brow. "You want me to lick your spoon?"

Among other things.

He nodded.

Then he stood and offered a taste of the dessert to her. Her warm, soft fingers curled around his hand and she guided the spoon to her mouth. She parted those pretty red lips and they closed over the perfectly prepared sorbetto. Her lashes fluttered as she moaned her pleasure and the last cell in his aroused body tossed its hands up in surrender.

When he started to withdraw the spoon, she clasped his hand and brought the utensil back to her mouth. Then slowly she licked off the smidge that remained.

Parker went up in flames.

Her dark lashes lowered in a slow blink as she looked up at him. "Did I pass?"

# Chapter 5

*I*f the look in Parker's deep blue eyes was any indication, she'd not only passed the audition with flying colors, she'd fired up something a whole lot tastier.

"You know you passed." He held her gaze as he set the spoon on the table and moved his hand to her waist. "But I'm an honest guy, and I have a ways to go before I make any decisions on who I hire. So I can't stand here right now and tell you you've got the job."

Her heart gave an unexpected twist.

She'd been hoping that tonight he'd be impressed enough with her cooking to tell her he had a place for her in his restaurant.

"And no matter how damned attracted to you I am"—his darkened gaze searched her face—"I can't promise you anything more than this one night. In any way."

The disappointment of not snagging the job tonight

dissipated when he openly admitted he was attracted to her. The feeling was on-fire *want it, need it, gotta have it* mutual.

"Parker?" Despite her outward confidence as her fingers toyed with a button on his shirt, butterflies battled like fighter planes in her stomach. "May I call you Parker? Or would you prefer I call you Chef?"

"Depends on what you're going to say next."

"I'm obviously attracted to you." And she was. Foolishly so. Common sense told her to stop. Back away. Keep this on a professional level only. But all the hormone related circuits in her body were clicking on full charge, and common sense became completely null and void. She wanted him. And she wanted him bad. "So how about we say the audition and the business part of tonight is over. Whatever happens next is strictly off the clock."

"Then please"—a smile that turned her inside out lifted his sexy mouth—"call me Parker."

"How about"—she trailed her fingers down the short row of buttons on his Henley shirt—"we just stop talking altogether?"

"I like where you're going with this." He lifted her fingers and kissed them.

"So we're on the same page?" she asked. "One night. A good time. Then tomorrow it's back to business?"

"Definitely." His hand on her waist slipped a little lower and lust darkened his eyes. "One night only."

"Right here?" she asked.

"Right now."

She slid her hand up his sleeve and enjoyed the warm, thick muscle beneath the soft fabric. "Then shut up and kiss me, *Parker.*"

His name left her lips on a brief sigh as he pulled her against his hard body, lowered his head, and did just that.

He pulled her closer, settled his hands on her butt, and urged her to the toes of her boots. His firm, warm lips opened against hers and he fed her deliciously wet, breath-stealing kisses. His tongue tangled with hers. Teased and tempted her to lose absolutely all control.

When she curled her arms around his neck, he rocked his long, thick erection against her, proving that anything going on right now only had to do with one man, one woman, and a whole hell of a lot of sexual promise.

He shifted her around until the dining table pressed into her backside. Then he moved between her thighs, lifted his head, and cradled her face in one hand while the other gently cupped her breast. "Right here?"

"As quickly as possible." She curled her fingers into the bottom of his shirt and pulled it up over his head. Unable to resist, she pressed her lips to the ripple of abdominal muscles. His warm skin smelled fresh, like soap, cotton, and desirable male.

Desire raged through her blood and consumed her as she looked up at him. "I want you, Parker. I want you now."

He held her face in his large hands. "I'm not looking for a fast fuck, Gabriella. My body might disagree, but I don't care if you have somewhere else to be," he added in a deep, sexy tone that vibrated against her breasts. "One night is all we have. So I'm taking my time."

Lust and heat darkened his eyes. And while he claimed to be in no hurry, he wasted no time in unbuttoning her chef's coat and tossing it to a chair before he laid her back on the table.

He looked her over, softly touching her here and there—the sensitive skin in the crook of her arms, the palms of her hands, her face, her breasts, and between her legs. When he leaned in and trailed a line of scorching kisses down the side of her neck, every cell and nerve in her body came alive. All she could do was grab his shoulders and hold on.

"By all means, take your time," she whispered. "I'm not going anywhere."

"That's good." His breath rasped hot and moist against her ear while his talented hands snuck beneath her dress. "But these panties are."

The significance of his words vibrated between her legs as he moved down her body, kissing her through the fabric of her dress until he stood between her legs wearing a smile dripping with naughtiness. Slowly he eased the dress all the way up her thighs until her black lace panties were exposed.

"Mmmm." He lowered his head and kissed her stomach, then he moved lower and kissed the inside of each thigh. "Even better than I've been imagining."

He'd been imagining her naked?

Oh, they were definitely on the same page.

His finger traced over the lace edges then dipped beneath to teasingly touch her skin before he curled a finger and tugged the scrap of fabric down her legs.

"The boots?" He lifted a dark brow. "They stay."

A shudder of anticipation rippled over Gabi's body as he drew the panties down over her boots and stuffed them in the back pocket of his jeans.

She grinned. "Keepsake?"

"Just the start." He planted several hot, slick kisses on her abdomen. "I plan to take a whole lot more before the night's over."

At any other time with any other man, she might feel self-conscious being spread out like Thanksgiving dinner. But the sexual heat in his eyes shoved her apprehension right off the table.

His hands slid up her legs and settled beneath her. Then he pulled her toward him until her bottom was at the edge of the table.

When he leaned down to kiss her mouth, the denim of his jeans touched her bare skin and his erection pressed against her mound. The pulsing heat tempted her to wrap her legs around him and rub against him until she came.

Before she could move he slipped from her embrace and paid attention to her breasts with his mouth over the fabric of her dress. Beneath his skillful caress her nipples peaked and ached for the warm, wet recess of his mouth, skin to skin.

He whipped the dress over her head and tossed

it on a nearby chair. He did the same with her black lace bra and before she knew it, aside from her boots, she was completely naked on the table where she'd just served him dinner.

"Damn." Smiling, he shook his head slowly. "I hope you're up for a long night."

"I hope *you're* up for it." She sat up, cupped her palm over his erection, and gave him a good squeeze. He pushed against her hand and she smiled.

"That should tell you I am."

"It does. But I'm also a very . . . visual person." She pressed her lips to his bare chest and swept her tongue across a flat brown nipple while reaching for his zipper. "And since your towel gave me only a hint, I'm eager to see the entire package."

"I'm all yours." He held his hands up in surrender.

She did appreciate a man who didn't mind handing over the reins when she wanted to exhibit a little control.

Like a slow tease, she lowered the zipper on his jeans and pushed the pair of black boxer briefs down his slim hips and perfect ass. His erection sprang free and she curled her fingers around him.

"Impressive." And he was. Very. Suddenly she felt very greedy.

For a moment he let her touch him, stroke him, and test the weight of his testicles. Then he took her hands off of him and laid her back on the table.

"Did I pass?" he asked, mirroring her earlier question.

Nodding, she licked her lips.

"Just a yes? Let's see if I can gain some extra points."

Without hesitation, he skated moist, hot kisses down the side of her neck and then he cupped her breasts in his hands. Her back arched when he licked, and sucked, then blew warm air across her peaked nipples.

When she moaned he smiled against her cleavage.

"Are you a good girl, Gabriella?" He covered a nipple with his mouth, sucked it hard, then released it with a pop. "Or do you like to get a little dirty?"

The question heightened her awareness and raised goose bumps on her skin. Her fingers shoveled through his long hair and she lifted his head.

"I want good." She pressed her mouth to his. "And dirty."

"My kind of woman." He slipped from her grasp to kiss and lick his way down her body.

Each touch of his mouth and tongue sent fire through her veins. She ached and throbbed for more. And just when she thought she couldn't stand the delicious torture, he was between her legs. He touched her, played with her, made her moan out loud. His fingers parted her folds, then he pressed his warm tongue against her clit.

Pleasure whipped through her abdomen and her back arched off the tabletop as his warm, slick tongue lapped up and down and slid into her core.

The more he licked and sucked, the more her heart beat like crazy. As the pressure built and heat skyrocketed, she became a writhing, whimpering mass of need. Release was only a breath away and Gabi feared he would stop and make her beg for more.

But he didn't stop.

Sensing she was on the edge, his hands dove beneath her butt and he lifted her closer to his mouth. His hot tongue swept in like a flash of fire, and she exploded.

Even as she came, he continued to lick. Her body trembled as she climaxed like never before. Easing the pressure, he continued to lick her until the trembling quieted. Then he lifted his head and those blue eyes looked up at her from across her body.

"That"—she rose to her elbows—"was amazing. But . . ."

He came upright and she sat up.

"I know you've got a lot more to show me." She wrapped her fingers around his erection, gave him a long stroke, and then she cupped his balls in her hand with a gentle squeeze. "And I want more."

A wicked grin crossed his lips as his hand covered hers on his dick. Together they rubbed the thick swollen head between her slick folds. Her sensitive flesh tingled as he teased her back to life.

Letting go of his cock, he grabbed the foil packet he'd laid on the table.

"Let me do that." Anxious to feel him inside, she rolled the coiled latex down his long shaft. Then she lay back on the table and held out her arms. "Now, show me how dirty you can be."

"Are you giving me permission?" He slid his hands up her thighs, her belly, and over her breasts. Desire rushed through her veins as he sucked one swollen nipple into his mouth, glided his tongue along the crest, and gave it a hard pull with his lips.

"I'm giving you a challenge."

And then they were face to face.

Skin to skin.

"Tell me what you want, dirty girl."

"I want you inside me. And I don't want you to stop until I scream."

"Fuck. Yes." His hands gripped her butt and tilted her hips. Then he pushed inside her, hard and deep.

Parker closed his eyes and groaned as he gripped her firm ass, and sank into Gabriella's heat with a surge of heart pounding pleasure. Tension wound low and tight as his thrusts sank deeper. He wanted to fuck her hard and fast. He wanted to hear her scream. He wanted to feel a hot orgasm shoot up the back of his legs and through his cock. But she felt too damn good to go fast. They had one night and he wanted this to last.

She moaned his name and wrapped her legs around him and drew him in tighter like she couldn't get enough. So he gave her more.

There was no space between them. They'd become one, moving together like a synchronized fireworks display. Hearts pounding in one feverish rhythm.

"More, Parker," she moaned. "Give me more."

His balls tightened at the sound of her plea, and he was determined to give her everything she wanted.

"Harder. Please. Harder."

Jesus, the woman was going to kill him.

Not that he minded going out like this.

He grabbed her hips and pumped harder. She was hot, slick, and tight, and she surrounded him like a fitted glove. The friction was crazy and when her inner muscles tightened around him, he almost lost control.

Almost.

He shifted inside of her to make sure he touched that inner spot he knew would send her over the edge. And he knew he'd found the right place when her breathing increased and her moans became desperate little pants of breath.

"Oh. Oh, Parker." She surged up, grabbed his ass, and pulled him in tighter. "Oh. My. God!"

A screaming growl broke loose from her throat as she came.

Heart pounding, he broke into out-of-control thrusting pleasure as they came together in a breath-stealing explosion that left both of them gasping for air.

They moved from the kitchen to the bathroom, where he'd bent her over and shown her how dirty and satisfying shower sex could be. Later they ended up in his bed, where she took control and showed him how fucking mind-blowing it could be with a woman on top.

Hours later, thoroughly sated and taking pleasure in the feel of the curvy woman in his arms, Parker finally closed his eyes.

He'd promised her one night only, but damn, she was one of a kind. It was going to be hard to let her go.

But that's exactly what he had to do. No matter how badly he might want to go back for more.

*g*ray clouds swollen with rain darkened the morning sky as Parker blinked his eyes open and stretched. The first thing he noticed was the fragrance of a woman. The second thing he noticed, as he reached for her, was that his bed was empty. The sheets where she should have been lying were cold. Which meant she'd abandoned them long ago.

Thunder—unusual for a November morning—rumbled across the sky as Parker swung his legs off the bed and pulled on a pair of jeans. He didn't bother to zip them up as he headed both shirtless and barefoot into the rest of the house to search for her. But before he even reached the living room he knew he was completely alone.

The kitchen had been spotlessly cleaned. Every dish, every pot, pan, spoon, and spatula had been washed and put away. The dining room table, where he'd laid her out and feasted on her body like a dessert buffet, was wiped down and the chairs were put back in place. There was no sign that she'd been there at all except for the faint lingering perfume of her warm, luscious body.

He didn't know whether to be pissed that she'd left without a word or to laugh because he didn't have to deal with an awkward morning after. Most of all he worried that she'd made it home safely. He reached for his phone to call and check, then realized he didn't have her number.

Tossing his phone on the counter, he smiled. He'd been treated to a delicious meal prepared by a delectable woman. He'd had an amazing, unforgettable night of sex. *And* he'd been spared the whole *don't call me, I'll call you* routine when the sun came up.

Holy shit.

Now he really had to like her.

Too bad he didn't have any idea of how to get ahold of her, because even though casual sex may have always been his game, he never left a woman's bed without her knowing how much he appreciated and enjoyed the experience.

Apparently Gabriella didn't use the same MO.

He crossed the room and glanced outside at the low-hanging clouds and the mist hovering over the river. It was a perfect day to sleep in, or at least stay between the sheets with someone warm and sexy. Since that wasn't an option, he needed to get moving.

Saturdays were normally a welcome and badly needed day off, but with Groomzilla breathing down his neck and the calendar reminding him that there were only a few weeks until Thanksgiving and then Groomzilla's wedding, Parker had to get his clothes on and get busy.

An hour later he stood in the center of his soon-to-be restaurant, zipping up his coat to ward off the chill, and helping the construction crew decide exactly where to break out the back wall for the patio doors Lili had suggested.

But even with the roar of a power saw grinding in his ears, thoughts of Gabriella moaning his name as she wrapped her legs around him did not dissipate as fast as he'd expected. Not that he didn't appreciate the women he'd been with in the past, but Gabriella had definitely upped the game. Without a doubt, last night had been the best no strings sex of his life.

*g*abriella dropped food pellets into Basil's bowl then leaned her elbows on the counter to watch him eat.

"You know, you really don't need to be such a Mr. Cranky Pants. I'd be more than happy to get you a friend if you'd give up the whole fight-to-the-death thing."

The flashy betta fish gobbled up a food pellet and fanned his red tail as if he disputed her comment.

"Yeah. That's what I figured."

Fortunately, humans seemed a little more receptive to pairing up. At least once in a while. Even this morning, her body still hummed from last night. Thanks to Parker, every cell, every nerve in her body was as alive as if she'd touched a wild current. His touch had been gentle, possessive, hungry, electrifying. His mouth had created sensations in her body she'd never known could exist. He'd been powerful yet tender. And she'd lapped it up like a starving woman.

The man had lived up to everything her fantasies had created.

Crawling from his warm embrace in the middle of the night had been nothing short of torture. But before she'd stepped foot in his houseboat, she'd made a mental list of things to do and things to avoid at all costs. She'd broken damn near every one of them.

For all intents and purposes, she needed to retract the crazy thoughts floating through her sexually satisfied mind. Thoughts like how she wouldn't mind a repeat performance.

But that couldn't happen.

Not only had he made it clear they had one night and one night only, she couldn't afford to expect or even want more. Not even if the hours they'd spent in each other's arms, wrapped around each other's bodies in positions she'd never even dreamed of before, were unforgettable. But no matter how mindblowing the sex had been, it had nothing to do with the work she wanted to perform in his restaurant.

Before she'd walked into his soon-to-be restaurant, her mission had been clear. She needed to keep it that way. If he were like every other man she'd ever met— men who were more than forgettable—and if it were easy to separate a sexual relationship apart from the professional one, then she'd be ecstatic to have him wrap his arms around her again. But she didn't dare to pretend that Parker Kincade was like every other man she'd ever met. He was the kind of man a woman wanted to hold onto.

And not just for the incredible sex.

Keeping her distance, keeping a career agenda in mind, was crucial. Even if she had to carry a baseball bat and whack herself upside the head as a constant reminder, that's what she'd do.

From this moment on, seeing Parker as a man she wanted to work for, not a man she wanted to lick up one side and down the other, became her pledge. Her solemn vow.

Even if it killed her.

"**W**ho the hell's crazy idea was this?" Sean Scott pulled his ball cap off his head, shook off the raindrops, and ran his fingers through short hair littered with sawdust before plopping the cap on backward.

If the project manager didn't have such a huge grin on his face, Parker might be tempted to rearrange it a little for him in defense of the person who'd suggested the architectural change. "My sister. The event planner."

"You mean the gorgeous blonde I saw walking out of here a few hours ago?"

"Yes. The gorgeous blonde you will be keeping your eyes *and* hands off of." Parker folded his arms. "*If* you plan to keep them intact."

"She single?" Sean pushed a little harder, wearing that same playful grin.

"And you should keep thoughts like *that* completely out of your head. Unless you don't plan to keep it on your shoulders."

Sean laughed. "I get that she's got five protective brothers who could kick my ass or kill me and bury my body so it would never be found, but I am *not* dead." He held up his hands. "Yet. So I'll just worship from afar if that's all right with you."

Parker knew he and his brothers could take care of any guy looking at either of their sisters with bad intentions. But Sean was a good guy. So Parker gave him a pass.

This time.

"In my books *afar* means out of touching range," he said.

Sean sucked in a breath. "That's a tall order, my man."

"So is a quick and painless death, but it can be arranged."

A comical shrug lifted the project manager's shoulders.

"Am I . . . interrupting?"

Before Parker even turned, the sound of a certain seductive feminine voice sent a shot of longing into his jeans. In his mind, he could hear it whispering naughty things and pleading for him to do that "again" and "harder."

"Damn, bro." Sean gave him a look. "You have

gorgeous women just falling out of trees around here or what?"

"Or what." He popped his fist on Sean's shoulder. "Get back to work before I make good on that promise."

"Yes, boss." Sean's response on his way out the door was totally tongue-in-cheek, but the way Sean had checked out Gabriella hadn't settled well with Parker.

At all.

And . . . yeah, that was definitely something he needed to get a handle on. They'd had one night. One fucking fabulous, hot, sweaty Friday night. But that didn't give him the right to get possessive. In fact, the whole jealous thing didn't even make sense. He'd never been that way in his entire life.

Holding a white pastry-sized box in her hands, Gabriella looked sweet and apologetic.

"Wow. That's awesome," he said to her.

Her head tilted just enough to send her long ponytail swinging against her back. "The cookies?"

"No. That you're real. Thought I just had this wild sexual fantasy and imagined you."

She came closer in a pair of skintight jeans tucked into the pair of boots that only reminded him of how the leather had felt against his naked hips as he plunged into her over and over last night. Or how the spiked heels had dug into his ass cheeks when she locked her legs around him and came. The pink hoodie she wore might be hiding the soft skin and lush amazingness above her narrow waist, but his mind—and his hands—had an excellent memory.

"Because I left in the middle of the night?" she asked, setting the box down.

"I prefer to call it *evaporated*. Like you'd never been there."

"Oh, Parker."

She came even closer and brought with her the scent of lemon and vanilla. He had to double his efforts not to grab her and plant his face in the sweet smelling curve of her neck.

"I can still call you Parker, right?"

When he nodded she reached up and touched his cheek. "Are you pouting?"

"Real men don't pout." He caught her hand in his and found her fingers cold from the chilly November day. "I was worried about you getting home safely and I didn't have your number to check."

"Well that was sweet. But as you can see . . ." She swept the hand he wasn't holding over her body. "I made it home fine."

He couldn't have stopped his eyes from roaming her mouthwatering curves if he'd tried. And he didn't try. Not even a little.

"I'm glad you made it home safe. But I'm a little confused why you're here now. I thought I made it clear last night that I wasn't ready to hire anyone yet." He let go of her hand and she tucked it in the pocket of her hoodie. "Or are you here for a different reason?"

"Don't worry. While I had a fantastic time, I'm not looking for a replay of last night," she said, and he was amazed at how badly her affirmation stung.

"But you're here now and I have to wonder why."

"Well." A saucy smile curved her lips. "If I learned anything at all last night, it's that I work very well *under* you."

Damn.

That she did.

She did a fucking fantastic job on top of him too.

"So even though I know you're not hiring just yet, I wanted you to know that I'm still very interested in working here. And I'd like you to keep me in mind."

Keep her in mind? Hell, he'd thought of little else since she'd walked through his door last night.

"I'm sorry to interrupt," a different female voice said.

Parker turned to find Lucy, his future sister-in-law, standing in the open doorway.

"Don't be sorry." He went to the door to greet her with a hug. "It's great to see you. What can I help you with?"

"I was actually looking for Jordan," Lucy said.

"Are you really sure you want to do that?"

"I'm sure." She sighed. "If only to keep him out of trouble."

"What's Groomzilla up to now?"

Lucy laughed. *"Groomzilla?"*

"Hey, he earned the name."

"And apparently he's still earning it." Lucy sighed

again. "This morning he mentioned something about *reindeer* for the wedding."

"Oh, God."

"I know." Lucy nodded. "Before I could ask if he was serious—actually I would have said *freaking* serious—he took off and I haven't seen him since. My fear factor is up around two hundred percent. He really is taking this wedding planning thing to the max."

"He could be anywhere up to God knows what by now." Parker knew that anything with Jordan was possible, and nothing was out of the question.

"I really didn't mean to interrupt," Lucy whispered, glancing over his shoulder. "But who's your friend?"

Parker wouldn't exactly call her a friend. Sexy, gorgeous, and confusing as hell? Yeah, she was all that.

"Lucy, this is Gabriella Montani. She's interested in a chef position here at the restaurant."

Gabriella stepped forward and shook Lucy's hand. "It's very nice to meet you. So you're planning a wedding?"

"Actually, my fiancé is doing all the planning."

"Really?" Gabriella grinned. "I like that."

Lucy sighed. "You wouldn't if you were engaged to Jordan."

"Tell her about the prom," Parker urged. The story was sweet and thoughtful, but so totally over the top it'd had Jordan Kincade written all over it.

"The prom?" Gabriella tilted her head and her long ponytail caught in the hood of her sweatshirt.

Before Parker could stop himself he slipped his hand under all that silky brown hair and lifted it away from the hood. But not before he probably, maybe, accidentally brushed his fingers across the back of her warm neck.

Gabriella gave him a confused look before returning her attention to Lucy.

"Jordan had asked me to the high school graduation dance but then he stood me up," Lucy said. "So a few months ago he created a prom just for the two of us."

"Well yay for him doing that," Gabriella said. "But boo for him standing you up."

"Believe me, he's made amends," Lucy said. "Many times over."

"So he's planning your wedding now as penance?" Gabriella asked.

When Lucy laughed again, Parker felt like a fly on the wall. He didn't mind being left out of the conversation. In fact, he rather enjoyed watching the two of them chat.

"Actually, he's doing me a favor," Lucy said. "I'm a teacher at the high school and have a couple of difficult students this year. So my extra time is really limited right now. Jordan didn't want to postpone the wedding, so he took over the planning duties."

"That is so sweet," Gabriella said. "It sounds like he'll make a wonderful husband."

Parker laughed. "Jordan's a former NHL hockey player. *Sweet* isn't quite the word to describe him."

"He *is* sweet," Lucy insisted with a smile. "And annoying. And full of himself. But mostly sweet. And apparently I've got to find him before he comes up with any more crazy ideas."

"Did you check up at the main house?" Parker asked.

"Not yet. I thought I'd come here first in case he was here pestering you." Lucy turned her attention back to Gabriella. "It was really nice meeting you. I'll keep my fingers crossed that the job here works out in your favor."

"Thanks. If you could put in a good word for me with the boss I'd appreciate it." Gabriella extended her hand and shook Lucy's. "Good luck with the wedding."

Lucy turned to go then stopped and said, "They're giving me a bridal shower in a couple of weeks. Maybe you'd like to come? You wouldn't have to bring anything. Just come have some fun."

"I'd love that. Thank you." Gabriella reached in her bag, pulled out a card, and handed it to Lucy. "Here's my number."

*WTF?*

Parker scratched his head.

How was it he'd had the woman screaming out his name when she orgasmed multiple times, but she wouldn't give up her contact info to him? Yet Lucy mentioned a bridal shower and *bingo*, she just gave it over?

As he waved goodbye to Lucy, he didn't understand

why Gabriella twisted him up over shit that shouldn't matter. He had too many things going on right now to worry about whether the woman he'd just had out-of-this-world-fucking-amazing sex with would give him her phone number or not.

Yeah. He was done with that crap kind of thinking.

"She seems nice." Gabriella tossed him a smile after Lucy left.

"She *is* nice. So back to why you're here."

"Cookies." She picked up the white box and opened the lid. Then she reached inside, took one out, and held it up. "And not just any cookies. Ricotta cheese cookies with lemon icing."

He reached for the cookie but she beat him to it and took a bite.

"I thought those were for me."

She chewed thoughtfully around a smile that tempted him to kiss it right off her face.

"They are." She offered the same cookie to him. "Taste."

Had he not spent last night with his mouth on hers and his tongue all over her body, he might hesitate. Instead, he wrapped his fingers around her hand, brought the cookie to his mouth, and sank his teeth into it. The light buttery and almond flavor with a hint of sweet lemon woke up his taste buds. Almost as deliciously as the woman who'd made the cookie.

"Good?" she asked.

"Wonderful."

"My *nonni* will be happy you approve. It's her recipe. In addition to my appetizer, entrée, and dessert skills, I thought you might also like a sample of my baking abilities. You know, just in case you decide to offer bakery goods on your menu."

He still didn't know what the hell he'd be offering on his menu, but he sure as hell wouldn't mind sampling *her* again. But that was against his rules.

"Do I get the rest?" he asked, because she still held the remaining bite of cookie in her hand. "Or are you just going to tempt me with it?"

She looked up at him from beneath those thick sooty lashes. "Do I tempt you, Parker?"

"Loaded question, Ms. Montani." In a last ditch effort to maintain professional control, he used her formal name. His good intentions went to shit when he leaned in and snagged the rest of the cookie between his teeth.

A smile curved her plump lips and he couldn't help but think of all the places that beautiful mouth had been last night.

Damn. It wasn't like he was some pubescent kid unable to control his urges.

He redoubled his efforts and let go of her hand.

"Thanks for the cookies. They'd make a nice addition to the dessert choices."

"Does that mean you'll give me the job?"

What he wanted to give her had nothing to do with the job. "So what do you think of the place?"

"Nice detour." She chuckled.

"I told you, I'm not ready to hire anyone yet."

"And I'm not ready to give up hope that there's a place for me in your restaurant. But back to your question." She set the cookie box down on a make-shift table of sawhorses and plywood. "I'm growing fond of the large hole in the back wall."

He turned and looked. "Last-minute design change. My sister suggested I put in doors and a patio for out-door dining and private parties."

"Your sister has excellent ideas."

"Stick around. You'll find out our family doesn't run short of opinions."

"That works for me. Because sticking around is exactly what I plan to do."

Parker could have taken her comment a hundred different ways and all of them could have been as innocent as the words had sounded.

But he didn't.

For some reason the idea of her sticking around excited him way more than it should. And that kind of thinking was a whole mess of trouble just waiting to explode.

Parker realized he couldn't help but wonder what Gabriella really had going on in that clever mind of hers. But like her phone number, she wasn't exactly forthcoming.

A hint of mystery could be fun, as long as he knew what road to follow. With Gabriella, he had no clue.

*W*hen Parker had brought her fingers to his mouth, Gabriella wanted to toss aside the good intentions she'd come here with today. Everything about this man kept sidetracking her.

Watching him at his food truck, she'd known he had the kind of devastating good looks that could melt a girl's panties right off her body. But she hadn't seen his keen sense of humor. She hadn't known the genuine love he had for the restaurant he was creating. Or the love he had for his family.

At this very moment she should only have one thing on her mind.

Proving herself.

Determined to stay focused, she took a breath.

When an army of construction guys in brown coveralls gathered in the large opening at the back wall of the building, she saw her opportunity to take a step back.

Literally and figuratively.

"Looks like there's a lot of work still to be done here," she said.

"Yep." Parker turned to look at the workers gathered in the opening. "There sure is."

"So put me to work."

His head snapped around. "What?"

She'd seen another chance to prove her worth and she seized it. "Put me to work. I know how to use a screwdriver, a hammer, a saw, and any kind of electric tool that makes a guy do that manly grunt thing."

"Oh really." He folded his arms. "And where did you learn these skills?"

"Habitat for Humanity. I've assisted on dozens of projects. Most recently I helped build a three bedroom house in Alabama after a tornado leveled an entire town."

"You're kidding."

"What." She held out her hands. "Don't I look like a hammer and saw kind of girl?"

"Not even close."

"Well I am. We built that place in a hundred hours. Handed over the keys to a wonderful woman and her small children. And we walked away knowing we'd just put a roof over a family's heads."

Parker folded his arms across his broad chest. "Looks like you're continuously going to surprise me."

"Hopefully in a good way."

"You're off to a damn good start." He tipped his head toward her feet. "Although I can't see how you're going to manage wielding a hammer in those."

"No worries. I always carry a pair of work boots and sneakers in my car. Along with a small toolbox. Just in case."

"I'm impressed." His smile increased to a grin. "Maybe the next time I have you naked I'll ask you to leave those on instead of the dominatrix heels."

A web of sensation tickled all those places he'd touched last night with his hands and mouth. Even though he'd been the one telling her they only had one night, he'd just hinted that maybe there could be a repeat. While her body said yes, yes, yes, she grabbed hold of her earlier promise and determination slid back into place.

As she turned to retrieve the boots from her car, she tossed him a look over her shoulder. "Who says there will be a next time?"

# Chapter 6

*H*ours later Parker's growling stomach got the best of him. The construction crew had called it a day, and the sun had disappeared below the horizon. Ready to call it a day himself, Parker went to find Gabriella, who'd disappeared into the kitchen area some time ago. He hadn't asked for her help. She hadn't asked to be paid. Instead she'd offered out of the goodness of her heart. Not many people would do something like that and he appreciated her help. Most of all it gave him an opportunity to see that while she was an excellent cook, she wasn't afraid to put in the hard work either. And even though he was a long way from making any decisions, she was exactly the type of person he wanted working for him.

She'd been working for hours without a break and he imagined she must be hungry too.

Last time he'd seen her she'd been talking with

Sean. She'd had a smile on the lips Parker had kissed last night and laughter flowing from the mouth that had moaned his name as she clenched her legs around him. Parker wasn't so sure he liked her sharing that smile and laughter with Sean. Then again, he had no claim on the woman and no intentions to make one. Right now all he could offer was a thank you for her hard work in the form of a nice dinner. Anything else was off the table.

Parker found her up on a ladder installing shelves on the back wall of what would eventually become his office. For a moment he stood back and watched her work. He regarded her focus and attention to detail. But that wasn't all he admired about her. She was much shorter in construction boots than high heels, but he damn sure loved her curves in those tight jeans.

Like a pro, she used the electric drill to screw in the anchors. Then she unhooked the tape measure from the pocket of her jeans and measured the space between the screws.

"Perfect." When she leaned away from the wall, gave a nod to her achievement, and high-fived herself, he chuckled.

Before she picked up the electric drill again he stepped up behind her, placed both hands on the ladder, and caged her in. "Thanks for your help. It looks great."

"No problem."

She turned in his arms. Thanks to the rung she

stood on, they were chest to chest. Had they both not been wearing such heavy clothes, her breasts would have pushed right into him and that would have made him damn happy.

"Told you I could handle it."

"Hey." He held up his hands. "I have two kickass sisters. I'm not the kind of guy who would doubt you because you're a girl."

"Well, that might be your first mistake of the day. In case you haven't noticed, I'm not a girl. I'm a woman."

"Oh." He settled his hands on her hips and lifted her down, but still held her close. "Believe me, I've noticed."

"Are we off the clock now, Chef?" She dragged a finger softly across the five o'clock shadow dusting his jaw. "Or do I need to report you to my boss?"

Had a smile not been playing on her pretty mouth he'd have backed away. He wasn't her boss. Not yet anyway.

Maybe not ever.

"How about we call it a day and go get something to eat?" he said.

"What makes you think I don't already have plans?"

"Do you?"

Her brown eyes sparkled as she shrugged and the now dirt-streaked pink sweatshirt brushed over her breasts. "Depends on what you're offering."

He moved his hands to the small of her back and impulsively drew her even closer. "What would you say if I offered you something that will make your mouth water and make you cry for more?"

"I'd say"—her eyes danced over his face and down his chest—"I like the way you think."

Thirty minutes later he delivered on his promise.

"*O*h. My. God. This is amazing."

Parker laughed as Gabriella sank her teeth into another juicy barbecued rib from Cranky Hank's Smokehouse. The sticky sweet sauce covered her fingertips and spread from the corners of her mouth like a wide smile. And she didn't even care.

That impressed the hell out of him.

Most women ordered salads then picked around the bowl to make it look like they were eating when they really weren't. Gabriella had dove into her plate with gusto and was making lusty sounds similar to when he'd been buried deep inside her body.

He was ridiculously turned on. In public. In a brightly lit restaurant. With several snoopy community members eyeballing him like they knew what was going on behind the zipper of his jeans.

"I thought you were a food purist," he joked. "Someone who doesn't believe in changing the taste by smothering or crisping the food to death."

"I am."

"Newsflash." He pointed to her plate. "Those ribs have been smothered in so much sauce they're dripping."

"So sue me." She shrugged. "Every once in a while I like to indulge in something that's really bad for me."

"Oh yeah? Like what, other than barbecued ribs?"

"Like . . . you."

"I'm bad for you?" He didn't know whether to take that as an insult or a compliment.

"Completely." She wagged her half-eaten rib at him. "Before I see you, I have all these good intentions. Plans. Purposes. But when I come within ten feet of you, some kind of weird chemical thing in my body takes over and shuts off all sensible thinking."

"Ten feet, huh. So . . ." He dug his fork into the shredded brisket on his plate without taking his eyes off of her. "What happens when you're within *two* feet of me?"

She gave him a saucy smile. "I end up naked on your dining table."

"I'm perfectly okay with that."

"Really? What happens when the next woman comes over to cook for you? Won't you look at your dining table and feel . . . awkward?"

Awkward? No.

Horny as hell? Oh yeah.

"No one has ever come to my house to cook for me before," he assured her. Unable to picture anyone other than her laid out on that table or any other table, he stabbed at the potato salad on his plate. "Can't imagine it will happen again any time soon."

"So I'm a first?"

And probably a last.

"You fishing, Gabriella?"

She shook her head. "Didn't bring my pole."

Miraculously he avoided blurting out a juvenile response of him having one ready for her. "Well obviously something is on your mind."

"Other than hoping to leave a lasting impression on you *and* your dining table?"

"Yeah. Other than that." He did like her honesty. And the suddenly uncomfortable fit of his jeans told him he was damn well ready to repeat last night right now. But getting kicked out of Cranky Hank's for having sex on the table would spread like gossipy wildfire throughout the valley and he'd never hear the end of it. Plus he wasn't a fan of doing jail time for indecent exposure.

Among other things.

When she sank her teeth into another bite of rib then licked the sauce from her lips, he changed his mind. He was more than willing to bear the brunt of the aftermath.

Pushing away her plate, she wiped her hands and face with the towelettes provided. "I guess I'm curious about what type of menu you plan to have at your restaurant. You haven't said and I'm wondering why you're keeping so tight lipped about it."

"I don't remember you directly asking me."

"Well, consider it asked."

"Truth?"

She nodded. "Always."

"I can't decide."

"Seriously?" She crumpled the used towelettes into a pile on the table.

"Yeah. Go figure. I've dreamed of having this opportunity for years. I thought I'd planned everything down to every minor detail. Like what type of salt I'd put on the tables, what brand of ovens I'd use, and what the serving plates would look like. But now that it's actually happening?" He shrugged. "I can't make up my mind. I feel like the proverbial deer in the headlights."

"Need some help with that?"

Parker hated to admit it, but he wouldn't mind another opinion. The restaurant wasn't something he could discuss with his brothers. Their eyes would glaze over around the time he brought up his ideas for entrées.

Gabriella knew food. And she could cook like nobody's business. He respected that about her.

"I don't know if *help* is the right word," he said.

"Maybe you just need to relax a little." She wadded up her napkin and set it on the table.

"I'm not sure I even know how to relax anymore," he said, even though she'd left him completely relaxed last night. "There's a lot riding on getting the restaurant open and making it a success. I thought I was ready, but with everything that's happened this past year, maybe I was wrong."

He hated admitting weakness. Especially to someone he didn't really know all that well. But there it was.

"Well no wonder your creativity is all tangled up. Right now everything is about business and construction. And you're too tired at the end of the day to dream." She reached across the table and settled her soft hand on top of his. "I've got an idea. How about we take this discussion back to the restaurant? Sometimes the atmosphere of a place will lead you in the right direction."

And sometimes the atmosphere of a place just made him want to remove her clothes with his teeth. Not that he apparently needed a specific atmosphere to reach that conclusion.

"You don't want dessert?" he asked.

"Of course I do."

When she looked up at him with a hint of suggestion in those deep brown eyes he wondered if she had a replay of last night in mind.

He sure as hell hoped so.

The moment they walked through the barn door, Gabi knew she needed to pull back on the reins of her enthusiasm. This wasn't her restaurant. It wasn't her dream. That honor belonged to Parker. And though she had a million ideas spinning through her head, she could only share a portion so she didn't override his passion.

Or worse, piss him off so he wouldn't hire her.

From the moment her father had told her she didn't have what it took to be a success in *his world*, she'd fantasized about taking over his restaurants in

New York, Chicago, and Las Vegas and completely making them her own. The truth didn't occur to her until she'd matured a little and her anger based notions dissolved.

Taking over what her father had already created would never prove anything.

Once she'd finally gotten that figured out she realized she needed to create her own culinary universe. Whether that meant someday she'd own a restaurant of her own or be the head chef somewhere fabulous, she had no clue. But the eager dragon that lived and breathed within her sometimes drove her too fast and too hard. And sometimes it drove people away.

Parker deserved to have his own dream come true. She could never be so selfish as to put her own wants first. Exactly what that meant she wasn't sure because that's all she'd been thinking of lately. But somehow, in the past two days, he'd become far more important than just a one-night stand.

The realization snuck up on her like a Halloween scare and she had to take a deep breath. Put things in perspective. The sexual chemistry they had was off the charts, but they'd made a deal.

One night.

And so, she'd do her absolute best to keep her desire, her overenthusiastic mouth, and her ideas on lockdown. And she'd do her best to support him in his quest to make his own dream come true.

Even if that meant hers had to wait just a little longer.

"Sorry it's so cold in here," he said, closing the

door behind him. He switched on a camping lantern supported by a makeshift table held up by two saw-horses. "The heating and cooling system hasn't been installed yet. Neither has the lighting. You sure you want to do this here?"

"Yes." She turned and found him standing there with his hands thrust into the pockets of his heavy-weight coat. Behind him a beam of moonlight shone through the window and glistened against his dark hair. He looked so good she wanted to crawl inside that big coat and wrap herself around his warm body.

"I want to do this here," she added. "The cold can help us imagine what it might be like when you have your grand opening in the next couple of months and the types of meals that will warm up your customers."

"Actually . . ."

He moved closer and everything inside of her that had wanted him last night at his houseboat wanted him right now in this cold, half-finished shell of a barn.

"The restaurant won't open to the public until mid-January. But everything needs to be completed before Christmas," he said. "Jordan and Lucy want to have their wedding reception here. Which doesn't make any sense at all when there's a perfectly pleasant event center on the property."

"Are you talking about Groomzilla?"

"The one and only."

"I don't care what you say, he sounds sweet. Like

he really wants to make it special for his bride-to-be."
Gabi could only hope that someday she'd be lucky
enough to find a man who would love her as much.

"He does," Parker admitted. "That's why I'm busting my ass to get it done on time."

"Because you love your brother."

"I love all of them."

"All?" There were more amazing-looking Kincade
men? Impossible. "How many more?"

"Four brothers. Two sisters. Oddly, until a few
months ago I only had one sister."

"But I thought your parents . . ."

"Died earlier this year. Our new sister, Lili, is an
adult. Our father had an affair with her mother."

"Wow."

His eyes narrowed. "Shocked?"

"No. I can just . . . relate. I mean, obviously I can't
compare the situations, but my father also had an
affair when he was married to my mother."

That much she could reveal without giving away
her father's identity. "I have two much younger half
sisters I'll probably never get to know." God knows
she'd tried. But she'd been refused by their mother,
who held as much animosity toward Gabi's father as
Gabi's own mother did. She really couldn't blame
either woman. Of course, he hadn't been able to stick
with that relationship either. He'd moved on and was
now cavorting around with a woman a few years
younger than Gabi.

While that might be embarrassing for her person-

ally, she couldn't help feeling more sorry for the innocent children he'd created that he'd never care for.
Never be a father to. The whole thing just made her
heart ache. Because even though she didn't know her
half sisters—may never know them—she knew how
it felt to be abandoned by your father.

"So I think it's wonderful that you're getting to
know your new sister," Gabi said.

"I'm sorry you have to go through that." Genuine
empathy darkened the tone in his voice.

"You too. You're lucky you have an opportunity
with Lili."

"It's not her fault our father cheated on our mother
or treated her and her mother like shit. It's not any
of our faults. So why should anyone be further
punished?" He shrugged his broad shoulders. "Her
mother recently passed away and Lili's all alone. The
vineyard is a family business. *She's* family. And she
has talents that fit. So we might as well all make this
work out together."

Gabi admired that Parker was the kind of man who
would welcome someone with open arms instead
of pushing them away. She liked that his thoughts
and emotions went beyond the surface, and that he
seemed to be the type of man who didn't rush to
judgment or want to punish someone for another's
doings. That showed real character.

When it came to figuring out his restaurant menu,
his mental roadblock might be bigger than he realized. He'd been through a huge emotional roller

coaster since his parents died. The pressure to get the restaurant done in time for his brother's wedding added extra stress. Also, running a busy full-time business that began before the crack of dawn each day was bound to cause anyone to stumble. More than likely the man just needed to relax a little so he could figure things out.

Or . . . maybe he needed just the opposite. Maybe he needed to get really riled up about something to get his blood boiling.

Her *nonni* often said that passion could be a great motivator. If that was the case, Gabi would happily volunteer to help the sexy man blow off a little steam.

"You do have a big family. That might be a little intimidating for her," she said of Lili. "I imagine it would take some getting used to."

"Oh." He snapped his fingers. "Can't forget we also have Ryan's little girl, Riley, and Aunt Pippy. Until Jordan and Lucy get married, she'll stay up at the main house with our teenage sister, Nicole."

"Pippy? Unique name."

"Unique woman." He chuckled affectionately. "It's a nickname for Penelope. She's a little on the quirky side. Thinks it's still the make-love-not-war era. Or at least that's what her psychedelic wardrobe, makeup, and jewelry tell us."

Gabi thought of her *nonni*, who was the complete opposite, and favored a long calico print apron that had gone out of style a century ago. "I think I'd like to meet your aunt Pippy."

"Careful what you wish for." Parker led her by the elbow deeper into the restaurant where it was a tad bit warmer. His unexpected touch sent a tingle up her arm and into her chest. "Sorry I can't offer you a chair, but I can pull up a bucket."

"I have a better idea. Let's go into the kitchen. Maybe the surroundings will give you some culinary inspiration."

"Whatever you want."

Now there was a dangerous thought.

"Might be warmer in there too." He grabbed the lantern and led her through the shiny new stainless door.

Might be a whole lot warmer if he'd just wrap his arms around her.

She glanced around the empty room that would eventually become a kitchen and ordered herself to stay focused.

"Show me where everything will go." She took a step back toward the wall to give him space. "I want to picture it in my head."

He looked at her funny.

Yeah. She definitely needed to pull back on the enthusiasm.

"It's a basic floor plan. The walk-in cooler goes there." He pointed. "Oven, grill, and burners here. Salad station there. Assembly station there. Pickup over there."

"Well you certainly have all that figured out." She folded her arms. "So what kind of food do you see plated at the pickup station?"

"I don't know." He scratched his head and sighed. "Don't get me wrong. I've done my homework. Done research on the target audience. Talked to a few local chefs who have a steady clientele. And I know my budget and expenses."

"Great groundwork. Have you chosen a name for the place?"

"Sunshine & Vine."

"I like that. It opens the door for all kinds of ideas. What style are you thinking? A flashy hot spot? Bistro? Grill? Café?"

"We won't be open all day or even every day. It will be specialized to dinners, desserts, and wine. Catering mostly to middle-aged adults with combined salaries over $150K. Eventually I'd like it to be a destination restaurant. Somewhere people are willing to drive a distance to get to."

"Then what's your menu style? Table d'hôte? A la carte? Static? Cycle?"

"Signature a la carte with daily specialties."

"Casual or fine dining?"

"Fine." He chuckled. "Do you ever take a breath?"

"Not when there's stuff to figure out. Cuisine style?"

He dropped his chin. "And there lies the problem."

"But you have everything else figured out."

His gaze came up and found hers. "It's not that easy."

"It *is* that easy, Parker. You've selected a name that invokes a classy atmosphere. You already have a built-in vineyard theme. Your restaurant is in an old wooden barn. You have a running creek within a stone's throw of the restaurant. From the looks of the construction going on with the rest of the vineyard, it looks like your renovations will add an Old World atmosphere. You know you're not creating a build-a-burger joint and you're not going to serve fried chicken and corn-on-the-cob. It should be easy."

"Well, it's not." When his jaw clenched she realized she'd pushed him. And that was good. Exactly what needed to happen to move him off his stumbling block.

He'd been answering all her questions mechanically, without the passion she knew he personified. She knew he had an eclectic style because she'd seen and tasted his food truck menu. She needed to keep pushing him through the obstacle that was keeping him from pulling his dream together and nicely tying it up with a bow.

"Want to know what *I'd* do with this place?" she asked, knowing he probably didn't.

"I'm sure you're going to tell me whether I want to know or not." He crossed his arms. "Right?"

"See what a smart man you are?" She cracked a smile to see if he'd give one back. He didn't, but the furrow in his brow did deepen.

"First of all," she said, "I'd really specialize it. If possible, I'd use some of the open property to create a restaurant garden. A place where you could grow fresh herbs and vegetables for the dishes you'll prepare. Pacific Northwesterners *love* organic."

"I don't know if the growing season here would sustain it all year."

"Then build a greenhouse to give things a jump start or extend the season. It doesn't have to be huge, just big enough to help tie things into what makes your place special."

His jaw-clenched silence said he was either contemplating her idea or considering choking her.

"As far as the menu goes, I'd go for traditional," she said. "Freshly caught seafood married with light and fresh pastas. If you have ranchers nearby you could serve local beef or free-range poultry. Light fare. Nothing too heavy. Celebrate your dishes with a dash of what you grow on those vines out there. Create entrées that reflect the surroundings."

"You've given this some thought." He spoke in not so much of a snarl as a grumble. Maybe because he hadn't been the one to come up with it first.

"I have a lot of spare time," she said. Thanks to being unemployed, a fact of which he was unaware and a fact she planned to keep private. If he hired her she wanted it to be because he knew she was qualified, not because he was doing her a favor so she didn't end up eating at a soup kitchen. "Tossing a frozen pizza in the oven or popcorn in the microwave for your employer doesn't take much brain power."

"Those are all interesting suggestions," he admitted. "And not at all close to what I've been mulling over in my head."

"You mean you don't have fantasies about popping

microwave kettle corn?" She flashed him another smile but he was still too deep in his own tangle of thoughts to reciprocate.

So she pushed some more.

"So what kind of menu have you been mulling over? Calamari and escargot? Bratwurst and beer? Tacos and margaritas?"

"Those aren't my style."

"Then what *is* your style? It's hard to tell. Your food truck menu is very . . . eclectic."

Both eyebrows shot up his forehead. "Is that an insult?"

"Not at all. I value creativity. Even if it sometimes seems a little . . . schizophrenic."

"The food truck business does great," he protested.

"I don't doubt that. I've sampled the menu and everything I've tasted is amazing. Although there are some days I'm not sure your customers are really there for the food."

His head went back like she'd slapped him. "What do you mean by that?"

"I mean they think you're hot. They go there to see *you*. To flirt with you. Hope for a date with you. Or maybe just some heavy petting in the back of your food truck."

"My customers aren't all women."

"I wasn't talking about *just* the women."

His brows pulled together.

"Kidding!"

"I don't even know what to say to that."

"Okay." Perfect. Now she had his mind off all the things that had it clogged up. "Then *say* your five top menu sellers."

"Easy. Pan-seared halibut crusted with roasted, crushed pumpkin seeds." He counted the dishes off with his fingers. "Pork chops with maple-apple chutney and bacon au jus. New York steak sandwich. Slow-roasted chicken and dumplings. And . . . I'd have to say the eggplant caponata and the ricotta stuffed tortellini would probably be a tie."

"What a wonderful, flavorful variety," she said.

"I like to change things up."

"And you've been successful at it."

"I have."

"So why are you so confused about creating the menu for Sunshine & Vine? The answer seems simple to me."

"That's probably because you don't have everything riding on its success."

"Ah. So now we get down to the truth." Unable to resist the worried furrow to his brow and the tight clench to his jaw, she wrapped her fingers in the front of his jacket. "You're afraid you'll fail."

"Maybe."

Absently, she stroked her fingertip down the icy teeth of the coat's zipper. "Were you this nervous when you first opened the food truck?"

"Not really."

"So you're more nervous this time because . . ."

"Because I'm building the restaurant on vineyard

property to help my family. To help make the family business profitable again. To help ensure that the future generations of our family can continue the legacy our grandfather started."

Family.

Her heart squeezed knowing how deeply he cared for them.

"You know what I think?"

"I'm afraid to ask."

She chuckled. "I think you're an amazing man. And I have no doubt that you and your restaurant will succeed."

"But mostly . . ." A slow smile tipped his delicious mouth as he moved in closer. The scent of warm man triggered all her womanly senses. "You think I'm hot."

She laughed. "As a wildfire burning out of control."

"That's pretty cheesy."

When he put his hands on her hips and brought her up against him she knew she'd not only hit some hot buttons, she'd ignited some sexual interest too. Totally not her intent. Still . . .

"And for you to pretend that you don't know you're good looking is even cheesier," she said.

"Then I guess it's a good thing we're standing in a kitchen, or all this cheesiness could get really messy."

Shoving her good intentions in a mental lockbox, she slipped her hand into the front of his jacket. "Is it?"

"Is it what?"

"About to get messy?"

"I think we're way past messy." He leaned his big warm body against her. "I think we're headed into virtual meltdown territory."

He cupped her face between his hands and tilted her head for a deep, lingering kiss that promised good and naked things to come. As his tongue slicked against hers and he led her into a sensuous dance that made her nipples hard, his erection pressed against the crux of her thighs and roused the lust patrol in her panties.

Kissing Parker was like all the best things coming together. If she thought about it too much, it would scare the daylights out of her. So she didn't think. Instead she wrapped her arms around his neck, lifted to the toes of her boots, and put everything she had into kissing him back.

Kissing Gabriella might be his current favorite thing. She was incredibly sexy and desirable. And as much as he might try to deny it, there was some kind of crazy chemistry between the two of them that made him act unreasonably and think irrationally.

Right now, he should only be focused on getting his restaurant done in time for Jordan and Lucy's wedding. But that wasn't stopping his hands from sliding beneath Gabriella's sweatshirt so he could touch her warm, silky skin and cup her more than ample breasts in the palms of his hands.

On a sigh her lips parted and she opened to him.

The sweetness of the barbecue sauce she'd had at dinner lingered on her tongue and he couldn't get enough. When her icy hands snuck beneath his shirt and touched his skin, he shivered, even as his dick grew harder. Right then, all he could think about was getting her heated up, naked, and under him.

"Parker?"

A female voice. *Not* Gabriella's.

His head snapped up. "Fuck."

"Who is it?"

"Nicki. My little sister." While Gabriella licked her lips, he tried to subdue the erection pushed against the zipper of his jeans. "I need to see what she wants."

"Okay."

"Stay here. Just like that." He pressed his mouth to hers once more before he broke contact and backed away. "I'll be right back."

"Okay."

"Promise."

When she gave him a nod he pushed through the door and out into the dining area when all he really wanted was to stay right there, strip her down, and make her sigh.

# Chapter 7

Parker found Nicole by the front door holding a flashlight and shivering in a pair of Ugg boots with a fuzzy hooded white parka over her cat pajamas.

"Nicki? What are you doing here? It's late."

"I've been working on a new song all night and I got stuck on the lyrics, so I thought I'd take a walk. I saw a light on in here and noticed your car parked out front. I thought you were still working, so I thought I'd drop by and say hi."

There were times when Parker looked at his eighteen-year-old sister and saw a young woman ready to start her adventure in life. There were other times—like right now—when he looked at her and still saw the little girl who used to tag along behind him and his brothers, wanting so badly to be a part of the pack.

The glittery pink tutus and tiaras she'd constantly worn hadn't helped her fit in with the boys. The fact that they were all so much older than her hadn't helped either. Tonight, with her pretty face surrounded by the fur on the hood of her jacket and the cartoon cat pajamas, she looked like a little girl again. Unfortunately she was a girl with a lot of baggage on her small shoulders, so he opened his arms and pulled her into a hug.

"I'm glad you came by," he said. "But you're shivering like you've been stuck in a freezer."

"Yeah. The weather is definitely getting colder. But the fresh air always helps me think. And I'm searching for the perfect line for the song."

"For Jordy's wedding?"

Nicki nodded. "I already wrote one, but the more I play it the less I like it. So since I have a few weeks, I decided to start from scratch."

"I'm sure whatever you create Jordan and Lucy will love it."

"I hope so." She shrugged as her gaze darted around the room. "Wow. You're really making progress."

"That's the plan. I guess both of us have Jordan's wedding on the mind." Currently an out-and-out lie on his part because all he could really think about was that Gabriella was waiting for him to come strip her down and heat up the kitchen.

"Do you think you'll have the place done in time?" Nicki asked.

Parker pushed out a breath. "I'm busting my ass to make it happen. As long as the construction crew stays on task, the equipment arrives on time, and everything passes inspection, I'd say there's a chance."

"I'll keep my fingers crossed."

"I'd appreciate that."

"The big glass doors are new from the last plans I saw," Nicki said with a nod toward the back wall.

"Yeah. Someone suggested it," he said. "I thought it was a good idea. Now we can have a dining patio on the back that will overlook the vineyard and creek and add a place for smaller parties and receptions."

"*Someone* who?"

Shit. He didn't want to bring up Lili's name. There was still too much animosity on Nicki's part. But at some point, Nicki had to deal with the truth. And though he wanted to protect his sister—hell, all the members of his family—from any further heartache, it didn't look like today was that day.

"Lili suggested it. She's family too. And just like anyone else, she's got a right to be a part of the development of the vineyard."

"That's not the way I see it."

"Shit, Nicki." Frustrated and tired of the recycled conversation, Parker shoved his fingers through his hair. "Why do you have to make everything an argument?"

"I'm not arguing." Nicki lifted her chin. "You're the one getting all defensive."

"Of course I am. Because how are we going to resolve this?" he asked her. "How can we all possibly work together to build a future if you won't even give it a chance? I understand your feelings—"

"No you don't."

"I do. Believe me, I do. But just like nothing you

ever did had anything to do with Dad's behavior toward you, Lili's in the same place. She didn't ask for him to be her father. She didn't ask for him to abandon her in the same way he abandoned you. She didn't have anything to do with the choices our father made. You've both been dealt a shitty hand. And you both have more in common than you're willing to admit. You should be pulling together instead of pushing her away."

Huge tears floated in her eyes. "Are you choosing her over me?"

"Of course not." He hugged her again even though he wanted to grab her by the shoulders and shake some sense into her. "There are no sides. That's what you have to understand. We're all in this together. Nobody likes what happened. Nobody likes the situation. But we're the only ones who can turn a negative into a positive, Nic. We can't let the choices or the sins of our parents become our own. We have to fight—to come together—and be there for each other. Otherwise it will destroy us all. Don't you see that?"

Nicole wiped her damp eyes with the sleeve of her coat. "You make it sound so easy."

"I know it's not easy. It's all kinds of fucked up. But life is what you make it. And unless you want to be miserable for the rest of your life just so you'll have more fuel for your songwriting, it's not worth the energy to stay pissed."

"I'd rather write happy songs."

"Then live a happy life." Parker hugged her again,

this time staying in the hold until he felt her body relax.

"You can let go of me now," she said with her face muffled against his coat.

"Nope."

"I can't breathe."

"Still a nope."

She slapped him on the arm and giggled. "You're such a dork."

"But I'm a dork that loves you. And I want you to be happy." He held her away so he could look into her eyes. "You need to start talking to the rest of us more, Nic. Don't hold all this in. We're here for you. Every stupid one of us is here for you. Anytime. Anywhere. We may not have all the answers but we'll try hard to find them."

"I know."

"And you should really try to open your heart toward Lili. Don't blame her for something that wasn't her fault. If you give her a chance, I think you might be pleasantly surprised at what you'll find."

Before she could answer, he pulled her back into his arms again until she nodded against his coat.

"Okay. I'll try."

"Love you, Nicki."

Her arms finally came up and she hugged him. "Love you more."

"Impossible."

After several moments of a swaying embrace, they eased apart.

"Now get back to the house and finish that song for Groomzilla," Parker told her. "And make some hot chocolate to warm up. Double the marshmallows."

"Yes, Dad." She gave him a little salute before she turned in her Ugg boots and left.

As he watched her go, Parker's chest tightened and he pressed his fist tight against the center, wishing he could protect her from all the ugliness in the world.

One day when he had his own children, he'd make damn sure his top priority was that he and their mother maintained an honest, loving relationship until the day they died. He believed in the power and the honesty of marriage vows. Without an absolute dedication to upholding them, everyone—especially the children—suffered. And that hard lesson, as he'd recently learned, was completely unacceptable.

He rubbed the center of his chest, willing the ache to go away. Holding back the urge to cry from all the lies, the losses, the lingering devastation for everyone involved. All his life he'd thought his parents had one of those marriages that nothing could shake, rattle, or destroy. He'd just never imagined how badly, once cracked, the foundation could shatter.

Inhaling a hard breath, he suddenly remembered he'd left Gabriella alone in the kitchen.

The woman had an uncanny understanding of things. And she'd hinted that she'd traveled some rough roads of her own. She had a warm embrace and a soft place that made his heart feel good.

Right now he needed to let this all go. He needed someone to hold. Someone to tell him everything was going to be okay.

Even if it was a damn lie.

He pushed through the stainless door, but the kitchen was empty. He opened the back door and stepped outside. The entire area as far as he could see was void of another living soul.

Gabriella was gone.

And once again he had no way to contact her. No way to know if she'd arrived home safe and sound.

Damn she was good at this disappearing act shit.

Maybe he should just let her go and forget the whole thing. After all, they'd agreed on one night.

And it had been one hot, crazy, unforgettable night.

Shaking his head, he pulled his cell phone from his pocket and tapped Lucy's name in his contact list. When his call went straight to voicemail he hung up without leaving a message. Then he tapped on another contact and called in the cavalry.

*S*haken to the core, Gabi drove her little car through the rolling hills of Sunshine Valley toward home.

She never should have eavesdropped.

The last time she'd had the displeasure of doing so had been when her mother had called out her father for having an affair. That argument had led to their divorce and the subsequent destruction of Gabi's entire world. She'd been a fragile, self-conscious suburban

Chicago high schooler at the time. An age where appearances were everything and gossip could shatter your spirit.

She'd once been a proud member of the popular crowd. A cheerleader. A member of the honor society. And though she'd personally never done anything to embarrass or hurt anyone else, she'd seen how some of her friends had treated others with less care and consideration. When the bomb detonated on her life, instead of understanding her situation and caring for her like friends should do, they'd turned on her like a pack of wild dogs.

At a time when she'd been devastated by her father's betrayal and her mother's subsequent withdrawal from any kind of participation in her life, she'd been completely shattered by those she'd once called friends.

This time her eavesdropping had been eye opening in a completely different kind of way.

Listening to Parker talk to his sister with so much love and passion opened up something inside of Gabi. She knew he was a decent person; otherwise she'd never have slept with him. But having the opportunity to actually watch, or in this case hear, his love and compassion broke something loose inside of her.

For years she'd compared every guy she'd dated to her father—and not in a good way. She always felt like she was waiting for the other shoe to drop, or for him to show the true colors he'd most likely been hiding. For a while she'd even made it a point to only date *leavers* because she knew eventually they would.

At the end of the day she hadn't needed a therapist to tell her she had daddy issues. Which was why she'd stopped dating altogether and bought Basil for male companionship. He could make all the threats he wanted by flashing his colorful tail, but in the end, she knew he'd never leave her until he went to the big fish bowl in the sky.

But if she were ever in the market for a forever guy, Parker would top the list. She knew he'd be the kind of man who'd commit to loving someone and he'd give it his all. He'd protect them and their hearts at all costs.

Gabi couldn't ever remember having that kind of love or security. And as appealing as it might be, she had a long way to go before she could even consider being in that kind of relationship with that kind of man.

No matter how good it sounded.

Falling in love wasn't anywhere on her radar. But she was human, and she tried to keep hope alive that not all men were dogs. Tonight, Parker had proven himself to be a prince. If she were to actually work side by side with him, the inevitability that she'd fall head over heels existed. He had everything going for him. He was gorgeous, kind, polite, caring, and protective. He had a plan for his life and he was going after it two hundred percent. He was responsible and funny. And he made love to her with care, consideration, and a whole lot of *hell yeah*.

So how could she *not* fall in love?

*E*arly Sunday morning Gabi took a cool shower to wake up. Last night her mind had refused to shut off and sleeping had become impossible. Even when she'd tried to turn her thoughts to something other than Parker Kincade, they circled right back around again.

She couldn't work *for* him.

She couldn't work *with* him.

She had to distance herself from him before she got too involved.

She realized that now.

Unfortunately she'd banked everything on Plan A and had nothing as a backup.

Currently she was unemployed with a savings account that would only cover a couple of months. That was it. A stupid move to quit her job for sure. But even without the prospect of working at Parker's Sunshine & Vine, she knew she couldn't have lasted another day working for an employer who not only didn't respect good food, he didn't respect her, or even himself.

The day she'd quit, the noose had tightened. If her life depended on it, she knew she couldn't make one more PB&J. Couldn't shove one more frozen pizza in the oven. Couldn't microwave one more bag of popcorn. And no way would she deal with having to thwart his wandering hands.

Now the holidays loomed. She had presents to buy, rent to pay, and fish pellets to provide for Basil who currently swam around in his bowl like he didn't have a care in the world.

She had to make a new plan.

One that didn't involve Parker or his restaurant. She had to find a way to make a professional name for herself to reclaim her pride. To prove her father wrong. And she had to keep a tight hold on her heart until she made that happen.

But on this dark and dreary Sunday, there was an opportunity for her to spread her love in another way and lift her spirits at the same time. When she felt good she thought clearer. Outside the box.

Yes, that's exactly what she needed to do.

She needed to stop thinking about herself and put that energy into helping someone else.

In full *go* mode, she went to the pantry and pulled out an armload of ingredients. Then she took out a few of the large disposable aluminum pans she kept on hand. She got busy turning on the oven and stove burners, and pulling everything to the center of the small kitchen island she'd purchased to give her more counter space in her dinky one bedroom apartment.

As she filled the pots with water, Basil swam up to the glass of his bowl, pursed his fish lips, and blew a bubble.

"Oh. So now you want to get chummy? Where were you when I needed a friend a few minutes ago?"

Basil blew another bubble then turned his tail and, once again, disappeared behind his plastic foliage.

"Careful, buster, or I'll replace you with a cat."

Just as she reached into the lower cupboard to bring out her big stainless mixing bowl, the doorbell rang.

She glanced at the clock and wondered who could be at her door before noon on Sunday. Surely it wasn't the nosy Mrs. Flagstone two buildings down. No doubt she'd be at church, praying for the souls of people like Gabi who only hit the pews on rare occasions. Then again, maybe Mrs. Flagstone had the right idea. Maybe if Gabi invested a little more time in prayer, her circumstances might change. But Gabi had never been the type to think it was okay to call on God to fix the mess that had become of her life.

She could do this.

God had plenty of other things to take care of.

When the bell rang again, Gabi had no choice but to answer.

She flipped the locks, swung open the door, and couldn't believe her eyes when she found a sexy, dark-haired, blue-eyed man leaning casually against her doorway.

"*H*ello, Houdini."

Parker knew he shouldn't start the visit with sarcasm, but the moment he'd opened his mouth it just came spewing out. He'd spent the entire sleepless night worrying about why she'd disappeared and if she'd made it home okay. Then he'd dealt with a construction crew who'd shown up at o-dark-thirty to begin installing the foundation for the heating and cooling system and they'd needed his help. Finally he'd managed to grab a shower up at the main house, where he'd had to dodge Aunt Pippy's efforts to force-feed him a plate of cinnamon rolls from Sugarbuns Bakery. And where she'd efficiently dodged him about the information she needed to reveal about his father's affair.

A short while later he'd managed to shoot out the door to zip back to Portland. No thanks to Google Maps, he'd spent the last twenty minutes trying to locate Gabriella's place in the maze of buildings and overgrown foliage that made up her apartment complex.

"What are you doing here?" she asked. Her wide eyes revealed that finding him at her door had been the last thing she'd expected.

"Aren't you going to invite me in?"

Her teeth snagged her lush lower lip while she gave his question some consideration.

Just when he thought she'd extend the invitation she proved him wrong. "How did you find me?"

"I sold my soul to the devil."

"You shouldn't have made the deal. Or the effort."

Too bad.

He wanted to know why the hell she kept disappearing. Especially last night when they'd obviously been on the same lust-driven page. Before he'd gone to talk to Nicole, everything had seemed fine. And yet, Gabriella had vanished without a word.

"Look." He eased his shoulder off the doorjamb and took a step closer. She smelled sweet and fresh like sugar and lemons. The crazy desire to bury his face in the curve of her neck and gently suck on her soft flesh until she moaned overwhelmed him. "We can stand here playing the fifty-questions game, or you can invite me in so we can talk."

"I'm busy."

He glanced over her shoulder at the empty apartment. "Really?"

"Really."

"Or are you really just trying to keep me out because you have another guy hidden in there?"

"I'm busy."

"Well, lucky for you, I'm a big helper." He pushed past her and walked into the small but tidy apartment. He was impressed that the place wasn't decorated like total Girlyville with lace and ruffles. Instead she'd cleverly filled the space with a traditional style in welcoming shades of brown and accented everything with pops of green from a healthy array of plants. Mostly herbs. So maybe when she suggested he create a garden for his restaurant she knew what she was talking about.

"Nice place."

For a moment she stood there as though trying to decide whether to close the door or kick him out. Finally, she sighed her resignation and shut the door. Clearly she hadn't been expecting company.

Least of all him.

A pair of yoga pants with a zebra print waistband and a hot pink sports bra accented her luscious curves. Her feet were stuffed into fuzzy house shoes. And her long, silky hair was pulled up on top of her head in one of those messy just-out-of-bed buns. Not an ounce of makeup covered her face and she wore a pair of dark-framed glasses.

She looked sexy as hell.

And he was definitely going to have a hard time keeping his hands to himself.

"I didn't know you wore glasses," he said, moving further into the apartment where several stockpots of water had started to boil and steam on the stove.

"You've only known me for a week."

"So . . . contacts the rest of the time?"

"The answer to that is pretty obvious. So let's go back to my original questions." She crossed her arms and tilted her head. "What are you doing here? And exactly how did you find me?"

"I have friends in high places with access to things like the address of a woman who keeps popping into my life then disappearing without telling me her phone number. I had to come see for myself that she's who she says she is and isn't just a figment of my imagination. And especially not that she keeps disappearing because she's involved with another man."

He glanced around the apartment again. "So are you? Because that's the only reason I can come up with that you keep disappearing."

"I'm not involved with *any* man. But aside from that, do I look like the kind of woman who'd be involved with more than one guy at a time?"

"Sweetheart, you look like the kind of woman who needs to be taken back to bed and shown a good time. But I'm thinking that if you already had a guy doing that, you wouldn't have come on to me."

"*I* came on to *you*?" Her dark eyes widened and her luscious mouth dropped open.

"That's my story."

"Well, your story could use a few revisions."

He shrugged, strolled into the small kitchen, looked into the boiling pots of water, and checked out the ingredients on the counter. "What are you trying to make?"

"Sense of what you're doing here," she said, clearly agitated, but not enough to put the effort into a full-blown hissy fit.

"Just wanted to make sure you got home okay."

"You expect me to buy that?"

At the sharpness in her tone, he looked up from the cellophane packages of noodles and boxes of panko breadcrumbs on the counter. "Yes."

"As you can see, I'm fine." She pushed back a strand of hair that had escaped the bun on her head.

"Is that my cue to leave?"

"Your cue to leave was the frown I gave you when I opened the door."

"Look. I'm sorry. I would have called. But I didn't have your number."

"I gave it to Lucy."

"Lucy was busy doing future-wife things with my brother."

The hint of a smile touched her lips. "In other words they were intimately engaged and you didn't have the heart to interrupt?"

"In other words, if I'd have interrupted, Groomzilla would have taken off my head and used it as a pumpkin decoration."

Her smile grew just slightly.

"Look. I'm not usually a stalker kind of guy. But you've shown up three times saying you want to work for me at my restaurant. You've cooked a spectacular meal for me. I've seen you naked. I've had my mouth on most of your delicious body. And I know the sounds you make when you come the first, second, third, *and* fourth time." He came around the kitchen island to stand in front of her. "So what part of all that says I don't deserve to have your number so I can make sure you're okay when you take off like the Road Runner with Wile E. Coyote on your tail?"

"When you put it like that, I guess you're probably right."

"You guess?" It wasn't anger, fear, or embarrassment that tinged her beautiful face with shades of pink, it was something else. And he needed to find out what.

When he moved close, settled his hand on her hip, and drew her toward him, she didn't resist.

"Last night when I went back into the kitchen and you were gone, I was genuinely worried. Not that we've ever had any kind of incident at the vineyard, but you were just . . . gone. Again. No goodbye. No *you're a jerk, Parker Kincade, and I never want to see you again.* Nothing. Zip. Nada." He shrugged. "So sue me. I'm a worrier."

"I'm sorry." She glanced away. "Bad habit."

"Of running?"

She nodded.

"Why?"

"Trust issues."

He searched her face for any sign of BS, but all he found was an expression of total honesty.

Now they were getting somewhere.

"Well *trust me*, Gabriella, you have no reason to run from me. Got that?" He settled both hands on her hips and lowered his head to kiss her.

Effectively dodging him, she edged her head back. "I'm not sure this is a good idea."

"Kissing?"

Again he received a nod.

"Kissing is a great idea." He captured her mouth to prove it.

A moment of hesitation lingered before she wrapped her arms around his neck and leaned into his body.

Reluctantly he ended the kiss, and not just because he didn't want her to think he'd only come here for sex. Even as mind-blowing as it had been. He honestly wanted to know what was going on with her, what was up with the array of ingredients on her counter, and why she tried to be so secretive.

"You want coffee?" She blushed like that had been their first kiss. Like he hadn't previously had his mouth on some of her most private places.

"Love some."

"Pumpkin spice creamer?" She opened the refrigerator door. "Sugar?"

"Black."

"Huh. I figured you for a fancy coffee kind of guy."

"Why would you think that?"

"Because it's obvious that you enjoy flavor. Black coffee is kind of boring." She removed a vintage sugar container in the shape of an English country cottage from the cupboard. "And you are far from a boring kind of guy."

"Thank you. I try to be as least uninteresting as possible. Nice to know someone noticed."

She poured his coffee into a Waffle House mug and slid it to him across the counter.

He held up the mug, read the logo, and laughed. "Somewhere you frequent often?"

"I wish. If we had one here I'd be tempted to go every day."

"So are you a fan of the waffles or hash browns?"

"Hash browns. Smothered, covered, and capped, thank you very much."

"I promise I won't judge."

"Have you ever eaten there?"

"Can't say I have." He sipped the strong coffee.

"Well, you don't know what you're missing. I myself am rather fond of dive bars and restaurants." She poured several boxes of noodles into the boiling water and gave each a quick stir. "So who's your friend in high places that hunted me down for you?"

"I could tell you but then I'd have to kill you."

"Tell me or I *will* kill *you*."

"Ease up, cowgirl. I called in a favor from a buddy in law enforcement who owed me one. Still had to bribe him with a steak dinner. By the way, you don't have any outstanding warrants."

"Funny. Why didn't you just pay one of those sites on the internet like PeopleFinder? It probably would have cost you less than the steak dinner."

"Finding you at any cost was worth it."

Great. Now he sounded like a total bullshitter. Or maybe he was totally telling her the truth. Chances were she was right. He probably shouldn't have come here. They'd had their one night. Still, if she was going to work for him, shouldn't he know a little more about her?

Good excuse.

She set down the wooden spoon and gave him a look. "I don't know whether to be flattered that you cared enough or ticked off that you invaded my personal info."

"I'm going to vote for the flattered option."

No smile crossed her lips as she studied him for an uncomfortably long moment. Then she said, "Jury's still out."

"I've got time. How about another cup of coffee?" He pushed the half-empty mug toward her for a refill then pointed at the stove when really, he should retreat and get the hell out of there. "So what are you making?"

"The ultimate macaroni and cheese."

"The *ultimate*?"

"Baked. Three cheeses. Topped with panko bread-crumbs. And the secret weapon." She reached inside the refrigerator, pulled out a slab of bacon, and held it up. "Bacon makes everything taste better."

"On that we agree. So is this for a party or something? Those are some pretty big foil pans."

"If you really want to know, why don't you ask your cop friend? Maybe he can do another bio search on me."

Regret tightened his throat. "Are you really pissed?"

Her shoulders lifted on a sigh as she pushed the refilled mug his way. "No."

"Good. Because I really did worry about you. Not just last night but after you left my house on Friday too."

"You did?"

He nodded.

Her expression softened. "I'm not used to having someone worry about me."

With one sentence she delivered another bit of telling information she probably hadn't planned to reveal. Before he could delve deeper, her cell rang. She glanced at the number and smiled.

"Sorry, I have to take this." She put the phone to her ear. "Nonni!"

Parker watched her face light up before she disappeared from the room and closed her bedroom door. Somebody cared about her. Not that he was eavesdropping, but without any effort he could hear her muffled side of the lively conversation.

In Italian.

Though he couldn't understand one damn word, he could tell it was a good call from the amount of laughter and vocal inflections. And yeah, she may have been talking to her grandmother, but hearing her speak fluent Italian was sexy as hell.

Several minutes later he heard her say, *"Addio, Nonni. Ci vediamo dopo l'anno nuovo. Io ti amo."* And he wondered exactly what she'd said.

Another couple of minutes passed before she came back into the kitchen with the tip of her nose pink as though she'd been crying.

"Everything okay?"

She nodded then dumped the macaroni noodles through a strainer. "Sometimes I just miss my grandmother."

"I know what you mean." Parker's stomach tightened. "I miss mine too."

"You don't visit her?"

"She died a long time ago."

"I'm so sorry." Her meaningful and understanding expression touched his heart and made him wonder how much loss she might also have suffered in her life. "Was she wonderful?"

"She was the best. She was always baking something or she'd be putting up jams and jellies for the local farmers' market. Or she'd be reading adventure stories to me and my brothers." Sweet memories of the woman flooded his heart. "Why don't you visit your grandmother?"

"I'd like to, but she lives so far away."

"Where?"

"In Italy."

"So that's how you found your cooking school?"

Her gaze shot up to his and he briefly wondered at the surprise he saw there.

"No. I found that all on my own. My *nonni* lives in a very small town where everyone knows everyone else's business."

"Sounds like Sunshine Valley, where everybody knows your name."

"In your case, that's a good thing. Right?"

"How's that?" All he could think of were the whispers that had caught fire as soon as Aunt Pippy spilled the beans to a long-winded friend about the vineyard's financial troubles and their new half sister.

"Word of mouth will be the best advertisement for your restaurant," Gabriella said.

"I hope so."

"I know so." She dumped the strained noodles into the large foil pans.

"I appreciate the vote of confidence." He waited for her to say something off-handed about her working there as his chef so it was a sure bet the reviews would be positive, but she left him hanging. "Tell me about your grandmother."

"Actually, I'd rather hear about your aunt Pippy. You made her sound like quite a character."

Another evasion.

She was quite good at throwing those around.

"She is. But she's something you have to experience for yourself." He pointed to the foil pans filled with steaming noodles. "What are you planning to do with so much ultimate mac and cheese?"

"I'm taking it to the women and children's shelter. The women there have escaped really bad situations with only the clothes on their backs. They literally leave with nothing. As often as I can, I like to fill their bellies with a little comfort food."

"That's a really nice gesture."

"It's the least I can do." She shrugged. "The holidays are coming up fast. I can't imagine how difficult it must be to live in a shelter at all, let alone during this time of year. Comfort food always makes me feel better. So I always hope it helps them a little bit too."

"You take them comfort food often?"

She shrugged. "As often as possible."

Parker set down his coffee mug and joined her at the counter. He took her chin in his hand and lifted her face. "I never knew you had such a soft spot."

"So the dominatrix boots fooled you."

"*You* fooled me. I want to know who you are when no one's looking. So, Gabriella." He brushed his thumb across her plush bottom lip. "Tell me. What are you hiding?"

Her eyes widened and then she barked a laugh that confirmed he'd hit the mark. "That's ridiculous. What would I have to hide?"

There was the million dollar question.

And honestly, why did it matter to him?

A few hours later Gabi and Parker left the women and children's shelter. After delivering several large pans of her ultimate macaroni and cheese, she noticed he'd become unusually quiet.

"It's tough to see that, isn't it," she said, not asked, because she already knew the answer.

He nodded, steering his SUV through the rain. "I had no idea. And literally no clue their living restrictions were so rigid. They weren't even going to let me in."

"That's because some of the women are too fearful of men and they're still in danger."

"And that's the reason each room has a double deadbolt?"

She nodded. "Sometimes their abusers discover where they are and try to break in to force them to come back. Or . . . worse."

Parker sighed and Gabi knew exactly the scenarios running through his head because she'd imagined them too. Sadly, he'd only seen a fraction of why she supported the women and children's shelter. By the deep furrows creasing his forehead and the corners of his eyes, she knew the visit had affected him a great deal. She understood. It broke her heart every time she went to the facility and heard the stories of the women who had to live there until they could get back on their feet and be safe. There were all kinds of abuse. Gabi had learned that not all were delivered in a physical manner. A lot came through words. She'd learned that passive-aggressive confrontations could be used in almost as painful a manner as a physical blow. But unlike a bruise, those wounds sometimes never healed.

The visit today gave her another snippet of insight to Parker. They'd only known each other a short time, and yet, she felt she knew him better than men she'd dated for months. Dangerously warm and fuzzy feelings squeezed her heart. She knew she had to be careful. It would be so easy to fall in love with him. Good thing she'd vowed to distance herself. Of course, now that he knew where she lived that might prove to be a bit more tricky.

"What we saw in there really hits home," he said.

"How so?" She turned her attention away from the sights on the streets and back to watching him. His hands were tight around the steering wheel, and though she couldn't see his eyes because he was looking straight ahead, she could tell that he was deeply troubled.

"Jordan's fiancée, Lucy, was one of those women."

"Oh my God." The thought sickened her. "No wonder your brother is trying so hard to give her everything he can for their wedding."

"He still feels guilty."

"But how could her bad marriage be his fault?"

"Because he stood her up for that graduation dance." He reached over and turned down the radio. "She met her ex in college and married very young. Jordan thinks if he hadn't treated her so badly that night, she wouldn't have hooked up with some loser who used her as a punching bag. He thinks maybe she didn't believe she was good enough to find anyone better."

"Surely he knows that's not true."

"Doesn't matter. That's how he feels. He loves her so much. And he's really not just trying to make up for fucking up so bad with her. He's just crazy about her. She's made him a better man. He knows it. And he's going to do everything in his power to make sure that he's good enough for her."

For a moment Gabi didn't know how to respond. She'd never met such a selfless man in her life. On the best of days, her father could never even come close. Even her own brother—who'd become her father's narcissistic mini me—stood on rocky ground with marriage number two. He wouldn't have a clue about sacrificing anything to make and keep a woman happy.

Gabi couldn't imagine what it would be like to have that kind of love. To have a man appreciate and cherish you like that. To have a man a woman could trust with everything.

Even her darkest secrets.

"I like your brother," she said.

Parker chuckled. "You don't even know him."

"But I can see him through Lucy's eyes." And that's all that mattered. When she looked at Parker, she knew he'd be a man a woman could trust like that. He valued the women in his life and he'd protect them at all costs.

He'd do the same for the woman he loved.

During the rest of the ride he became increasingly quiet and Gabi wished she knew exactly what was going on in his head.

Once they reached her apartment, he parked his SUV then held his jacket over her head to guard her against the pounding rain as he walked her to the door. The gesture was sweet and maybe even a bit old-fashioned, but she totally loved it.

In the world she lived in, the men she knew were too wrapped up in themselves to care about anyone else. Parker was like a beacon of light in that stormy sea. He was smart, sexy, talented, and compassionate. By the time they reached her door, it was all Gabi could do not to ignore her earlier vow, wrap her arms around him, pull him inside, and tear off his clothes. But when she unlocked the door and stepped into her living room, he remained at the doorway.

"Aren't you coming in?"

To her surprise and dismay, he shook his head.

"Why not?"

"I think maybe you had the right idea all along." He stepped closer, cupped her face in his big hands, and gently kissed her lips. Then he looked down into her face, his blue eyes troubled. "I like you, Gabriella.

A lot. And there's nothing I'd like better than to come inside with you and show you exactly how much."

"But?"

"But . . . I'm seeing a different side of you."

"So . . . what? You think I'm an axe murderer or something?"

He gave her a faint smile. "I just think you deserve a guy who has more to offer than I do."

She doubted anyone could lay claim to that. "Why do you say that?"

"Because you're a forever girl who needs and deserves a forever guy. I can't be him. And I don't want you to waste your time. Believe me." He swept the pad of his thumb across her bottom lip. "Running away from me was the right choice."

The first time she'd run because they'd agreed to one night only. Bailing in the early morning hours had saved both of them from an awkward situation. The second time she'd run because it became pretty clear that she'd never be able to keep things between them casual. But like the flip of a coin, right now, she wasn't so sure she wanted him to walk away. No. On second thought, she was pretty sure she didn't want him to walk away. Finding a forever guy hadn't been on her list, but she'd damn sure take one right now if it was Parker.

"Why don't you come inside so we can talk this over?"

The slow shake of his head told her he thought coming inside was a bad idea.

"I made a mistake coming here. But I do think

you're a gifted chef, Gabriella. After Thanksgiving, if you're still interested in working at the restaurant, come by and we'll do a proper job interview. Application, resume, references, the whole shebang."

He said nothing more, just turned and walked away.

This morning she'd been positive that working for him was a bad idea because she was afraid she'd become too involved. Now, she was only sure of one thing—she was already too involved. Her heart ached in a way that had nothing to do with proving herself in the culinary world. Because what the hell good was success if you had no one to share it with?

# Chapter 8

$P$arker had barely made it back to his houseboat, pulled a bottle of very appropriately named Rock Bottom Ale from the fridge, and collapsed on his sofa before his cell rang.

"We've got her cornered," his brother Declan announced, sounding more exhausted than victorious.

"*Her* who?" Parker asked, too tired to think.

"Our elusive and sneaky aunt. Ethan caught her tiptoeing out the door with a packed suitcase. Apparently she thought she could escape again without having to tell us the story about Mom and Dad."

Fuck.

Parker was drained. He didn't have an ounce of energy left to even nuke a microwave dinner. He was dog-tired and his emotions had been tangled up in a knot since he'd left Gabriella's apartment. Not that he'd wanted to leave. He'd wanted to go inside, toss her over his shoulder, and carry her into the bedroom. He'd wanted to slip between the covers and make love to her for the rest of this rainy, shitty day.

But on that trip to the women and children's shelter, she'd confirmed everything he'd begun to imagine about her. Aside from her fire and sass, she had a heart and soul that saw no end. And though she might very well be the kind of woman he'd like to spend eternity with, he needed to be honest. He didn't have the time or the energy to put into a relationship right now. He was spread too thin in too many directions to be good for anyone. She deserved to have someone more like Jordan. A man who was willing to drop everything, to do whatever it took to devote however much time was needed to make her happy.

He couldn't put himself out there like that.

Not now.

Not in the near future.

Maybe not ever.

And if he couldn't commit, it would be unfair as hell to drag Gabriella into this mess he called life.

"Did you chain Aunt Pippy to a chair?" he asked Declan.

"Didn't have to. She has a brother sitting on each side and one in front of her. Lucy and Brooke are standing by in case she uses the excuse that she has to use the restroom. No chance of her escaping out the window."

Parker nearly laughed as he pictured his two future sisters-in-law standing as potty room guards.

"What are they going to do, go into the bathroom with her?"

"They say if they have to they will. Nicki's in her room upstairs determined not to come down until we force her. And Lili is on her way up to the house now. We're just waiting on you."

Parker longingly eyed the bottle of ale in his hand, then without taking a drink, set it down on the table. "I'm on my way."

*W*ith the box of cookies Gabriella had made him in his hand, Parker stood outside the door of his childhood home listening to the ruckus inside that sounded like an unruly crowd at an MMA title match.

Someone needed to call in a referee.

The longer he stood there, the more the voices escalated. In the time it had taken for him to drive from Portland, the situation had somehow turned into a shouting match. While arguments and disagreements were not unusual for his family, he didn't like the caustic tone he heard. Most differences were thrown out there with a sense of levity that helped calm down those in battle. Tonight's clash felt as cold and bitter as the wind that blew at his back.

He snatched a cookie from the box, stuck it in his mouth, and pushed all thoughts of the woman who'd baked it from his mind. Chomping his teeth into the flavorful bite, he steeled himself against the inevitable and opened the gates of hell.

What he found on the inside of the house was even crazier than what it had sounded like from the outside.

Face redder than when she wore too much blush, Aunt Pippy sat trapped in the middle of the sofa with Ethan on one side and Declan on the other. Brooke, Declan's fiancée, was perched on Dec's lap so he couldn't get up and strangle anyone. Jordan and Ryan stood in the center of the room arguing with fingers pointed while Lucy held the back of Jordan's sweatshirt in a death grip. Nicki stood on the bottom step of the stairs interjecting her arms-folded opinions at high volume. And Lili sat in a lone chair, wary eyes darting side to side, searching for the best escape route.

Even Nicki's kitten Fezik got into the act by attacking the tail of Lucy's dog Ziggy. The only person absent from the chaos was Ryan's nine-year-old daughter, Riley.

Parker wanted to run back out the door. It would be easy to do since no one in the mix had even noticed he'd come in. But he couldn't be a coward. This shit had to stop.

He swallowed the remains of the moist cookie, put two fingers to his mouth, and whistled as loud as he could.

The yelling stopped and heads swiveled in his direction.

Judging by the glares he received, it was a good thing they weren't holding weapons.

"Thank fuck you're finally here," Jordan exclaimed.

"Language!" Aunt Pippy, Lucy, Brooke, and Nicki yelled at him in unison, then everyone began arguing again.

Frown lines deep, Ryan turned toward Parker. "I've tried to get a handle on this. So can you reach into that bag of snark you usually tote around and find something to break this up?"

"Pretty sure it's going to take a sledgehammer."

At that moment the shrill of Nicki's screech sliced down his back and he'd had enough.

He whistled again. "Stop!"

When he had everyone's attention again, he could think of only one method that would work in this situation.

Shame.

"You should all be ashamed of yourselves," he scolded. "You're at each other's throats and you've got Lili scared to death. What's yelling and arguing going to accomplish?"

His question was met with icy silence.

"Everyone sit the hell down. Take a breath. Take a shot of whiskey." He pointed. "Not you, Nicole. The rest of you . . . do whatever you need to do to pull yourselves together. Now!"

"Thank you, Parker," Aunt Pippy said, brushing her carrot orange hair off her forehead like she'd been in a back alley brawl.

"You're not off the hot seat, Aunt Pippy. So above all, *you* need to take a breath. Because you have a lot of explaining to do."

Rightfully so, their aunt hung her head.

She'd been the only one with the knowledge of what had happened between their parents all those years ago, of what had caused such a rift that their father would cheat, produce an illegitimate daughter, and then steal money from their family-owned business.

She'd been the only one who'd known why their father would risk everything he'd worked hard for, his family, and the legacy his own father had created decades ago.

She'd been the only one who could tell them the truth so that they could—hopefully—mend the gaping wound left open after their parents' deaths and move on.

She'd been the only one who could help them heal, and she'd been avoiding them like a cat burglar at the Louvre.

"I'm not the oldest. So pulling this mess of a family meeting together is Ryan's job." Parker set the box of cookies down on the coffee table and looked at his brother. "Unless you want to defer."

"I'm good." Ryan's broad chest lifted on a harsh intake of air to clear the obvious ire from his system. "Thanks."

"Then the floor is all yours." Parker took the chair next to Lili, gave her a smile, and felt mildly relieved when she returned a tentative version of the same gesture. He took her hand and gave it a reassuring squeeze. Glancing across the room, he then crooked his finger at Nicki.

She shook her head.

Damn stubborn girl.

With a little more insistence and a glare, he crooked his finger again.

A long hesitation followed before his baby sister finally rolled her eyes and stomped across the carpet in the living room like a two-year-old in the midst of a tantrum. Parker tipped his head, indicating for her to sit in the empty chair on the other side of him. After Nicki flopped down in it like she'd just run a 100K marathon, he reached over and held her hand too.

And there he sat, the only glue between two sisters who'd barely uttered a word to each other that wasn't heated or accusatory. While his heart pounded and ached, everyone else in the room looked at the three of them and suddenly seemed to realize how much was at stake.

He'd be damned if he'd let go of the two fragile flowers in his immediate care. Not until they both realized that whether there was love or tension in the air, they were all bonded by blood.

And no one could take that away.

"Parker's right." Ryan spun his gaze around the room. "We should all be ashamed. We're a family. Every single one of us belongs here. And regardless of what household we were raised in, each one of us deserves to know the truth so we can make things right."

All eyes then shot in Aunt Pippy's direction. By the look in her eye, she was finally resigned to tell

the story that would either make or break them and
their fragile beliefs.

"Time to do the right thing, Aunt Pippy," Ryan
said.

Their aunt looked at each and every one of them
before she spoke. Parker's chest tightened as the sister
on either side of him gripped his fingers tight.

"For the record, your mother and father *never*
wanted any of you to know about this." Aunt Pippy
stated the obvious, suddenly looking much older than
the fiery orange hair and globs of makeup would
have you believe. "And honestly, I'm tired of trying
to keep their secret. They managed to keep it buried
for twenty-five years. But since they're gone now
and their secret seems to be hurting everyone they
loved and tried to protect, I guess you're right. It's
time."

Everyone leaned forward. Waited. Listened.

"Things fell apart shortly after Ethan was born.
No fault of yours, sweetheart," Pippy said to their
youngest brother, who flinched but said nothing in
return. Parker could see the distress on his face and
he could almost hear Ethan wondering if not blaming him was just one more of the lies their parents
had told.

"Your father wasn't the first to cheat," Aunt Pippy
announced.

Parker's head snapped back so fast his neck cracked.

"That dishonor went to your mother, who felt that
with five rambunctious boys, your father paid more

attention to all of you than her. In essence, she was jealous of the lives she'd created. It didn't stop her from being a good mother, but her attitude and her affair with a local man did irreparable damage between her and your dad."

Unable to loosen the invisible fist gripping his heart, Parker glanced around the room. Not a single person was looking up. Not a single eye was on their aunt. Everyone seemed to have a sudden interest in the floor, and Parker knew they were all trying to grasp onto the dirty hand they'd just been dealt.

They'd all been blaming everything on their father when he wasn't the only one at fault.

"After a couple of years of sleeping on the sofa and the cold shoulder, your dad couldn't take the silent treatment and the long dragged-out fights anymore, so he went back east to spend some time with Uncle Richard. He figured while he was away he'd have the peace of mind to figure out how to save his marriage. His biggest fear was losing you boys. He loved you more than life itself."

Now there was something Parker could believe. Their father had always taken time for him and his brothers, and he truly seemed to enjoy the time they spent together.

"While he was there he met Lili's mom, Natalie." Pippy's clasped hands began to flex and tighten. "She paid attention to him. Listened to him. She tried to be the open heart and the soft shoulder he'd needed from your mom. She was a good, sweet woman." Pippy shrugged. "It doesn't seem so far-fetched that they then fell in love."

Parker felt Lili tense. She tried to pull her hand away but he held on and tightened his grip. Then he leaned over and kissed the side of her head. A stuttered breath lifted her shoulders and Parker knew this was as devastating for her to hear as it was for the rest of them.

"But your dad knew he had to come back and try to save his marriage, if only for the sake of you boys. It wasn't long after he came back that Lili's mom informed him that she was pregnant."

Aunt Pippy paused, dropped her head into her hands, and slowly shook it back and forth.

"God, he was so torn apart. He loved you boys, he still loved your mom, and he loved Natalie too. Though he knew what he'd done was wrong, he couldn't help being excited about Natalie's pregnancy. He didn't know what to do. A few weeks later, Natalie—bless her heart—told your dad she'd lost the baby so he wouldn't feel the need to make such a dramatic life-changing decision. With five boys and a longstanding marriage, she knew where his loyalties needed to lie. So she broke it off with him for good and he . . . was heartbroken. A few months later your dad had to take a trip back east. He looked her up and discovered that she'd given birth to Lili."

Pippy paused again and swiped at the tears hanging on her bottom lashes. The action smeared her mascara and she came up looking like a raccoon.

Lucy handed her a box of tissues. She plucked out several and blew her nose.

"My mom told him he didn't need to feel responsible," Lili said in a shaky voice. "That's what she told me just before she died. She told me that even though she loved him, she made him promise to stay with his wife and sons."

"That's right." Aunt Pippy gave a nod. "And walking away from you, Lili, was the hardest thing he'd ever done. Don't you ever think that because he wasn't there, that he didn't love you. Because he did."

On his other side, Parker felt Nicole start to tremble. He looked at her and her emotions were right there on the surface for everyone to see. He knew she wanted to scream "But what about me?" Because, in essence, their father had abandoned her too. He leaned in and kissed the side of her head. It wasn't much of a reassurance, but at the moment it was all he could do not to fall apart himself.

"When your father came back home he told your mother everything," Pippy said. "She was livid, and she threatened to take you boys away and the vineyard too. He told her that he'd never leave her because he still loved her and he loved his sons. But he also admitted that a huge chunk of his heart had been left with Natalie and Lili."

Pippy sniffed. "After a time, your mother thought everything would go back to normal, but it didn't. There was just too much damage for it to heal. Like a lot of other women desperate to save their marriages, your mother thought if she had another child it would make things better."

"But having so many children is what seemingly started the problem in the first place," Jordan pointed out.

Aunt Pippy nodded and brushed her hands over her paisley print dress. "But she thought having a *daughter* this time would take your daddy's mind off Lili. So she talked your dad into going to a doctor for artificial insemination and using sperm separation for gender selection. At that point your dad was numb. Basically he went along with it to keep your mother happy and to save an argument."

Nicki's sob tore everyone's attention in her direction.

"It's okay, Nic," Ethan reassured her from across the room. "Just hang on. We need to hear the truth. Okay?"

Nicole didn't answer, but she gripped Parker's hand tighter and he could tell she was barely holding onto her composure.

"I'm sorry, honey," Aunt Pippy said to her. "I know this is hard to hear. And no matter what you think, your daddy loved you. He was just so torn up inside he didn't know how to react anymore. He withdrew into a shell of the man he'd once been. I can tell you I'd never seen him like that before and I didn't know how to help him. I know your mother was my sister and I was supposed to be on her side. But it was a tough side to be on when I had to watch a man's emotions shrivel up the way your daddy's did."

"I noticed a definite change in him over the years," Ryan said. "He became quieter. More withdrawn. I just thought maybe that was a part of aging."

"Now you know why." Aunt Pippy shook her head. "When he started siphoning money from the vineyard he fell into a deeper well of self-hate. Even though he couldn't be a part of Lili's life and had seen her only one time, he wanted to support her in any way he could. So he sent money even though no court ever ordered him to do so. Natalie refused it time and time again, but he insisted.

"Nicole, I know you feel like your daddy abandoned you too, and for the most part, you're right. But your mother spoiled you rotten, and your father allowed for that, thinking it made up for what he couldn't give you emotionally."

For a long drawn-out silent moment everyone in the room looked back down to the floor like it held the rest of the answers to their questions.

"I've got one last thing to say and then I'm done. Unless someone has questions." Their aunt looked pale and drained, despite her raccoon eyes. "No one in this room with Kincade blood in their veins should ever doubt that they were loved. Your parents weren't perfect. They made a mess of what they had, but they tried to make it work. In the last few years they'd finally started to communicate like a husband and wife again. They took that Hawaiian vacation to try and rediscover the love they'd once had many years ago. Unfortunately they never got that chance."

Aunt Pippy stood, and in a stern voice said, "It's

a week and a half until Thanksgiving. A time when families come together. Don't let their mess destroy your lives. Don't let it make you afraid to fall in love. Don't let it make you afraid to disagree with the ones you love. Just remember to look at the person you're with—whether it's a brother, a sister, or a spouse—and let yourself be honest with your feelings. Talk things out. Embrace the other's differences. And at the end of the day, remember, you're all in this together. You all have each other to rely on. Yes, you've all been lied to, cheated, or robbed in one way or another in the past, but please, don't let that dictate your future."

A collective exhale rippled through the room as though someone had let the air out of a bunch of balloons.

"Questions?" Pippy looked at them all. No one said a word. "Good. Because I need a glass of wine and a long nap."

Her age never appeared more obvious than when she creaked across the room and climbed the stairs. No one moved a muscle until they all heard her bedroom door close. Then Nicole and Lili looked at each other. Unsure of what was going on in their minds, Parker held tightly onto their hands. A second later he let go when they got up, grabbed each other in a bear hug, and started crying together.

Sisters united.

Parker's eyes welled up with tears.

A second later the entire family formed a group hug.

And they cried.

For the past, for transgressions that had created broken hearts, and for the loss of everything they'd once believed.

But now it was time to move on.

Together.

# Chapter 9

Pushing a cart with a wobbly wheel through the grocery store to the Muzak version of "Home for the Holidays" did not put a spring in Gabriella's step. Just the opposite. She clung to the metal cart and shuffled down the bread aisle like she'd have to face the grocery gremlin at the endcap filled with cans of pumpkin pie mix.

Shopping for a Thanksgiving dinner she'd have to eat alone while being eyed by the ever-cranky Basil the betta fish held about as much appeal as going on a honeymoon alone. But that was the hand either fate or Gabi had dealt herself.

When you were alone, the holidays sucked.

As if the ever-present romantic or warm, loving family commercials weren't bad enough, the store aisles packed with Christmas tinsel, lights, ornaments, and artificial trees had started popping up way before Halloween. Gabi hadn't been prepared for the empty feeling it left in her gut. So she'd decided that this year she'd at least put up a tree. She'd celebrate with a spiked hot chocolate and she'd light cranberry-apple scented candles and watch *Christmas Vacation* while she baked cookies for the women and children's shelter. She'd do what she could to wipe away the loneliness the holidays always brought to people like her who had no *plus one*.

But first, she had to make it through Thanksgiving.

While she perused the meager selection of turkey breasts—because why would she bother buying an entire turkey—several mothers with their adorable pack of kids in tow joined her in the poultry section. Gabi watched in total amazement and appreciation of the women who managed to control their children, who appeared to have octopus arms as they reached for this and grabbed for that off the shelves.

None of the mothers lost their cool. They merely gave their children the stink eye accompanied by a tight smile. Like magic the kids behaved. Well, at least for all of five seconds before they started octopus arming again.

Gabi chuckled and wondered if that's what it had been like for Parker's mother when she'd taken all five of her boys shopping.

Parker.

He was never far from her mind. In fact, he was mostly all she thought about since he'd walked away from her door two weeks ago. Two long damn weeks ago when he'd cut off any hope for intimacy and distantly instructed her to come by after Thanksgiving for a job interview. And for all of those two weeks she wondered how in the world they'd gone from licking each other's bodies to such a formal situation.

True, they'd initially had an understanding that their fling was for one night only. But after that there had still been kissing, and touching, and it had felt like something between them had changed. She hadn't intended to let her heart get involved, but, boom, there it was. Her heart had snuck its way into the mix and made things difficult.

She'd had a priority that had nothing to do with snuggling. But Parker made her want to forget that priority. He made her want to make the time to snuggle. He made her want to care. Made her want to forget about all the crap that had happened in her past and start fresh.

None of that mattered because the choice had been taken away.

He'd made it clear it was to be business only between them from now on.

The problem was, she missed him.

At the end of the turkey aisle, a young couple held hands as they selected a giant gobbler. Gabi teared up then released a derisive scoff.

God. Her emotions were squirting all over the place like a can of Silly String. Damn holidays. They always got to her. All she could think about was how during that special time of the year, families got together. They laughed, talked, celebrated their differences and their unity. Just like those damn television commercials. Everything was shiny, twinkly, and bright. Snowflakes, peppermint, and puppies. Falling in love, romance, and diamonds.

Swallowing the holly jolly overload ache in her heart, she reached into the grocery cooler and grabbed the package with the smallest turkey breast.

"Gabriella?"

Gabi looked up to find Lucy, Jordan Kincade's fiancée, pushing a cart in her direction.

"I thought that was you." Lucy rolled her cart up next to Gabi's and flashed a friendly smile. "How are you?"

"I'm good." *Liar.* "How are the wedding plans going?"

Lucy rolled her eyes. "Jordan wrangled his sister Lili into helping him. When I heard something about pirates, I ran out the door."

"Pirates?"

"I think he was talking about his hockey player buddies. At least I *hope* he was talking about his hockey player buddies."

"I don't know." Gabi grinned. "A pirate wedding could be fun. Everyone could gift you with treasure chests full of gold and jewels. You could drink grog instead of champagne. And instead of saying *I do*, you could say *arrgh* and swear a lot."

Lucy laughed. "Alpha male that he is, I'm sure that would be right up Jordan's alley. Maybe you'll have to come and see how it all turns out."

Gabi didn't want to gush that she'd love to go because she figured the invitation was only incidental and that a real invitation would not be arriving in the mail. "I'm sure whatever he comes up with you're going to love."

"I will. But I'd be just as happy going to the courthouse for a short and sweet ceremony. Jordan lived in the spotlight for so long it doesn't bother him, but I'm not really big on public attention."

"Just gaze into the eyes of the man you love. The next thing you know you'll be alone in the honeymoon suite."

"Or the Jolly Roger."

They both laughed and Gabi realized she could probably be good friends with this woman.

She wanted to ask about Parker, but she wouldn't. Instead she asked, "So what are you doing shopping here instead of in Sunshine?"

"Sometimes I just need to get away from the whole small-town thing," Lucy explained. "Not that I don't love it, but when you're a teacher you know every kid and all their parents. A twenty-minute shopping excursion can turn into several hours depending on how many people you run into. If I shop here I get to stroll anonymously down the aisles and complete my list in record time."

"Sounds like good planning."

"I'm a teacher. Planning is what I do." Lucy leaned a hip against her shopping cart. "Today I'm picking up stuff for Thanksgiving dinner. We all tossed some dinner and dessert items into a hat and everyone chose one to make. That way no one has to cook all the food and end up exhausted before it's even served."

"A potluck Thanksgiving. I like that idea."

"Who are you spending the holiday with?"

Gabi shifted her gaze away from Lucy and tried to find something in the store to deter the conversation.

Then Lucy looked down into Gabi's cart. "Is that a turkey breast?"

Gabi was sure she didn't mean it to sound so accusatory.

"I really don't need an entire turkey."

"Does that mean you're going to be alone for Thanksgiving?" One of Lucy's teacherly eyebrows lifted and dared Gabi to lie.

"I won't exactly be alone."

Lucy folded her arms and seemingly kicked into mama bear mode. "So who are you spending Thanksgiving with?"

"Basil."

"You're spending the holiday with a spice?"

"No. Basil is my . . ." *Crap.* "Betta fish."

Gabi could almost hear Lucy's teeth grind. Then the woman reached into Gabi's cart, pulled out the package of turkey breast, and tossed it back into the cooler.

"Absolutely not. You're having Thanksgiving dinner with us. After all, if you work for Parker you'll be like family."

Chances for that were slim to none.

"I think the Kincade family table will be full enough," Gabi said, appreciating the offer.

"Nonsense. There's always room for more," Lucy said. "Say you'll join us."

Even though it was probably ridiculous to contemplate spending a family holiday with a family she didn't know, Gabi caught her bottom lip between her teeth and considered it. "Don't you need to call someone and ask for permission before you bring home a complete stranger for a family holiday?"

"It's not just a family holiday. It's a day to give thanks," Lucy insisted. "Personally, I'm thankful that this year I don't have to spend another holiday alone. I don't know what your history is or why you're spending it alone but none of that matters. What does matter is that the season of giving should really start with the giving of heart and friendship, don't you agree?"

Taken aback by the enormous generosity, Gabi could only nod.

"Besides, you're not a complete stranger because you're with Parker," Lucy said.

"Oh." Gabi's heart stumbled. "I'm not *with* Parker. I just want to work for him at his restaurant."

A knowing smile touched Lucy's lips. "You sound like I used to. I was so bent on *not* claiming the feelings I had for Jordan I told everyone who'd listen that he and I weren't together. Even though I knew Jordan and I were already connected by heart. And from the way Parker looked at you in the restaurant that day, I'd say you might have already crossed that bridge."

Gabi curled her fingers around the handle of her shopping cart and tried to respond but only managed to stutter.

"Of course, I say all this now that we're getting married, but there was a time I considered wrapping my hands around his holly jolly overload neck and strangling him." Lucy smiled.

"He does seem a bit . . . strong-willed."

"I believe the term is *maxed-out alpha male*." Lucy chuckled. "Truthfully? I know I'm lucky to have found the kind of love I have with Jordan. And I guess I just want all the people I care about to be as happy as I am. Declan found Brooke. Parker found you. Now all I have left to wish for is Ryan, Ethan, and Nicole. Oh. And Lili."

"Lili the half sister?"

Lucy nodded. "See, you already know who everyone in the family is. So you're no stranger at all. Say you'll join us. Everyone is supposed to arrive at the main house at four o'clock. Bring a dish if it makes you feel better. Just say you'll come and then actually show up."

Gabi could say no, but that would be entirely stupid when spending the holiday alone sounded horrible. Basil wouldn't mind the diss. And she really, really wanted to see Parker again.

"I'd love to join you. But you'll be sure to let Parker know I'm coming, right? I'd hate to barge in and surprise him."

What if he brought a date? How horrible would that be? Before she could recant, Lucy smiled.

"Of course I'll tell him." Lucy gave her a hug. "See you Thursday."

As Gabi watched her new friend push her cart in the direction of the huge pile of vacuum seal wrapped turkeys, she tried to contain the excitement in her heart.

She didn't have to spend Thanksgiving alone. She'd be spending it with Parker.

Hopefully he wouldn't kick her out the door.

Thick gray clouds swollen with rain hovered in the sky and threatened to douse the Thanksgiving Day festivities with a good soaking. Status quo for much of the fall and winter weather in Sunshine. Still, Parker had hoped for sunny skies, or at least less of a biting wind.

With his car heater blasting, he tried not to chuckle as he drove past the gates to Sunshine Creek Vineyard and the huge inflatable turkey and pilgrims. Or he should say, the fully pumped-up male pilgrim and the partially inflated female, who was bent at the waist of her white apron and appeared to be going down on the blown-up dude in the black Puritan hat.

Aunt Pippy strikes again.

Everyone had a quirky person in their family; the Kincades laid claim to Aunt Pippy. When she'd first cleared the air about what their parents had done and what they'd been through, they'd all felt like strangling her, but now he and all his siblings were bonding like he'd hoped. And they'd all agreed that the real tragedy was the misery their parents had created for themselves and had been forced to live with most of their adult lives. Dinner today—their first Thanksgiving with Lili and without their parents—was bound to be different.

As he continued up the winding road to the main house he intentionally kept his eyes away from the direction of his restaurant. He'd promised himself he wouldn't go there today. With so much work still to be done before Jordan and Lucy's wedding, it was tempting. But today was family eat-drink-and-be-merry time. Not work-until-you-sweat time.

With the vast assortment of cars and trucks clogging the driveway, he parked as close to the house as possible then retrieved the casserole dish of praline topped sweet potatoes from the backseat. For his food truck fare his imagination could take flight with whatever the hell he felt like cooking that day. For the holidays, he loved traditional. But that hadn't stopped him from also making a dish of chili corn pudding for his brothers, who were always fans of hot and spicy. Along with the diced green chilies, he'd tossed in a handful of finely chopped habanero, so they'd be grabbing their bottles of ale to douse the flames.

Before he even opened the front door he heard voices. Fortunately they weren't raised in anger like the last time he'd been there. Now he caught a hint of excitement and laughter. As he came through the door, everyone in the vicinity stopped and unanimously said, "Parker!" then they went right back to what they were doing. A grin burst across his face. His family drove him nuts, but he wouldn't have it any other way.

As he came inside, the house was deliciously warm with the scent of turkey, stuffing, and pumpkin spice. Inhaling all the goodness, he set the casserole dishes on the long buffet. A moment later little Riley, his adorable niece, dashed into the room and lifted her arms to him for a hug. Tall like her father, she had her mother's blond-haired beauty. Fortunately her mother's selfishness didn't seem to swim in her DNA.

"Uncle Parker, know what I made?" She grinned and he noticed a tooth was missing. "You're gonna love it."

He ruffled her long curls and chuckled at her enthusiasm. "Tell me."

"I made pumpkin and turkey Rice Krispies treats."

"Wow. That's pretty clever." He tilted his head, pretending to be puzzled even though he knew exactly what she'd meant. "I'm not sure I'd ever think to put all those flavors together."

"Uncle Parker." She rolled her eyes and giggled. "I made them in the *shape* of pumpkins and turkeys."

"Oh. You fooled me." He wrapped her up in another hug and the moment he let go she darted off toward the kitchen.

One by one his brothers welcomed him by breaking out the whole *fist-bump, one-armed bro hug* thing. The ladies in the house each gave him a full-on hug. And for sheer entertainment purposes, Nicki's cat Fezik scampered through the house, chased by Lucy's golden retriever Ziggy, and Brooke's mini Australian shepherd Moochie.

Chaos.

God, he loved it. Good thing too, because in this family it ruled the day.

A knock on the door revealed Sean, his project manager, whom he'd personally invited to the dinner. They chatted for a few minutes about the evils of watching the Thanksgiving Day parade unless they were chained to the TV with their eyes forcibly propped open. When the conversation started to swing toward the restaurant construction, Parker held up his hand, signaling the topic was off limits for the day.

The house was full and loud. Plates and bowls of food started to appear and fill up the banquet table. Autumn leaves and mums in fall colors decorated every available space in sight. And true to her out-rageousness, Aunt Pippy popped out of the kitchen decked out in a fluorescent orange jumpsuit, a turkey print vest, and a roasted turkey hat on her head.

Still, something was missing.

It didn't take a genius to realize that the *something* was his parents. And even though they'd left behind so much sadness and tribulations, they were still his parents. And he missed them.

His thoughts took a dramatic left turn and Gabriella entered his mind. He wondered what she was doing today. Who she was spending the holiday with. Hell, he just wondered how she was doing. Not for the first time since he'd dragged himself away from her apartment did he realize he missed her too. He missed her smile. Her laugh. Her wicked sense of humor. And yeah, he missed her sexy curves. Not to mention he missed having his hands on those curves.

Walking away from her might have been the smart thing to do. Then again, it might have been the biggest mistake of his entire pathetic life.

But for now, with so many other things going on, he didn't have much time to think about what could have been if they'd met another time. Yeah, and that was a damned lie. He thought about her all the time. Especially when he crawled into bed at night.

He could imagine her sweet scent, the way she touched him, and especially the way she kissed him like she never wanted to stop.

He wondered if she liked a more traditional Thanksgiving dinner or if she preferred haute cuisine. He wondered if she liked pumpkin or apple pie, light or dark meat, and if she favored her cranberries fresh or jellied. He wondered why any of that mattered and why he'd even let it cross his mind. Because the truth of the matter was, she might have been the one with a running problem, but he'd been the one to walk away.

Refocusing his attention back to the people in the room, he found Sean trying to sweet-talk Lili about something. His sister smiled as though she enjoyed the attention Sean was giving her while she placed silverware at each place setting. A spark of big brother protectiveness fell on Parker's shoulders and he had to stop himself from interfering. With a shake of his head, Parker realized that Sean was a pretty standup guy and Lili was a grown woman. And even though Parker might want to treat her like a child and discourage any ardent admirers, it was really none of his business.

As long as they treated her right.

Carrying a big basket of homemade rolls, Aunt Pippy walked by on her way to the buffet and gave him a peck on the cheek. "You're looking especially handsome today."

"Figured I'd put on something other than jeans," he said of his dark gray slacks and light blue shirt.

"You're missing a tie."

He laughed. "Ties are for weddings, funerals, and court appearances."

"Well, in any case, stay away from the dogs. They'll shed all over you and you want to look nice."

He didn't much care how he looked, he was more interested in how good everything was going to taste. Thanksgiving provided most all of his favorite foods in one sitting. As a bonus the dessert table nearly overflowed with pies, cakes, and Riley's clever Rice Krispies treats. His sweet tooth was going to be in freaking ecstasy.

Ryan rolled up with a bottle of winter ale and handed it to him. "Happy Thanksgiving."

"Thanks. You too." Parker took a drink. "Looks like Riley's an aspiring chef."

Ryan wore his love for his daughter on his sleeve, so Parker wasn't surprised when his brother's face lit up with pride. "She's a good kid."

"She's a *great* kid. You're doing a terrific job with her."

"It's a challenge. Sometimes I feel like she's the adult with the way she watches over me and makes sure I'm taking care of myself."

"I think growing up fast is kind of normal when a child is being raised by a single parent."

"It's not fair though." Ryan's broad shoulders lifted. "Her mom called this morning to wish her a happy Thanksgiving."

"Did she now."

"Yep. Know what Riley said?"

"I suppose she's too young to tell the woman to eff off."

"Well, that's kind of what she said, only in kid terms. I was proud of her. At the same time I know I should have told her to be more respectful."

"Ryan? Your ex completely abandoned that little girl. I don't think Riley needs to be more respectful. Respect isn't given, it's earned. Don't you think it's up to your ex to be more of a mother than to just call once in a blue moon and on holidays?"

"Yeah."

"Then let Riley say what she wants. She'll feel better about it rather than being stifled because of what someone else thinks she should do. Give her some independence now and she'll grow up to be a strong woman."

"You know what you need?" Ryan asked.

"The list is too long to choose just one thing."

His brother chuckled. "You need to have some kids. I think you'd be a great dad."

"Got too many things in the way to even be thinking about that. Plus there's that little problem of finding the right woman first."

"Thought you'd already found her." Ryan took another drink.

"Says who?"

"Don't you listen to family gossip?"

"I do my best not to. That shit gives me nightmares and I'm just now getting over my fear of closet monsters."

Ryan laughed and Parker was glad he could get his brother's mind off the wicked witch he used to be married to with a bit of humor. Diverting attention away from himself was always an added plus.

The doorbell rang and conversation stopped as Lucy ran to answer the door. Parker took a look around the room and saw that everyone seemed to be here, so he was perplexed by who might be calling on a holiday. However, it wasn't unusual for someone in the family to invite individuals to a cookout or even to the harvest dinner they celebrated with when they brought in the grapes. But usually the holidays were just family. Then again, with Jordan and Declan getting married, maybe future family members had been invited. By the looks of things they had plenty of food to share.

Ryan gave a nod toward the door. "Wonder who that could be."

"Don't know." Parker shrugged. "But I'm guessing with all these weddings, we're going to need a bigger table."

Jordan suddenly appeared, snagged Parker's half-empty beer out of his hand, and replaced it with an old-fashioned glass filled with scotch on the rocks. "Looks like some of us are going to need a stronger drink."

"What the hell?" When the front door swung wide open, Parker knew exactly *what the hell.*

Sweet little Lucy didn't look remotely ashamed of her obvious matchmaking efforts as she winked at him over Gabriella's shoulder.

"Remember all the shit you've been giving me about getting married?" Jordan leaned in. "If Lucy has her way, the shit will be coming at you soon, little brother."

With an evil laugh Jordan walked away, taking Parker's bottle of beer with him. Ryan had the audacity to stand there and chuckle. And all Parker could think was, damn the woman looked good in that dress.

*I*t had taken more than an ounce of courage for Gabriella to knock on the Kincade family's door. It wasn't like her to turn up at a private holiday celebration when she barely knew two members of the family. But having a chance to see Parker again was something she hadn't been able to pass up. Unfortunately the dark slash of his brows pulled tight over his vivid blue eyes clearly implied he hadn't known she was coming and he might not be all that happy about it. Looked like Lucy had pulled a fast one on him. It was everything Gabi could do not to turn and run.

"Come in and meet everyone." Lucy took her by the hand and led her into the room where it seemed like everyone except Parker had been prepared for her arrival. "And don't worry, Parker's frown isn't directed at you."

"I'm not so sure about that."

Lucy briefly stopped and looked at Gabi. "Well, even if it was, would you be sorry you came?"

"Not at all."

"Good. Because I'm glad you're here." She flashed a smile and gave Gabi's hand a squeeze. "Now let's go stir things up a little, shall we?"

As a unit, the Kincade brothers were a visual force to be reckoned with. Each one more gorgeous than the next. Yeah, she might be partial, but in her eyes, Parker stood at the top.

The sweet aroma of a holiday home wafted through the air as Gabi tried to keep her attention focused on those she was meeting. Forgetting names was not the lasting impression she wanted to leave. Making a fool of herself by gawking at Parker wasn't her plan either.

She handed over the casserole dish containing the honey maple roasted carrots she'd made after debating whether to go traditional with her share of the potluck meal, or to think outside the box. Familiar with Parker's palate but not knowing the rest of his family, she'd decided to play it tasty but safe.

Just like she planned to do with Parker.

"Everyone, meet Gabriella," Lucy said to the room. "I ran into her at the grocery store the other day and when I found out she was going to be all alone for the holiday, well, I just knew she should spend the day with us."

Gabi was grateful for Lucy's kindness, and she was sure she hadn't meant to make Gabi feel inadequate about spending the holiday alone, but there it was. Even to her own ears, she sounded pathetic. Determined not to *be* pathetic, she plastered a smile on her face and thanked everyone for allowing her to crash their party.

A quick glance across the room told her Parker didn't feel any more comfortable than she did.

Lucy continued the introductions by adding that Gabi was a chef and had high hopes of working at Parker's new restaurant. "But no business talk today, you two," Lucy said, tossing her gaze between Gabi and Parker. "Everyone just needs to enjoy themselves and eat too much."

As the Kincades and Sean all stepped up to greet her, Gabi began to feel a little more relaxed. Ethan, the youngest brother, handed her a glass of wine, and with a few quick jokes immediately made her feel more at home. Though strikingly handsome and interesting, somehow Sean missed the memo that Gabi had eyes for Parker. With a light touch on her arm, he quickly offered himself up as her unassigned escort.

Parker had yet to cross the room and come her way. Still, his gaze had not left her once. Well, that wasn't necessarily true. He'd thrown a few blue-eyed daggers in Sean's direction—all of which went completely unnoticed by everyone except Gabi. Normally daggers, or anything sharp for that matter, weren't a good thing, but Gabi took them as a sign that the evening held possibility.

A woman with electric orange hair, purple metallic eyeshadow, and a roasted turkey hat came out of the kitchen and clapped her hands.

"Bring your appetites. Dinner is ready."

Gabi had no doubt this was the infamous Aunt Pippy.

"We do all the family meals buffet style," Brooke, Declan Kincade's beautiful fiancée, said with a grin. "That way you can sneak between people who are taking too long loading up their plates."

Gabi looked at the long buffet table and what seemed like miles of side dishes and desserts. She'd been too nervous to have an appetite, but everything looked so delicious she couldn't wait to dig in. "Do you think anyone would notice if I went straight for dessert?"

Brooke laughed. "No. But that's a great idea. I may have to join you."

Sean took it upon himself to seat her and Lili, and then he placed himself between the two of them.

"Nice maneuvering," Ethan commented as he sat between his sister Nicole and Aunt Pippy. "Wish I'd thought of it first."

"Hey." Nicole playfully whacked him on the arm.

"Yeah. What are we, limburger cheese?" Aunt Pippy said.

"Ryan, as the oldest, you're at the head of the table," Pippy said when he started to take a seat near the center of the table next to his adorable daughter. "Riley's next to you. Sorry for the confusion. Guess I should have made the seating arrangement more clear ahead of time."

"I'm sorry." Gabi apologized, even though she was thankful to the depths of her heart for sitting among this wonderful family. The bad memories since her parents' divorce had blocked all the good times. If there were even any to remember. "I've probably thrown you off."

"Nonsense." Pippy waved a hand. "I counted you as soon as Lucy told me you were coming."

Gabi snuck a look at Parker. By the narrowing of his eyes, she knew he was surprised to have it confirmed that, yes, he'd been the only one who hadn't known she was coming. Gabi was impressed that a family the size of the Kincades could keep a secret. As plates were filled and laughter flowed, it was nice, for a change, to sit with those who displayed love and used humor as a form of expression.

At the head of the table, Ryan offered thanks for the food and family. Grateful they hadn't done a roundtable what-I'm-thankful-for, Gabi sipped her wine and was eager to respond when the family drew her into a conversation.

"So what makes you want to work for our brother?" Declan asked as he tore apart a steaming homemade dinner roll.

Maybe initially she'd wanted to work for Parker for purely selfish reasons, but things had changed. Yes, she was still eager for an opportunity to spread her wings and earn a paycheck, but if her feet were held to the fire she'd have to admit that working alongside Parker offered an inspiring workplace. Today she was definitely more interested in facing the future with the man sitting across the table than dwelling on the past and the man who'd ruined it.

"Are you kidding? Have you tasted his food?" Hoping to break the ice a little, she grinned at him. "He had me at paella."

He smiled at that and she breathed a little easier.

"So what do you think you can bring to the table?" Jordan asked her, poking his fork through a glob of sweet potatoes, unaware he'd made a pun until Lucy elbowed him and laughed.

"A challenge," Gabi said, and then smiled when he lifted a brow. "I don't believe in trying to out-cook someone, especially when it's the man who signs your paychecks. But I would hope that I could be a good sounding board for his creativity. I know how special opening his own restaurant is to him. And I respect that. But I'm also not afraid to assert my opinion when an opportunity arises."

Parker lifted his wine glass. "I'll drink to that."

Gabi took a bite of moist turkey and sausage stuffing. The flavor rolled across her tongue as the table conversation picked up.

"I think Parker should be one of those TV chefs," Nicole said. "He's got the looks, the talent, the personality. He's the whole package. Maybe I'll send his name in the next time they have the casting call for *Food Network Star*."

"Please don't." Parker gave his sister a smile. "I love you, but if you do something like that I might have to kill you."

"No desire to become famous?" Lili asked him.

"I can barely keep up with the life I already have," Parker said.

"I don't think being a celebrity chef is all it's cracked up to be." Gabi hadn't meant to speak out, but the idea of Parker being ruined by the kind of life being a celebrity chef offered sent a shiver down her back. When everyone looked her way, she hoped she wouldn't open her mouth any wider and stick her entire foot in.

Though she knew for certain what happened when fame and fortune showed up at your door, she didn't want any of the nice, normal people at this table to know who she was related to. She didn't want to spoil anything.

"Guess I've read too many entertainment magazines," she explained.

"It does seem like a lot of those celebrity marriages end in divorce," Lucy said. "And we'd never want that for Parker."

"Parker hasn't even finished his dinner, let alone planned anything as extravagant as marriage," Parker said. "Let me at least get through dessert first."

Everyone chuckled and, thankfully, the conversation jumped to the recent grape harvest and the plans for the new bed-and-breakfast cottages being constructed.

Sean piped in that when the project was all done, the place would make people feel like they were strolling down a small European cobblestone street.

"Like Belle's little town in *Beauty and the Beast*?" Riley asked.

"Afraid I haven't seen the movie to compare," Sean said.

"Well that's disappointing," Lili chided with a smile. "How can you call yourself an architect if you aren't familiar with the wonders of Disney design? It's every child's, every woman's idea of perfection."

The smile on Sean's face said he knew he was being teased, so he didn't take any offense. "I think my university forgot to add Disney to the master's program."

"Wouldn't that be a fabulous job?" Brooke commented and Gabi wondered if Declan's fiancée had gathered any inspiration at the Disney parks for her new family fun center.

"Can I work for Disney, Daddy?" Riley asked Ryan, who patted her hand and said, "Sugar, you can be anything you want to be."

"That's it!" Excitedly, Jordan slapped his hand down on the table. The plates and silverware jingled as he leaned in and kissed Lucy's confused face.

"Dude." Ethan chuckled. "You been smoking something funny?"

"No. But I just figured out the theme for our wedding reception."

"Oh dear God." Parker sighed. "Groomzilla's at it again."

"Jordan." Lucy patted his arm. "Today is about the holiday. Not our wedding."

"But, baby." Jordan cupped Lucy's face in his hands and kissed her sweetly. "I just figured it out. You're my princess, and I want you to have the fairy-tale wedding you deserve. We could do Disney. A different princess theme for each table at the reception. Doesn't that sound like a great idea?"

Gabi grinned, remembering what Lucy had said at the grocery store about being happy if they just went to the courthouse to get married. So watching how the smart schoolteacher handled the big man who used to knock equally big guys around on the ice was going to be fun.

"Exactly how many brides' magazines have you been reading?" Lucy asked.

"It's my fault," Lili said. "I told him the reception might be easier to plan if he came up with a theme."

"You're forgiven." Lucy smiled at her future sister-in-law then looked back at her groom-to-be. "How about we just go with a Christmas theme? The wedding takes place the week of Christmas. Everything will already be decorated. Problem solved."

"That's not very personalized." Jordan's happy smile fell like a soufflé.

Obviously aware she'd burst his bubble, Lucy sighed. "Then do whatever makes you happy."

"I want *you* to be happy." Jordan lifted Lucy's hand and kissed the backs of her fingers.

"Okay. Then do whatever you think *I* want."

Declan groaned. "Good God, get a room, you two."

"If the restaurant doesn't get done on time there won't be any reception. Themed or unthemed," Parker said, tossing a look in Sean's direction.

"It'll be done," Sean reassured them and then nodded at Parker. "As long as *you* keep helping out on the late-into-the-night projects."

"Of course." Parker jabbed his fork into a carrot from the side dish Gabi had brought. "I can sleep when I'm dead."

"No dying." Nicole jumped back into the conversation. "At least not until you give me my Christmas present."

The lively conversation continued through the rest

of dinner and well into dessert. Finally, when everyone got up from the table to stretch and attempt to let
the lump of delicious food in their bellies settle, Gabi
helped clear the table and clean the dishes.

She liked being able to help. But even more, she
liked the energy and the warmth of being a part of
this great big loving family.

Even if it was only for a day.

After dinner the men shifted into the den, flipped
on the big screen TV, and pulled up an NFL game.
With their favorite team at first and goal, everyone
sat down and started whooping and hollering for a
touchdown. Parker took the opportunity to sneak out
of the room and go in search of Gabriella.

He'd been completely floored when she'd shown up
at the door. She looked so good in that body hugging
dress with her pretty hair down and curled around
her face. For a moment he'd held his breath just so he
wouldn't blurt out something stupid. Like give away
the fact that he'd missed seeing her these past weeks.
Hesitant to bring any attention in his direction from
nosy relatives, other than a few words at the table, he
hadn't talked to her.

The house was big, but eventually he caught up
with her in the hallway where she was blessedly alone.

"Fancy seeing you here," he said, blocking her only
path to escape.

"Sorry about that." She gave him a timid smile.

"When I ran into Lucy at the store, she wouldn't take no for an answer. She promised she'd let you know I was invited."

"Nope. Total surprise."

She looked down to the coat he held in his hands.

"Put this on," he said with a lot more snarl than he intended.

"That doesn't belong to me."

"Doesn't matter."

Her eyes narrowed. "Are you telling me to leave?"

"I'm telling you to put on the coat."

"Newsflash. You're not the boss of me. If I'm going to leave I'll do it of my own free will. I was invited here and—"

"Just put on the damn coat, Gabriella."

He held up the black wool garment and, without further argument, she slipped her arms through the sleeves.

"Can I at least thank Lucy for inviting me and tell everyone goodbye?"

"No." If he gave his family an inch they'd make a big deal out of nothing. Sometimes on the sly worked much better with this nosy bunch. And he had too much on his mind, too many questions. He didn't need to be deterred by even more.

Once Gabriella had the coat on, he tugged the front closed and buttoned the top. "Hood."

Frowning, she flipped the hood up over the top of her head.

What seemed like hours later, he settled his hand

on her elbow, then guided her through the empty living room and out the door. Her boot heels clicked on the walkway as he led her through the drizzle and away from the array of cars littering the driveway.

"I'm parked over there." She pointed a long finger tipped with glittery festive orange polish toward a little blue Kia.

"Right." He pulled her in the opposite direction. "But we're going this way."

She looked up at him through the dark and blinked her long thick lashes. "And this way leads to where?"

"Sunshine & Vine."

"We're going to the restaurant?"

"Where did you think we were going?"

"I thought you were kicking me out."

He stopped, turned her to face him, and settled his hands on her arms. He fought the desire to pull her closer, wrap her in his arms, and kiss the hell out of her. Because that's all he'd been thinking about from the moment she walked into the house. "Why would I do that?"

She gave him a defiant look. "Because you're pissed off."

*"Pissed off?"*

"Look." She gave him a stubborn lift of her chin. "I know I invaded your territory, but—"

"You didn't invade anything. I was just surprised when you walked through the door."

"So you're not mad?"

Judging by the hard thump of his heart, he was as

far from mad as a guy could get. But before he gave in to the desire burning through his blood and covered her luscious lips with his, he slid his hand down to hers and intertwined their fingers.

"Come on. Let's go."

She blinked her pretty—and confused—brown eyes. "To the restaurant."

He shook his head. "To complicate the hell out of things."

# Chapter 10

$D$rizzle turned to rain, but the foul weather on the walk down the hill to the restaurant did nothing to discourage Parker's desire. In fact, it might have done just the opposite. In his mind he pictured more pleasurable things. Sweetly scented things. Naughty things. And heating it all up with a good amount of passion.

By the time he unlocked and opened the restaurant, he was ready to slip his hands beneath the black wool coat Gabriella wore and pull her hard against his aching body. He didn't know who the coat belonged to and he hadn't cared when he'd grabbed it off the hall tree and tried to escape before anyone saw them. Everyone would figure things out later. By then, hopefully he'd have things figured out too. Because right now, his body was doing all the reasoning. And it certainly wasn't leaning toward the right thing.

Instead of giving in to instinct and removing the sweater dress that hugged all her delectable curves, he removed her wet wool coat and tossed it over a sawhorse near the door. Then he dropped his dry work coat over her shoulders.

"Thanks." Standing there in the dark, her fingers curled into the Sherpa lining and she gave a little shiver.

"Guess I should have driven you over."

"I'm a Portlander." She gave the long damp curls down her back a little shake. "I'm okay with walking in the rain."

As they stood there in the darkness with only a hint of light bouncing off the raindrops on the window, he looked at her long and hard. The more he looked the more he liked what he saw. He liked that she spoke up for herself. Liked that she'd been brave enough to accept Lucy's dinner invitation. Liked that she was a woman who obviously knew her own mind. What he didn't like was the way she turned him upside down until he didn't know if he was coming or going.

"That was a very nice dinner," she said, looking up at him with drops of moisture tipping her long eyelashes. "I really appreciate Lucy's invitation."

Curious, he asked, "What would you have done if you hadn't come here?"

A shrug lifted her shoulders. "When I ran into Lucy I had a turkey breast in my grocery cart. I'd probably have roasted that and then had dinner watching the Hallmark Channel or something."

In his mind he could see her inside her little apartment sharing Thanksgiving dinner with her cranky little fish. The scenario hit him in the gut as hard as if one of his brothers had thrown a punch. Even when he'd been at his worst as a teen, he'd had family to share the holidays with. No one should have to be alone when the rest of the turkey-eating nation were together.

"My family enjoyed having you at dinner," he said.

"They did?"

He nodded. "I wondered how this year would go without our parents here and my mom leading the way. Even though she and my father apparently had their issues, she managed to set their differences aside and made a big deal out of the holidays. It was nice to see, in their absence, that our family is strong enough to continue with tradition."

"It must be really hard for you without them here."

"It is." An ache spread throughout his chest. "I wish I could tell them how sorry I am just one more time."

"Today's a day to be thankful. What are you sorry for?"

"For being so selfish and treating them and the rest of my family like shit when I was a teenager."

"But so much time has passed. Isn't that all just water under the bridge?" She tugged the coat closer. "You all seem to get along so well now."

"We do. But there was a time when I blamed my parents, brothers, and sister for everything that was wrong with me. I was impatient and selfish. In my mind, the world revolved around me and I thought I should have been getting a lot more attention. Ryan was older and had his own life going on so he didn't have anything to do with me. Jordan was completely focused on hockey and seemed to be gone most of the time. Declan was always quiet and a little withdrawn. Ethan was this happy-go-lucky kid who didn't want to hang out with someone who preferred darkness and anger. And Nicole was the little princess who stole all my mom's attention. Eventually all of them went in the other direction when I came around."

"I can't picture you like that."

He scoffed. "Believe me, I was even worse than I'm describing."

"What did you do to get into trouble?" she asked.

The memories dog-piled on him and he wondered how he'd painted himself in this corner—confessing all his dirty deeds—when all he really wanted to do was touch Gabriella and all her soft curves.

"I got in with a bunch of other guys who felt like I did. They had resentment and hostility growing out of them like spider webs and I got caught up in it." The despair of those days still turned his stomach. "I got into drugs and alcohol. And I was thrown in jail for driving under the influence."

"That must have been really hard for you and for your parents."

In her eyes he found no judgment, only compassion.

"Sitting on that concrete block in the jail cell changed everything. At first I was pissed I'd been arrested. I blamed the cops because, of course, I was innocent. But there was one officer who came into the cell, sat down, and talked to me. He didn't get all preachy. He just said that he understood what I was going through and that I was young and had the opportunity to turn my life around."

"He sounds like a nice guy."

"He was. And believe me, I was belligerent and did not deserve his kindness. But when my parents came to bail me out, and I saw the torment in their eyes, I understood what the officer had been saying. Because I was a juvenile and a first-time offender, the court gave me a chance. My parents gave me an ultimatum. That's how I ended up at Life's Kitchen in Idaho."

"I'm not familiar with that. Is it a cooking school?"

"It's that and more. They not only taught me how to cook, they taught me the skills I needed to secure employment and become financially independent. More importantly, they taught me personal development. At Life's Kitchen I gained a sense of direction. I found what I loved to do. And that gave me the confidence I needed to turn my life around."

She gave him a warm smile. "And you *have* turned your life around."

"I have." The pressure eased from his chest and shoulders.

"Then take today and be thankful that those days are behind you, and that you're part of a loving family. Not everyone can do that."

"I am thankful."

"Good."

"And I'm sorry that you almost had to spend Thanksgiving alone."

"I wouldn't have been alone." She lifted her chin. "Don't forget I have Basil."

"Sweetheart." He tucked his finger beneath her chin, wanting to kiss her so bad it hurt. "That bubbly little dude doesn't count."

For a long moment they looked into each other's eyes as a sensual energy wound around them.

"You know, I can't figure you out," he said honestly.

"And why's that?"

"Because you're like no one else I've ever known. You can act like a total badass, but you've got this great big heart hiding behind all that sass. You're a talented chef who spends half a day making macaroni and cheese for a women's shelter. But then you come in here, pick up an electric drill, and put some of these construction guys to shame. You dress like every man's fantasy and yet you seem most comfortable in jeans and a sweatshirt. You're one part sex goddess and one part girl next door. So which one is the real Gabriella Montani?"

She sighed. "I could tell you but that would be boring."

"Come on. I came clean with you about my past."

"And I appreciate that. It makes me feel . . ." Her fingers reached out and touched the front of his shirt.

"What?" Damn, she wasn't even touching his skin and yet he could feel her.

"Thankful." Her tenuous smile said she'd been about to say something else. And he was disappointed she didn't. "So how about you show me what's new around this place. I assume that's what we came here for, right?"

"Right." Totally a lie. "Give me a sec. We still don't have lighting."

He turned on the work lantern, waited till it pumped up to full brightness, then held it up. "So what do you think?"

Her high heels tapped on the wood floor as she strolled around the room. "You've made some good progress."

"It's getting there. We've finally reached a point where I don't have to help out as much, and I can start focusing on the details."

"Like?"

"Furniture. Lighting. Table settings."

She hid a gasp behind her fingers. "You haven't selected furniture yet?"

"I've been too busy doing stuff like pounding nails and building shit."

"Which makes me ask why you're even having to do all of that. It seems like you have an adequate construction crew."

"I hate giving up control."

She glanced over her shoulder at him with a smile. "You don't seem to mind it so much in bed."

Heat swept through his veins as the memory of her on top of him with her head thrown back in ecstasy grabbed him below the belt. "That might be the only place I'll let go."

"Well, it's a good thing you'll have more time to focus on the details now."

"That's the problem. I really don't. This time of year the food truck business usually slows down because there are less people walking outside during lunchtime, so I hire out for special events. I've got several lined up over the next couple of weeks. We're also planning Jordan's bachelor party."

"So no rest for the wicked?"

He flashed a grin that probably gave her a hint of the *wicked* things going through his mind. "Not in the foreseeable future."

"How can I help?"

He took a step back. "Why would you want to do that? You don't work for me. And—"

"Maybe I just want to see you achieve your dream. Maybe I really like Lucy and Jordan and just want to see them have the reception they deserve." She closed the small space between them. "Maybe I just . . . like you, Parker Kincade. And maybe I just want to make you happy."

A delicious vibration danced through his veins. "I am happy."

"With what exactly?" A slight tilt of her head made her dangly silver earrings jingle.

"Happy that you're here."

"Me too."

"I didn't want to leave that day at your apartment, you know."

"You didn't?"

"No. What I really wanted to do was this." He cupped her face in his hands and kissed her. Her lips were soft and warm as she parted them to let his tongue slip inside her mouth.

When she wrapped her arms around his neck, his work coat fell from her shoulders and her full breasts pressed into his chest. The chill in the air pebbled her nipples so hard he could feel them all the way through two layers of fabric.

Wanting, needing, desperate for more, his mouth left her lips and trailed down the side of her neck. He inhaled her like a bottle of fine wine. She smelled like pumpkin spice, rain, and warm, lusty woman. Gently he sucked her flesh into his mouth and her head fell backward, giving him better access.

"I need this, Parker. I need *you*," she whispered roughly. "You're all I've been able to think about. I need your mouth on me. Your hands."

"Great minds think alike." He hadn't brought her here for this, but the hell if he'd walk away now.

"I need you inside me," she said.

God. He did love a woman who knew what she wanted.

She pushed him back with one hand and started removing the clingy sweater dress with the other. "I've needed you since that night on your houseboat."

"Are you sure you want to take that off? It's cold in here."

"Then heat me up." When she was down to nothing but black lace underthings, high-heeled boots, and goose bumps, she reached for him.

He caught her hands in his. "Who says you get to call the shots?"

Challenge widened her eyes, but her smile never faltered. "I don't like to give up control either. Only for you."

Clasping both her wrists in one hand, he moved in close and picked up where he'd left off. His mouth moved down her neck and across the swell of her breasts that were pushed above the black lace bra. A deep moan rumbled in her chest as he slipped his tongue beneath the lace edging. Needing to touch as well as taste he let go of her wrists and cupped her breasts in his hands. Lifting them slightly, he pulled the lace down with his thumbs and sucked an erect nipple into his mouth.

"Mmmm. You taste as good as you smell," he said against her soft skin while he slid a hand between her legs and cupped her moist heat. "I'm betting you taste this good all over."

"I'm betting if you don't do something more than taste, this could turn . . . ohhhh. My. God."

He loved the way she moaned so full of passion as his fingers snuck beneath the laced edge of her panties and slid home. He moved them the way he knew she liked with a slow, circular motion, and then a teasing dip inside. "Are you heated up enough now?"

"Almost."

He gently pinched her clit between his thumb and finger then retracted for another rub. "How about now?"

"How about you take those pants off and make sure."

He licked the side of her throat again and moved his mouth back down to her nipple. "I'm pretty happy where we're at right now." Which was a fucking lie if he'd ever told one. He wanted inside of her so bad his dick was throbbing an SOS message.

"Really?" She reached between them. Her fingers covered his erection and she squeezed. "Because *this* very big part of you is displaying some dissatisfaction."

Unable not to, he pushed against her hand. When she squeezed him again his eyes nearly crossed.

"I think some equal attention is necessary." Reaching around, she slid her fingers into his back pocket, pulled his wallet out, and handed it to him. "And we need to make it fast."

Before he'd removed the condom from his wallet, she had him unzipped and both his pants and boxer briefs pushed down over his hips. Hastily, she grabbed the foil packet he held between his fingers, tore it open, and rolled the latex over his erection.

Damn that was sexy.

Nothing made a man feel more wanted than when a woman couldn't wait to have him inside her.

He cupped her sweet lace covered ass in his hands, lifted her, and laid her back on the makeshift worktable.

"Hurry, Parker." She slid her fingers down into the lace that covered her mound and touched herself.

"Fuck. You keep that up and I'm not going to make it."

"Then take them off." With the hand that wasn't busy, she curled her fingers into his still-buttoned shirt and pulled him down until they were nose to nose. "Take *me*."

"Greedy woman."

With both hands he pulled off the little scrap of black lace and exposed her. For a moment he watched her fingers dip between her slick folds and rotate faster. She made him so hard he almost burst.

"You're so fucking beautiful. So fucking hot." Unable to stand the pressure, he fisted his cock and gave it a couple of hard pumps to release the pressure. Then he pulled her fingers away and replaced them with his own as he guided himself inside her slick channel.

As badly as he wanted to pump fast and hard, and come even harder, he entered her slowly, enjoying the feel of her body stretching to give him room. He swept the pad of his thumb around her clit and watched as her eyes fluttered closed.

"All of you." Her words came out in a breathy pant and she locked her legs around his hips. "I want all of you, Parker. Hot. Hard. And fast."

"I thought I was the one in control." Hell, neither

one of them was in control. Still, he gave her what she wanted, pumping into her steadily harder and faster. Her whimpers and moans increased in intensity. He watched her nipples harden. With her panting breaths and an "oh God" thrown in here and there, he knew she was on the threshold and he was right there with her. He increased the pressure of his thumb on her clit, drove harder, and was rewarded when he felt her inner muscles clench around him.

She inhaled a sudden gasp and her body gave a long, satisfied shudder.

When he knew she'd flown over the edge, he allowed himself to let go too. A hot tingle shot up the backs of his legs and into his balls. When he came, it was more intense than ever before and made it almost impossible to stay on his feet. He had to lean down, wrap his arms around her, and kiss her softly swearing mouth just to hang on. Her body pulsated around him as the orgasm subsided and he was able to take a real breath.

For several minutes they stayed like that, her tight in his arms, their hearts pounding together.

Yeah.

He'd fucking died and gone to heaven.

*W*hen speech became possible, Gabi sighed. "Can we do that again?"

He chuckled and kissed her mouth. "Absofucking-lutely."

Still semi-hard, he pumped into her a couple more times and she sighed. "We *definitely* need to do that again."

"You're lying here naked. Not that I mind. But aren't you cold?"

"Cold?" She wrapped her arms and legs around him and squeezed. "Best heater in the world right here."

She opened her eyes and found him looking down at her with an emotion she couldn't quite name. And frankly, she was so freaking content right now she didn't even want to try.

He eased out of her and an immediate chill flushed over her body.

"See." He pointed at her pebbled nipples. "You are cold."

"I wouldn't be if you'd stayed in place."

"Have to get rid of this first."

When he left the room, she knew he was disposing of the condom. "I hope you have plenty more of those in your wallet."

Though she could barely see through the darkness, he came back into the room grinning. The humor in his heart verified it when he said, "Sex maniac."

She leaned up on her elbows and returned his grin. "Is that a complaint?"

"No, ma'am. Uh-uh. Not even a little." He picked up his Sherpa lined coat and held it up for her to slip into as she eased off the sheet of plywood. Thankful for no splinters in her ass, she slipped her arms into

the sleeves and pulled the coat together. It was so big
it hit her about mid-thigh, but her bare legs definitely
felt the chill. She turned to find him looking at her
intensely.

"What?"

"You are the sexiest woman I have ever seen." He
wrapped his hands around her upper arms and drew
her in for a meaningful kiss.

"And knowing that all you have on under that coat
is a black lace bra?" He exhaled a breath. "Yeah. We'll
definitely be doing *that* again."

"Will you think of me the next time you put on
the coat?"

"I can promise you I won't even be able to *think*
the next time I wear it. I'll only be picturing you
zipped up inside of it wearing those hot damn boots
with that fuck-me-again look in your eye."

Earlier tonight Gabi had felt like the proverbial
outsider while she dodged Parker's glares. Though
she'd never given it much—or any—thought before,
hot sex was definitely a great icebreaker.

"So . . . back to you." Gently she touched his face.
"I offered to help. Tell me more about what *you* need."

He settled his hands on her hips and pulled her
tight against him. "Dangerous request."

"Hey. I'm the one who just said I wanted to do
that again." She leaned in and kissed him, liking that
she felt comfortable enough to do so. "So if you're
ready . . ."

"For you? Always."

"Parker Kincade, you do know how to say just the right thing to a lady." She wrapped her arms around him and returned the kiss, which became increasingly hot before she leaned her head back. "But let's focus on your *other* needs for right now. There's plenty of moonlight left for the rest."

"It's raining pretty hard." He tipped his head toward the door. "We might have to stay locked in."

"Do you have a construction crew showing up in the morning?"

"Unfortunately."

"Then let's figure out the rest. And maybe we could continue this . . . discussion, back at either your place or mine where it's warmer?"

His head tilted and the lantern light gleamed on his dark hair. "Is that even a question?"

"I'm trying not to be greedy."

"By all means. Please be greedy." He drew his finger down the side of her face then caught his fingertip on her bottom lip. "But we go to either your place or mine on one condition."

"Uh-oh." *Please don't say it's only for one more night.*

"We sneak back into the main house and steal some leftovers before we go. And once we get where we're going . . . *you* stay put. No running this time."

Whew. Heartbreak averted.

"Until you're done with me?"

"Baby, I'm not going to be done with you any time soon."

She liked the sound of that. "And you won't disappear either?"

"As the old saying goes, not a snowball's chance in hell."

"Then you have a deal."

Other than another amazing time exploring his body and what he could do with it to make hers sing like a freaking opera star, exactly what she was agreeing to was uncertain. She may be swimming in dangerous waters. But, if she was going to go down with Parker, oh what a lovely way to drown.

# Chapter 11

*G*abi pulled the restaurant supply catalog from his hands then rolled over in bed, propped herself up on her elbows, and scanned the products on the page.

"Can I look too?" Parker wanted to sigh with contentment as they lazed around in bed the morning after Thanksgiving. It might be Black Friday with shoppers everywhere in downtown Portland, but he'd chosen to give his food truck staff the day off. He just never imagined he'd be spending it in bed with Gabriella. "Or are you going to hog the magazine like you did the pumpkin cheesecake?"

She smirked. "I warned you I wouldn't share."

"I know." He turned over and, lying beside her, mirrored her position. "But I had planned to spread it all over your body and lick it off slowly."

"Really? Because there's still a slice left." Another sassy grin lit up her face. "I hid it in the vegetable drawer."

"So you're holding out on me."

"I'm lying next to you naked. Does that seem like I'm holding out?"

Parker laughed, pushed the catalog out of her hands, rolled her over, and moved on top of her. He'd never shared *playtime* in bed with a woman before. He liked it.

He liked *her*.

And he hoped they could keep things just like this. Fun. Sexy. Casual. No strings sex with the benefit of each other's company on occasion or whenever time allowed. He knew that came off as selfish. Even more reason to make sure she felt the same way, because he'd never want to be a user. And that conversation needed to happen. Soon. But at the moment a certain part of him was getting insistent about dabbling in a little more of the *no strings sex* part.

Kisses turned hot and Parker made good on the pumpkin cheesecake promise.

Afterward they showered together. Since he was in no hurry for her to leave and she didn't seem in any hurry to pull another disappearing act, they ended up on his sofa. Outside the rain poured down. Inside he'd turned on the gas fireplace for ambience and buttoned up Gabriella in one of his flannel shirts. That she was naked beneath the soft material turned out to be very inspiring.

Settled cozily into a corner of the couch, she stretched out her shapely legs and propped her feet on his thighs while she continued to peruse the restaurant supply catalog. Parker sipped his steaming cup of whiskey-laced coffee and knew they needed to talk. To completely clear the air and make sure they were both on the same page. At the same time, they had such a good vibe going he didn't want to kill it. And so those words just stayed put inside his selfish brain.

"Hmmm." She tossed the catalog in his direction and he caught it with one hand. "I don't like any of those."

"How can you not like anything? There are hundreds of products to choose from. You can even mix and match tabletops and bases."

"Everything looks too generic."

"Most restaurant stuff is. Which is why they build thousands at a time. Which is why you can get such great prices."

"I know." She reached for her coffee mug, leaned back, and took a sip. "And that's the problem. Do you really want Sunshine & Vine to be generic? Don't you want it to be a reflection of your personality?"

"My personality?"

"What. You don't think you have one?"

"Of course I do. It just tends to vary on a day-to-day basis." Which translated to mildly aggravated, rationally frustrated, and wildly pissed off.

"That's only because you're under so much stress to get the restaurant done on time." She sipped her coffee again. "But you really need to think about the overall experience. These days food is personal. It seems everyone's a critic. Everyone likes things differently. And those who enjoy food as an experience—which is exactly the type of clientele anyone can hope for—

are lucky enough to have chefs who like to explore the possibilities. Chefs who aren't afraid to push the envelope on flavor. And that envelope is how you should see the design of your restaurant."

Parker blinked. She was preaching to the choir, but in his chaotic life, he'd forgotten the words to the sermon. Imagination and finding your essence were lessons he'd learned at Life's Kitchen when he'd been that troubled teen hell-bent on self-destruction. Lately he'd just been so happy to make any kind of progress he'd lost focus on the end result.

"Look at The Tasty Spoon," she said of his food truck. "Aside from the hunky guy who mans the kitchen, the exterior is part of what initially draws people to *your* food truck instead of the next one. It's bright and it looks like fun. Which, to the layman's eye, probably means your food will be fun. You managed to incorporate your logo in an inventive way that's synonymous with your personality and the creative dishes you serve."

"That was probably an unconscious doing on my part." Talking like this with her was enlightening. Not only did she help him put things in perspective, she managed to bring back the initial excitement he'd had in the prospect of opening his first restaurant.

"And that's fine. It worked." She swung her feet off his thighs and curled up by his side. "But that doesn't mean you should create the restaurant the same way. It doesn't mean you have to live up to everyone else's expectations either."

"Okay, fairy godmother, you lost me."

"Sorry. I can't help but get excited."

"I like it when you're excited."

"And I'd be happy to show you how truly excited I can get." Playfully, she nudged him with her shoulder. "But can we stick to talking about your restaurant for a little while longer?"

"Should I set a timer?"

"No." She laughed. "But you can tell me how you classify your style."

"Jeans, T-shirts, shoes when necessary. Easygoing unless a certain sexy someone wants to talk business instead of tearing off my clothes. Then I might get a little crazy."

"Save that crazy for later," she said. "I can put it to good use."

"And now you're teasing me and you expect me to stay on task?"

"Yes please."

"Evil woman." He leaned in and nipped her shoulder. "I might be sorry I asked, but how do *you* see me?"

"Naked."

He laughed. "You are such a tease."

"Guilty." She cupped his face in her hands and kissed him. "You really want to know what I see in you?"

"If you say a shallow male who only thinks about sex I'll cry . . . guilty." He sighed. "But go ahead anyway."

Her dark eyes glimmered. "I see a guy who has too

many layers to define. On one hand you're sexy casual with the jeans, the T-shirts, the longer hair, the perpetual five o'clock scruff. *That* Parker looks like he should be spending all his time kicked back on the beach with a Corona in one hand and a hot chick in the other. But last night at dinner, you looked more traditional. Sleek and classy. Like all you had to do was throw on a tux and you'd give George Clooney a run for his money. Like you could either be a jetsetter or someone in control of what everyone else does."

"Wow. That's a pretty deep look."

"I can go further if you want."

"You're scaring me enough now as it is." Not that he saw himself as either of those kinds of guys, and not that she really scared him, but he feared she may be one of those rare individuals who could look deep and really figure things out.

Yeah. That was scary as hell.

"I only want to help," she said, and he knew she meant it.

"Okay, then go ahead. Just kick those closet skeletons out of the way first."

"I'm not digging *that* deep. We'll keep the conversation in reference to the restaurant. For now."

"Oh good. Because I was about to go make this Irish coffee a double shot."

"Silly boy. Shall we continue?"

"Fire away."

"Have you come up with a final decision regarding your menu?"

"I've tried. But . . ." Yeah. He'd tried. But lately his

mind had been going in too many directions to narrow it down. Not only was he physically exhausted, he was mentally cooked. He figured since the restaurant wouldn't officially open until after the New Year, he'd have time to settle down and work it out. But it seemed the more time went on, the less he'd been able to shove one more thought inside his head.

"I'll take that as a no." Gabriella stroked her fingers down his arm. "If you want to discuss, maybe we should back up a little."

He stretched his arm out on the sofa behind her and tucked her closer to his side. "No. Let's keep moving forward. Maybe I can clear some things up."

"Okay." She chuckled. "So I know you're using the natural wood in the barn and you've created a spectacular focal point with that brick wall on the back, but what are your design plans for the interior?"

"I just figured I'd go with a clean, casual look, minimal wall deco. Maybe a few plants to play off the rustic wood." He shrugged. "Nothing fancy."

"But casual won't really play to your desired clientele. Casual won't make your restaurant become a destination for diners when all the other restaurants in Sunshine are laidback."

"You're right." With less than three weeks until Jordan's wedding and under two months to open the restaurant for business, Parker knew he had to get his shit together. Not only did he have to decide what he wanted, he had to order it and make sure it was delivered and installed on time.

"Since the exterior of your restaurant is an old

barn, diners are probably going to expect informal dining. Fool them."

"How do I do that?"

"Why did you choose the name Sunshine & Vine?"

"Because it's in Sunshine and in a vineyard."

"I get that. But don't you think someone might associate it with the famous intersection of Hollywood and Vine?"

"Never even entered my mind."

"Well it should. Old Hollywood was glamorous. It had just the right amount of sparkle and shine. Glitz and glamor. The exterior of your restaurant is a beautiful old barn, so provide the ultimate surprise with the interior. Beneath those rustic exposed wood beams, give your clientele a touch of Hollywood sparkle and mix it up with country chic. Give them the elegance of white linen tablecloths with black cloth napkins and glittery chandeliers. Then bring in a bit of country with a touch of corrugated metal— maybe on the front of your hostess station or even on a section of wall—and add in fresh wildflowers or herbs in a stylish vase for each table. Make it unique and completely your own style of sexy casual."

He thought about it for a moment, and he realized that all along he'd been imagining a country chic thing without the clichéd angle. But he could see how adding a bit of simple elegance to the touch of country would pair perfectly together. Like fine wine and an artisan focaccia.

"You're a genius." He cupped her face in his hands and kissed her.

"Will you please tell my potential boss that for me? I'm planning on asking for a big salary."

Her laughter lit him up on the inside.

"I can give you *big*. Right now."

She giggled as he pulled her beneath him and slipped his hands beneath the red flannel shirt.

A soft sigh whispered past her lips as he touched her in all his—and her—favorite places. And though his mind was close to letting the sensations in his body take over, he did have one more thought.

"Are we good with this?" he asked.

*"This?"*

"Keeping things casual. Fun. No strings. I know initially we agreed to one night but, obviously, we obliterated that deal. And"—he dropped a kiss to her lips—"I really like you."

Her slight hesitation cooled the rush of blood pumping through his veins.

"Sure." She looked him in the eye and gently pushed a lock of his hair off his forehead. "We can keep this casual."

Relief eased the pressure in his chest. "I'm glad."

She arched her pelvis into his erection. "I can tell."

He laughed, and then proceeded to show her exactly how much he liked her.

Later as he held her in his arms while they both began to doze off, realization hit him like a baseball bat in full swing. Trying to remain casual with this woman was going to be a lot more difficult than choosing restaurant furnishings or planning a menu.

# Chapter 12

*L*ate Friday afternoon Parker drove Gabi back to her car, which had remained parked near the main house at the vineyard. Not that she'd been all that eager to leave his cozy houseboat or his warm embrace, but there were two solid reasons she needed to go. One, she had to feed Basil. If he didn't get his pellets before a certain time he got really cranky and flashed his tail at her like a matador's red cape. And two, Parker wanted to keep this, whatever it was between them, casual.

She'd told him they would, even though she already knew she probably couldn't. She'd already switched trains on that track. Especially after the night and day they'd shared.

Parker was an affectionate man who didn't think twice about losing his man card because he liked to snuggle. He made love with a selfless passion that rang every bell in her system—more than once each time. He made her laugh. He made amazing eggs benedict. And he gave her something that had been completely unexpected.

He made her feel necessary.

With the exception of her *nonni*, no one in her life—no man especially—had ever made her feel needed, or for that matter, wanted. From her father all the way to her recent employer, not one had made her feel as though she ever had anything relevant to say or any purpose to exist.

Feeling wanted was a new concept.

And she liked it.

For a change, something other than the need to prove herself existed. So when Parker had shown up unexpectedly at her apartment door on Friday evening with a bowl of steaming hot penne pasta made with parmesan and zucchini, she eagerly invited him in.

Late into the night as they lay in her bed in each other's arms with the covers pulled up around them, Gabi had never been happier. Yet something still bothered her. And even though they'd agreed to keep things casual, she cared about him. Seeing him pushing himself to the brink of exhaustion every day worried her.

"Can I ask you a question?" she asked.

"Yes." He kissed her forehead. "I still believe in Santa Claus."

She chuckled. "Not what I was going to ask but

good to know. And if you're on speaking terms with him, can you put in a good word for me? Because I think I might be on his naughty list."

"Baby, with what you just did to my body, I *know* you're on his naughty list."

"But it was so worth the stocking full of coal."

"I second that." He kissed her forehead again. "So now that we know who's going to get a present from Santa and who's not, what else did you want to know?"

"Why do you feel the need to take on so much to make everyone else happy? And why do you drive yourself to exhaustion?"

"I told you about my past. I owe my family everything. And even though I'll never really be able to repay them, I have to keep trying."

The admission came out with such pain and guilt that he remained silent for a moment. Gabi slowly stroked his forearm without saying a word, hoping he'd continue, not blaming him if he didn't. Reliving those days must be extremely hard. Lord knew when she thought about everything her teen years had brought, it was like hitting a wall at full speed.

"I'm really sorry you went through all that," she said.

"Not everyone's life is a carnival. But I can't blame anyone else; I brought it all on my stupid self."

"You were young."

"And selfish."

"That's not so uncommon for teens."

"Yeah, but now that I know what my mom and dad were going through at the time with their marriage . . ." He blew out a breath of air. "I'll bet they wanted to kill me."

"That's not who you are now," she said, unaware of what his parents had really gone through. "I like who you are. And you've become the man you are because of that experience."

"You're a hell of a lot more understanding than I am."

Her chest tightened. "You mean if you found out some dark secret of mine you wouldn't want to know?"

"Honesty is really important to me." He tightened his arms around her and gave a questioning look. "I've spilled my guts. You got something you want to share?"

"No."

She did, but she couldn't. No, make that she wouldn't. He'd been the one to request they keep their relationship strictly casual. If she shared her past too, that might put them in a different relationship category. He had enough going on to listen to her sob story, so she decided to just keep this all about him.

For now.

"I guess I can understand why, at one time, you might have felt the need to make up for your past," she said. "But that was a long time ago. You were a boy then. You're a man now. Responsible. Intelligent.

Talented. And from what I can see, you're a great brother. I can't imagine anyone in your family would want you to still feel like you had something to prove. Or to push yourself so hard to please them. They just don't seem like those kind of people."

"You mentioned you had two half sisters from your father's affair. Any other siblings?"

She nodded. "I also have an older brother."

"Are you close?"

She snagged her bottom lip between her teeth while she tried to figure out how to answer that without being too revealing. She didn't want to spoil the rest of the night. Parker needed honesty. In this case, a partial truth was better than a complete lie.

"I'd like to be close, but that really isn't possible. My parents went through an ugly divorce a long time ago that split up the family."

"I'm sorry." He hugged her tight.

"Not your fault." Not her fault. Nobody's fault but her father's.

Maybe she really needed to heed her own advice and stop trying to make up for the past. Even if the mistakes weren't her own.

"So . . ." She trailed her hands down his sexy abs. "How about we get back to the *fun* part."

"Yes, ma'am." With a waggle of his eyebrows, he ducked under the covers.

Gabi knew she was in way over her head. Because while he performed magic beneath the sheets, she had to remind herself that they'd agreed to keep this relationship casual. Fun. No strings. Mission impossible in her books. Because whether she liked it or not, her heart was already tied up with a bow.

*S*aturday morning, Gabi had a hard time waking up Parker. She'd never seen anyone sleep so hard. He'd barely moved an inch all night. For hours he'd held her close, almost in a viselike grip. Not that she minded. But since he was the one who kept insisting they keep things fun and casual, she decided to tease him.

"I'm thinking of buying some velvet ropes."

Eyes wide, mouth full, he looked up from munching on the Mediterranean omelet she'd made for him. "Excuse me?"

"What. Are you against a little bit of friendly bondage?"

He swallowed hard. "Did we just move to a different level?"

Gabi folded her arms, leaned against the counter, and grinned. "You don't seem all that opposed to the prospect."

He got up from the table and came to stand in front of her. "Is that what you're into?" He settled his hands on her hips and drew her close.

"No, I was just teasing you because you hold onto me so tight when you sleep."

"Hmmm." He nuzzled her neck. "Maybe that's just because you're so soft and warm."

"And you sleep so hard. I could barely wake you up this morning."

"That's because I'm exhausted." He captured her

lips in a quick kiss. "Not that I'm complaining about the sex."

"I should hope not. You're enjoying yourself too much to complain."

"Yeah. I'm definitely willing to take one for the team. But what I meant was that I think I'm ready to admit that all the long hours of work, worry, rinse and repeat, are getting to me."

He stepped back and ran a hand through his hair, messing up the long dark locks that now fell to the tops of the broad shoulders on which he carried so much weight.

"I guess everything just finally caught up with me."

She stepped closer, reached up, and pushed back the lock of hair that fell over his forehead. "You need to stop working so hard."

"Are you worried about me?"

"Yes," she said. "And I know that's crossing the keeping-things-casual line, but I can't help it."

His dark brows came together as he searched her face.

Just when she thought he'd jump in to reinforce their agreement, he grinned.

"So . . . no velvet ropes?"

A little sigh of relief lifted her worried heart. "Never say never."

*L*ate in the afternoon, Parker's phone chimed with an incoming text. He pulled it from his pocket and read Ethan's message.

Me and the brothers are at main house getting ready to watch Alabama take on LSU. Beer. Football. Cussing. Get your ass up here.

Parker looked around at the construction activity in the restaurant and reluctantly decided Sean had things under control. He took a deep breath, texted his brother back, and walked away.

What could go wrong?

Just because he wasn't there every second to watch over everything didn't mean it would all fall apart. It wasn't like he was some kind of control freak micromanager. Maybe his being around was only getting in the way of reaching the completion date on time. Maybe all this time he thought he'd been helping where really he was only hindering the process.

He zipped up his Sherpa lined coat and ducked his head against the wind and the snow flurries as he headed up the hill to the house.

If Jordan could take the time away from playing Groomzilla, then it couldn't hurt for him to take a break. Right? Unfortunately he had too much invested to see things that way. It wasn't just time and money. For him the restaurant was a symbol of healing. It was a sign that the family was whole and that they were going to be able to put the past behind them.

Together.

Even so, taking an afternoon off wasn't going to destroy everything he'd been pushing hard for. And ever since he'd pulled his head out of his ass, he savored the time with his brothers. Even if some of those times came with yelling at the TV or yelling at each other.

Trudging up the hill, his boots slipped on the icy path. Falling and breaking his neck wouldn't be any damn help to getting things done, so he took smaller steps.

Finally he opened the front door and his ears were immediately assaulted by his brothers cursing over the roar of the college stadium crowd and the announcer's game commentary. He and his brothers would be a divided group, with half pulling for Alabama and the others rooting for LSU with a shitload of *fuck you*s and *shove it up your ass*es volleying around the room at full speed. But that's what made watching football so much fun in the Kincade household.

The moment he walked into the den, Ethan gave him a nod and Dec slapped a cold bottle of beer in his hand. They both scooted over on the sofa to make room. Ryan and Jordan hogged the recliners while the rest of them sat shoulder to shoulder. As the Alabama quarterback threw a bullet into the end zone and it was caught by the wide receiver, Parker and his brothers all came up out of their seats with various four-letter exclamations on the perfection of the pass.

When they all sat back down, Jordan looked over his shoulder at Parker. "About fucking time you took a day off."

If Parker rolled his eyes any harder they'd have

stuck at the back of his head. "How can I take a day off when your pussy ass alter ego, Groomzilla, keeps pushing me to get the restaurant done in time for his reception?"

"Someone has to keep you on your toes. I've got a wedding checklist I have to stick to, you know."

Next to Parker, Declan chuckled and said, "Know what I'm buying him for his bachelor party?"

"What?"

"Feminine hygiene products."

As the brothers laughed, Jordan flipped them his middle finger without taking his eyes off the action on the big screen TV.

"I thought about buying him a French maid outfit so he could really turn into Lucy's bitch," Ethan said.

Jordan's middle finger remained raised.

Parker laughed. "Guess I'll buy him an apron then."

"Hey." Jordan shot him the stink eye. "*You* wear an apron."

"Yeah. But not the kind with ruffles."

In the recliner, Ryan snorted. "Damn it's good to have everybody back home."

"Yeah," they all said in unison, even though Jordan's middle finger remained fully extended.

As the Alabama kicker sent a perfect PAT through the uprights, Declan looked at Parker and said, "My fiancée's coat is missing. You know anything about that?"

"It was Brooke's coat?"

"Yeah. She took the spare one home."

"Sorry."

Dec chuffed. "That contented look on your face says you aren't sorry at all."

"Yeah." Ethan swung his gaze around. "That look says you got laid. Plenty."

"You jealous?" Parker asked.

"Fuck yes."

Parker raised his bottle and took a drink. Even though it would be easy to brag, he didn't like talking about his sex life with anyone. What happened between a man and woman in bed was their business. But if he even tiptoed into that discussion with his brothers they'd want to know more. They'd want to know where things stood between him and Gabriella. They'd want to know his intentions. And he'd have to tell them he had no intentions. Which made him kind of sound like an ass. Like he was using Gabriella for sex and then when he was done with her he'd toss her aside. But it wasn't like that at all.

He wanted to be with her. He just didn't want her to expect him to be with her.

Shit. Did that even make any sense?

"She's a nice girl," Ryan said. "Don't fuck it up."

"Jesus." Parker slugged down a drink. "It's not like I have some kind of love-'em-and-leave-'em reputation."

"You sure about that?" Ethan asked.

"Yes." He was sure. Wasn't he?

"What about that Katrina chick?" Declan wanted to know. "You know, the one you met at the Seahawks game last year? The hot blonde with the big . . . personality? The one—"

"Yes," Parker interrupted. "I remember. What does she have to do with anything?"

"One week of some pretty hot stuff, from what I remember," Dec said. "And then you were over it."

"That doesn't make me the love-'em-and-leave-'em type. We just didn't have anything other than sex in common."

"And then there was Madison," Ryan reminded him. "Nice girl."

"Again. Nothing outside of the sheets."

"But you do have something more with Gabriella, right?" Jordan wanted to know. "I mean, you're both chefs. That's a lot of *in common*."

"Yes," Parker admitted. "We have a lot going on."

"Like I said." Ryan sipped from his beer. "She's a nice girl. Don't fuck it up."

Apparently while Parker had been trying to focus on just enjoying his time with Gabriella, his brothers had been paying a lot closer attention than he'd ever have guessed. It wasn't like he planned to fuck anything up. He just . . . what? He really liked her? He enjoyed the hell out of being with her? He couldn't wait until he could see her again? Yes. All of that. But right now he just needed to focus on the pile of shit he had to get done. He wasn't ready to hang drapes, start planning a wedding, or start making babies. Not that he would mind all that somewhere down the road. But right now he just

wanted to enjoy the occasional spare moments he
had with a woman who made him smile, made him
laugh, and made him feel damned good all over
without feeling guilty if he had other things to do
than pay attention to her.

Was that too much to ask?

*B*y the time Parker left her apartment the day
before, Gabriella had successfully helped him place
an online order for the booths, tables, and chairs.
She couldn't be happier that she'd helped him over
a hurdle he could now check off his list. Hopefully
with at least one thing off his mind he'd be able to
sleep a little easier.

He still had so much to do before Jordan and
Lucy's big day, and Christmas was sneaking up fast,
not to mention his day-to-day work with the food
truck. As she'd spent the quiet afternoon working on
some issues of her own, an idea had popped into her
head. No matter how much coffee she drank or how
many projects she invented, she couldn't tame the
thought. So she decided to act.

Hopefully, to Parker it wouldn't seem like she was
interfering, especially now that she'd put the idea
into full gear. All she really wanted to do was help
the man she'd quickly come to care about very much.

Main Street in beautiful downtown Sunshine had
come alive as Gabi drove toward Sugarbuns Bakery.
Christmas greenery now lined the street and shim-
mery candy canes adorned every light pole. Each

mom and pop store was decked out in garlands and lights. Festive wreaths brightened the doors. And at the intersection of Main and Burgundy, the Back Door Bookstore had perched a life-sized Santa on the cast-iron bench outside their window. In his white-gloved hands he held an array of children's books and a sign that said "Books Ignite Imagination."

Not wanting to reach her destination with empty hands, Gabi parked in front of the pastel pink building in the center of town and went inside. The mouth-watering aroma of Sugarbuns's locally celebrated cinnamon rolls greeted her along with the jingle of the bells above the door.

"Welcome to Sugarbuns. I'm Pearl." The woman behind the glass display case flashed a broad smile. "Today's specials are chocolate almond rum ring and southern butter almond coffee cake. We also have fresh almond crescent cookies and, of course, our cinnamon rolls. What can I get for you?"

Gabi scanned the display cases and her mouth watered. "My stomach says one of everything."

Pearl chuckled. "You won't believe how many times I've heard that. Haven't seen you around before. New in town?"

"I live in Portland. I'm going up to visit the Kincade family and I didn't want to show up empty-handed."

"Ah. The Kincades. Lovely people. Which one are you friends with?"

Friends or lovers? Gabi hoped they could be called both. "Parker."

"So you're the one." Pearl gave her a nod. "Gabriella, right?"

"How did you know?"

"Their aunt Pippy is a good friend of mine. She came in here just this morning talking about how her nephew Parker had found his girl."

Accustomed to large-scale gossip and slander but completely unaccustomed to small-town chatter, Gabi didn't know how to respond. So she took the long road. "If she meant that I'm the *chef* who'd like to work with Parker in his new restaurant, then yes, I'm the one. And yes, I'm Gabriella."

"Good to meet you, darlin'." Pearl stuck her hand across the display case for a handshake. "Have to say those Kincade boys are dropping like flies off the *available* list. Can't say I'm surprised though. Who wouldn't want to catch one of them? I might be old but I'm not dead."

"I'm not really . . ." Hmm. Gabi was rarely caught so off guard, but she didn't know how Parker would want her to counter since, in his mind, their relationship was to be fun, casual, and no strings only.

"Oh." Pearl waved her hand. "No need to confirm or deny. I'll get verification once the wedding cake is ordered."

And *there* was her conversation detour.

"Speaking of wedding cakes. Have Jordan and Lucy placed an order for theirs yet?"

"Oh sure. Jordan placed the order weeks ago. And changed it. Then changed it again." She chuckled.

"I keep expecting Lucy to show up and set things straight, but I hear she's put him in charge of everything. Though I can't imagine what she's thinking. He's not really the type to be in touch with his feminine side. If you know what I mean."

Gabi nodded. "But he's trying really hard to make Lucy happy."

"Well, if you promise to sneak a little bug in his ear, I can tell you exactly what kind of cake and design his bride-to-be would *like* to have."

Like fate had stepped in to help her with her goal today, Gabi grinned. "I'll take that little bug and a dozen cinnamon rolls to go."

When Jordan and Lucy opened the door to the main house at Sunshine Creek on Sunday morning, Gabriella knew she'd caught them off guard.

"Hi. Can I come in?"

"Of course." Looking a little puzzled, they both stepped back and she went inside the warm living room that still smelled like pumpkin pie.

"It's good to see you again," Lucy said.

"Especially since you and Parker disappeared so quickly Thanksgiving night," Jordan added, a smirk tilting his very masculine lips.

A flush crept up Gabi's cheeks.

"It took us several minutes to realize that Brooke's coat hadn't been lost," he added. "It got kidnapped."

"I could explain," Gabi said, trying to keep her

embarrassment intact. "But I'm not sure how willing your brother is to spill the beans."

"Oh, please give me and the brothers something to give him shit about." Jordan laughed when Lucy poked her elbow into his ribcage. "What? It's what we do."

Gabi smiled at their playfulness and familiarity. A girl always hoped for that kind of relationship with her man. "You're probably wondering why I just popped up on your doorstep."

"You're welcome here anytime." Lucy smiled. "Would you like some coffee or tea?"

"Actually, tea would be great. Herbal if you have it. I'm afraid of the consequences if I have any more coffee. I've already been running at Nascar speed this morning." She held up the pastry box. "I brought you some cinnamon rolls from Sugarbuns."

"Perfect. Let's talk in the kitchen," Jordan said. "Easier to eat and less chance for an interruption."

"Too late for that."

Gabi turned at the voice coming down the stairs. Today their aunt Pippy was decked out in a white Elvis jumpsuit with a red pleather belt and sparkly silver ankle boots. Earrings that looked like a complete solar system dangled from her ears. Gabi might question her fashion sense, but never her colorful personality.

"Don't get started yakking about my nephew without me," Pippy said. "I've already got everyone on alert."

"Alert?"

"Next brother taken off the market," Jordan told her. "According to Aunt Pippy we'll all be off the available list by the end of next year."

"*You'll* be off the list by the end of *this* year," Lucy reminded him, then brushed his cheek with a kiss.

"Which is exactly why I'm here." Gabi settled into one of the big wooden chairs at the table and pulled her notepad from her purse. All eyes were directed at her. Any other day she'd feel nervous about setting herself up to be a big buttinski. In this case, she didn't even flinch. She'd do anything to help Parker.

"It's no secret Parker and I have been spending some time together. And whether I actually end up working for him or not remains to be seen." Gabi took a breath, amazed at how fast he'd become important to her. "But that's not why I'm here. Right now I come strictly as a friend who's concerned about him. Even though I'm pretty sure he wouldn't want me to say anything."

"What's wrong?" Instant worry creased Lucy's forehead. "Is he sick?"

"He's overworked and exhausted. And he's not getting any sleep because his mind won't shut off long enough for him to relax. Between the family business, the food truck business, adding his physical efforts to building the restaurant as well as trying to make it all come together, and trying to figure out how to help you have the perfect wedding reception, he's not really making things happen like he might normally do."

"I've noticed he does look tired," Pippy said.

"Me too. I never wanted to add to his worries." Lucy poked Jordan in the side. "You need to stop being so hard on him."

"Hey. I didn't know he was overloaded," Jordan said.

"Well, pay attention." Lucy softened her stern tone with a squeeze on Jordan's arm. "Please."

"I want to help him without imposing my ideas or just pushing him aside and taking over," Gabi said. "So I thought maybe if you and Lucy could give me some ideas on what type of rehearsal dinner and reception menu you'd like to have, we could X two things off his to-do list. That way he could focus more attention on actually getting everything done on time without any added stress. It will also bring you two together as a team to get what you both want for your wedding, not just one person trying to decide for the other."

"I'd really like that." Jordan sighed with relief. "Being a wedding planner is not all it's cracked up to be. Even when you have a sister who's trying to take some of the heat off."

"I'm sorry." Lucy looked up at her fiancé with apology in her eyes. "I can take back the duties if you want. Or . . . we could just skip all the hassle and go down to the courthouse."

"Absolutely not." Jordan kissed Lucy's forehead. "It's not a hassle if, in the end, I get to be married to you. I just want you to have the best."

"I know you do." The smile Lucy gave her fiancé

melted Gabi's heart. "And I love you for that. But I'd really be just as happy if it was just you and me and a preacher."

"And I love you for that." Jordan returned his bride-to-be's smile. "But it ain't gonna happen that way. And you know why."

"Can we at least agree to scale it back just a little?" Lucy asked. "If only to take some of the pressure off Parker."

"If you insist."

Lucy looked relieved as she said to Gabi, "Sounds like you really care about Parker."

"I do." Why deny it. "I haven't known him that long but . . . . I want him not only to succeed, I want him to be able to enjoy the success without feeling like he's been dragged over a bed of hot coals."

Jordan and Lucy exchanged a look. Then Jordan said, "I honestly didn't know I was adding extra pressure on him to have the reception at the new place."

"He doesn't see it as extra pressure," Gabi said. "He loves you both and he wants to be able to give you the very best. He's just so tired he doesn't really know what the best might be right now."

"He's very good at hiding what's really going on inside his head," Lucy commented.

"Typical male," Aunt Pippy said. Then she looked at Gabi. "It's very considerate of you to want to help him."

"He matters a lot to me." Yep. It was out in the

open now. She might as well tell them she thought she was falling in love too. Open up the whole can of worms instead of just letting a few escape. Somehow, with the speed of a sexy smile, Parker had become an essential part of her life.

And it had absolutely nothing to do with working for him at his restaurant.

"I'm going to offer to work a few days in the food truck for him until things settle down," Gabi added. "He'll probably say no, but—"

"But you're not really a take-no-for-an-answer kind of girl," Pippy said.

"Exactly."

"Yep." Pippy gave a sharp nod as she reached into the open pastry box and scooped up a cinnamon roll. "Kincade boys are falling off the available list like dust off a chalkboard."

Gabi wanted to tell Parker's aunt that her feelings were one-sided. That Parker had stipulated they keep things "casual," so there were really no worries about him falling off the hot, sexy, available Kincade brother list any time soon.

Shifting the conversation back to the reason she'd shown up on their doorstep, Gabi said, "I thought maybe if I could help you narrow down some selections for your rehearsal and reception meals, I could pass them along to him. Then I could make sure all his supplies are ordered."

"Sounds like a great idea." Lucy laid her hand over Gabi's. "And thank you for wanting to help him out. The last thing we want is for him to be too exhausted to celebrate with everyone else."

"My thoughts exactly."

Gabi pushed the top of her pen down then scribbled a little on the notepad to make sure it worked. "By the way, when I stopped by Sugarbuns for the cinnamon rolls, Pearl said you were having a difficult time deciding on your cake flavors. Might I suggest a red velvet cake with Italian buttercream? It's elegant and flavorful and the deep red color fits in with the Christmas theme." She gave a wink to Lucy, having been informed that red velvet was the bride-to-be's favorite.

Lucy sighed. "Sounds perfect."

"That's it." Aunt Pippy lifted her hand as though she was being sworn in. "I'm throwing in my vote that Gabriella is *perfect* for our Parker."

Tangled up in emotion, Gabi had no idea if that was true. Even if she hoped with all her heart. But she was willing to let Parker take his time to figure things out.

# Chapter 13

Dust floated down from the exposed beam where an electrician was drilling holes for installation of the chandeliers above the booths. Eventually. If Parker could ever commit to making a choice.

And that was a damn big *if*.

That morning over coffee, Gabriella had encouraged him to sit down and make a decision on booths, tables, and chairs. By the time he pulled out his credit card and hit SUBMIT on the website, a huge relief settled over his shoulders. He could now mark three items off his enormous checklist. And he had her to thank for it.

What they'd accomplished together had fallen more into the business/serious category instead of the fun/casual category in which he wanted to maintain their relationship. In truth it had felt more like a partnership. Like a musical collaboration that had gone so well he wondered how everything else might work between them.

It also raised a bigger question.

Did it make sense for a guy who'd said he just wanted a fun and casual fling to keep showing up at her door and spending the night in her bed?

Did it make sense that when he woke up wrapped around her like an octopus he realized he slept better than when he slept alone? That every worry in his head seemed to evaporate when he had her in his arms?

Did it make sense for a man who claimed to want no strings to constantly be thinking about ways to show her how much he cared even if she wasn't exactly forthcoming with many tidbits about her personal life?

Until she'd pointed it out, he hadn't realized he was so strung out with no end in sight to the things on his checklist and not enough days to make it all happen. There were conversations he needed to have with Jordan so he could get a handle on the rehearsal dinner and reception. Conversations he needed to have with Lili to find out her marketing plans and ideas for incorporating the restaurant into the bigger scheme for the vineyard. And there were conversations he needed to have with himself. Because when he was with Gabriella, nothing about her felt just casual or no strings.

"Hey there."

He turned at the sultry sound of her voice.

"I was just thinking about you." Despite the construction crew surrounding them, he wrapped an arm around her waist and reeled her in for a kiss.

She blushed. "I like the way you think."

"Sweet. How about I get rid of these guys and we go see how hot we can make the kitchen without an oven."

She chuckled and touched his face with cool fingers. "As awesome as that sounds, I have something to show you."

"Even better." He tossed her a grin. "Let the removal of clothes begin."

"Whoa. Back the truck up, cowboy. The clothes are staying on." She returned his grin with a sexy one of her own. "For now."

"I'm highly disappointed. But I will hold you to the *for now* part later after everyone leaves. So what's up?"

"I hope you won't get mad, but I know how busy you are. So I took the liberty of talking with Jordan and Lucy about what type of entrées they'd like to have for the rehearsal dinner and reception."

She scrunched up her shoulders and nose like she expected the heat of his wrath.

"Are you serious?"

"I'm sorry. Are you mad?"

"About you." A truth that was becoming fact very fast. "Let me see what you came up with."

She handed him a small notepad filled with elegant writing and doodles of hearts and flowers.

"They want the rehearsal dinner to be informal since it's going to be just family and a few close friends who'll share in the wedding duties. It will be cold outside, so they mostly want to keep it simple with some comfort food and plenty of time for the wine and conversation to flow."

He looked at the suggestions on the list. "Pizza and pasta?"

She shrugged. "That's what they want."

"Sounds good to me. And for the reception?"

She pointed to a section below a line of doodled hearts. "They want to go with something more unexpected than a regular sit-down dinner," she said. "They're looking for something a lot more fun and less formal."

"Instead of signature drinks they want Popsicle cocktails and a specialty coffee bar?"

She nodded. "Preferably with blue and white décor."

"Yeah, but . . . Popsicles?"

"That was actually Lucy's idea. I think she's still trying to give Jordan the opportunity for his Disney *Frozen* theme. Maybe you could have white chocolate dipped sugar cookies for the coffee bar."

"And food?"

She pointed to the notepad again.

"Food stations?" He looked up. "Are they serious? My brother with the over-the-top personality wants food stations instead of a sit-down?"

Gabriella chuckled. "I think Lucy has shown him the error of his ways."

"Damn she's good. She must have the magic key because once Jordy gets something in his head he's like a dog with a big juicy bone."

"All I know is that there were some looks exchanged between the two of them and he caved like a man truly in love."

"That he is."

"Jordan pointed out that no one attending the wedding will need to be sold on the idea of coming to your restaurant once it opens. He said they'll all come regardless. Even if he has to"—she lowered her voice to try and sound like his brother—"bust some heads. So there's no real need for you to have an elaborate menu for the reception."

"Jordan said that?"

She nodded.

"Bullshit. What's the real reason? Because he has been busting my ass to get this place done on time."

"Honestly? They don't want you working the whole time. They want you at their wedding and their reception as their brother, not their hired chef and waiter. Jordan said he's used the reception as an excuse for you to get it done. Otherwise—his words, not mine—you'd be dragging your feet and the restaurant wouldn't come about for another couple of years."

He scoffed. "No faith asshole."

"Is he?"

"No." Parker sighed. "He's probably right. Damn him. The wedding definitely added a sense of urgency."

"So what do you think?"

"I think it's spuds and mac and cheese for all."

"Great." She clapped her hands together. "Then I just have one little request."

"Yes." He looped his arm around her waist and pulled her close. "I will take off my clothes and you may have your wicked way with me."

Her laughter rippled through his heart and danced across his skin. And damned if it didn't feel amazing.

"I'm not asking you to hire me on a permanent basis," she said, "but I'd really love for you to consider letting me help you with both the rehearsal dinner and the reception. Just . . . give me a chance to prove myself. I know I don't have a lot of experience with big events, but I promise you can trust me. And I promise . . ." She clasped her hand to her heart. "I promise I won't let you down."

Raw emotion shone in her eyes. Total and complete sincerity. How could he ever tell her no?

And how in the hell could he continue to believe that he could keep things casual with a woman like her?

"I do trust you." He kissed her. "And I know you won't let me down." He kissed her again. "Offer accepted."

Her eyes widened and a smile burst across her face. "Really?"

"Really."

When she cupped his face in her small hands and kissed him with such passion and promise, Parker knew he'd have to hold on tight to the reins. Because he could feel himself falling right over the damned cliff of his good intentions.

*D*ecember descended with bone-chilling temps and constant snow flurries. As Gabi stood in the center of Sunshine & Vine's kitchen watching deliveries of cooking equipment being rolled off the truck and loaded in, she wished the weather would either blizzard or stop. But currently it wasn't the weather bothering her.

Something didn't seem right.

She looked at the kitchen floor plan then looked at the space. Looked at the floor plan then looked at the space. She looked at the floor plan one more time and . . .

"Holy shit."

Clutching the plans in her hand, she went in search of Parker and found him at the top of a ladder getting ready to crawl up into the newly refinished rafters of the barn.

"Stop!"

Frowning, he looked down to where she stood. "I'm not going to fall."

"Good. But that's not why you need to stop. Come down here, I need to show you something."

"Problem?"

"Huge."

"Shit."

In record time, Parker came down the ladder and followed her into the kitchen.

"What's up?"

She pointed to the new broiler/grill, which had just been slid into place. "See that?"

"Yeah," he answered like she'd just told him the sky was blue.

"Now look up."

His eyes trailed north and landed on the ventilation problem. "Damn it. They installed it in the wrong place. I didn't even notice."

Gabi knew he would have if he weren't so tired. He'd spent the night at her apartment after falling asleep spread out on her sofa with his head in her lap while *Big Bang*'s Sheldon performed his now infamous *Penny, Penny, Penny* knock. Gabi had tried to talk Parker into letting her take over the food truck for him that day, but he'd told her there was too much of a learning curve to jump in on a solo flight. Especially since the truck had been hired out for a holiday party at one of the nearby offices. So he'd taken the shift himself before he showed up at the restaurant to put in more work hours.

"Something has to change," she said, pointing to the vent. "Otherwise you won't meet code on inspection."

"Damn it."

The delivery guys sensed something was wrong and stopped what they were doing.

"If you switch the grill with the deep fryer and

pasta cooker, it will be an easy fix," Gabi said. "But it will mess up the flow of the work area."

"So the only other solution will be a timely and costly relocation of the ventilation." He closed his eyes and with two fingers put pressure on the bridge of his nose. "I'm so screwed."

"Hold your horses." She set the floor plan down on a nearby counter. "Did you sign off on the work?"

"I . . . don't think so."

Her eyebrows hiked up her forehead. "You don't think? Or you know?"

He dropped his hand. "I can't remember."

The troubled expression darkening his eyes told the whole story. The man just needed to slow down and get some rest before he completely imploded.

"Can you do me a favor?" she asked.

"Sure."

"A few days ago you said you trusted me. Can you trust me right now with this situation?"

"I can do more than that."

"You can?"

"Yes. Gabriella? You're hired."

Those two words were better than the fanciest wrapped Christmas present.

"What's my job title?" she asked, barely able to contain her excitement.

"What do you want it to be?"

The question threw her. But she'd learned that if you don't ask for the moon, you won't get the stars. The first day she'd walked in here she'd been full of herself and overly confident. She'd been prepared to bullshit her way through whatever was necessary to obtain her goal. But right now, all she wanted was an opportunity to learn and prove herself. And above all she wanted to help Parker and his family achieve the goal of opening this restaurant on time.

"Broiler or sauté cook?" she asked.

"Bullshit." His eyes narrowed. "You'll be my sous chef or you'll be nothing."

"But . . . Parker." She curled her fingers around his forearm. "That's your second in command."

"You don't want the job?"

"I do, but I haven't even given you a job application or my resume. Or references."

He captured her face between his hands and looked right into her eyes. "I trust you, Gabriella."

Yep. Christmas morning. Happening right here.

"I won't—"

"Let me down. I know." He swept his thumb across her bottom lip. "And if you can make this ventilation problem go away, I'll give you a raise." With a smile he turned to go back into the front of the restaurant to finish whatever he'd been doing up on that ladder.

"We haven't even talked about how much money you're going to pay me," she called after him. "So how much of a raise will I get?"

He gave her a tired laugh. "If you have to ask, I've been doing it wrong."

She smiled. If she'd known he was talking about the perks of being his good-time girl, she'd have asked for more.

Spying a stack of invoices on the counter, she

shuffled through until she found the one for the ventilation contractor.

"*G*abriella literally saved the day," Parker boasted while they enjoyed dinner that night at Declan and Brooke's new house just a few miles away from the vineyard. The home was filled with Christmas spirit in the form of twinkling white lights, garlands of green, and an enormous decorated tree in the corner of the living room.

Admiration filled Parker's soul as he looked across the table at Gabriella. "Thanks to her, not only did it *not* cost me a dime to get the ventilation fixed, but they discounted the original price because it was their screwup. So now, instead of me having to fight a big battle to get things fixed before inspection, the restaurant opening is still on schedule."

"Way to go, Gabriella." Brooke fist bumped her.

"Parker has enough going on," she replied. "I was happy to be able to help."

"Don't be so modest." Parker slipped his hand over the top of hers on the table just because he had to touch her. "She also got all the meals figured out for Jordy and Lucy's rehearsal dinner *and* the reception."

"Wow." Dec laughed. "Looks like Christmas miracles do exist."

"You're not going to believe the menu they came up with," Parker said, sticking his fork into Brooke's delicious homemade lasagna.

"Lobster and caviar?" Declan asked with a grin, knowing their brother had always indulged in the finer things when he'd been an NHL player.

"Nope. Food stations with stuff like baked potatoes, mac and cheese, and French fries."

"Not that there's anything wrong with that," Dec said, "but, you're kidding. Jordan has been driving all of us crazy with this wedding planning stuff. I figured he'd go over the top."

"I think he might have finally realized that Lucy really wants to scale everything down," Gabriella said. "I get the feeling she's not much of an extrovert."

"She's not. She's a very private person." Brooke sipped her wine then set her glass down. "Which is why I think it surprised everyone that she and Jordan are such a perfect match. Because he's totally an extrovert."

"Opposites attract." Parker shrugged, wondering if that was true, why he and Gabriella seemed to do so well when they had so much in common. "Right?"

"Not always." Brooke grinned. "You two seem to be doing okay."

Instantly, Parker felt the pressure to explain their relationship. How could he do that when he was still trying to figure things out?

"That's because we're just keeping things fun and casual." For reassurance, Parker looked to Gabriella for confirmation. "Right?"

Her gaze immediately went to her plate where she pushed a piece of lasagna around with her fork. "Right."

Parker felt like an ass when an awkward silence brought the conversation to a halt. Dec and Brooke gave each other some kind of secret handshake look. A look reserved for couples who were in sync. Couples with a future together. Parker didn't know that look. Had never felt it or shared it with another woman. But the fact that now Gabriella wouldn't meet his eyes told him he'd stepped in it big time. And that left him feeling confused. They'd both agreed on the type of relationship they expected. They were both on the same page. Weren't they? But if that was true, why did he suddenly have a huge lump in the pit of his stomach that had him pushing away his half-eaten plate of food?

"I like the new place," he said, quickly changing the subject and hopefully taking the heat off the moment. "You've got lots of room to grow here."

"That's because we're getting married in a few months." Declan frowned at him as though he'd just enrolled in the idiot-of-the-month club. "And we plan to have a big family."

"And Moochie wants us to get another dog to keep her company because we're both at work so much," Brooke added.

"Sounds like you've got it all figured out," Parker said.

"Yeah. Some of us are lucky that way." Declan's glare intensified. "The rest of us should get a clue."

Parker didn't know how, but the evening had just gone from pleasant to how-fast-can-I-get-out-of-here.

When Gabriella offered to help Brooke clear the table, Parker knew by the intensity in his older brother's eyes that he was about to get a verbal spanking. And as soon as the ladies left the room, Dec proved him right.

"You're not serious."

"About what?" Parker asked.

Dec tilted his head toward the kitchen where Gabriella and Brooke were cleaning up.

"Cut me some slack. We haven't known each other that long. You knew Brooke for four years before you finally got a clue."

"Right. And I almost lost her because of my stupidity." Dec leaned back in his chair. "You willing to take that chance?"

At that moment, the ladies came back into the dining room, saving Parker from having to give a response. But the question lingered. And in all honesty, he really didn't have an answer.

When Parker drove Gabriella back to her apartment to drop her off, his mind was still working overtime thinking about what his brother had asked.

He'd met and bedded plenty of women. For the most part they'd all been nice and he'd enjoyed spending some time with them. He'd even dated a few for a couple of months. But none of them had ever stirred up any feelings in his heart.

And that's where the real problem lay.

With Christmas only a couple of weeks away, the stores, shops, and even the streets were bursting with holiday cheer that naturally brought a sense of family, home, and love. Every music station had deviated from their normal playlists to either classic or ridiculous holiday tunes. He still wasn't sure how dogs barking to "Jingle Bells" or Grandma getting run over by a reindeer was meant to add to the holiday, but apparently he didn't think like everyone else. Almost every TV commercial promoted the holiday with romantic scenes of champagne-filled flutes, a roaring fireplace, and a man proposing to a woman in the snow with a Christmas tree lit up in the background.

Unless you were dead, you couldn't ignore the impending holly jolly. And if you were a guy in any kind of a relationship—casual or otherwise—you felt the pressure to do something big for the girl you were dating. Countless men proposed on Christmas or New Year's Eve. But he and Gabriella were just getting to know each other. So how would this all play out? Would they see each other Christmas day? Or would they each do their own thing separately?

Other than figuring out what gifts to buy his family, or how many holiday parties to book for his food truck, he'd never given the holiday much thought. His family usually came together at some point during the day to exchange gifts, but then they spread out to celebrate in their own way with whomever they chose. Many of those times he'd call up friends or whomever he'd been dating at the time. Other times he spent the rest of the holiday alone.

As he walked Gabriella to her door, realization hit him like a wallop from Jack Frost.

Everything had changed.

When he hadn't been looking, Gabriella had become *someone* to him. Someone he enjoyed. Someone he liked to spend time with. Someone he wanted to be with. Especially on a holiday that celebrated all things warm, glittery, and, yeah, romantic.

When she opened the door to her apartment, Parker noticed that everything looked the same. Other than a lonely poinsettia plant in the center of her dining table there wasn't a single sign that the holiday was near. Did she even plan to celebrate? Would she be alone? The idea of her being locked up inside this little apartment on Christmas with nothing but a Siamese fighting fish to keep her company burned a hole in the center of his chest. She'd mentioned that her family was estranged since her parents' divorce. In essence that made them both parentless for the holidays.

"You want a glass of wine?" Gabriella asked him as she tossed her coat on the back of a chair. "I've got chardonnay and cabernet."

"Chardonnay will be fine." As he came inside, he glanced around her apartment again. "No tree?"

She opened the refrigerator door and shook her head.

"No decorations?"

Popping the cork on the bottle of wine, she again shook her head.

"Are you hiding from Christmas?" he asked.

In the process of removing a wine glass from her cupboard, she looked at him over her shoulder. "Hiding?"

"Yeah." He pointed to the lone poinsettia on her table. "Is that as festive as you're going to get?"

"I've got all kinds of decorations."

He looked around the apartment again. "Where?"

"In the closet." She poured their glasses half full then handed him one.

"So you just haven't put them up yet?" he asked.

"They've been in the closet since the day I bought them. I got them at an after Christmas sale about five years ago."

"Five years?"

She nodded.

"And they've never been out of the boxes?"

"Nope."

His stomach twisted. "Why?"

"Because after watching my parents battle it out in the courtroom and seeing them be granted their divorce—two weeks before Christmas—I just haven't ever felt the spirit. I kept trying—thus the purchase of the decorations—but the mood just never materialized. Know what I mean?"

"Yeah."

He stuck a hand in the pocket of his coat. Sighed to try and release the pressure in his chest. The ache in his heart.

Gabriella took another sip of wine and watched him over the rim of the glass.

*Fuck this.*

He didn't know what his family had planned for the big day; maybe the thought of everyone being together without their mom and dad was too much. No one had made an attempt to plan anything yet. He didn't want to end up spending the holidays alone and he didn't want her to spend them alone either. He didn't know where this fun, casual, no strings thing between them was going, but right now they enjoyed each other's company. They enjoyed each other's bodies. And soon they'd be working side by side. That, at least, gave them something to celebrate.

"Grab your fish. And point me toward the closet where your decorations are hidden." He didn't mean to growl, but it had still come out that way.

"Why?"

"Because you and your little bubble blowing friend are coming to my house." He set down his wine glass and curled his hands around her arms. "You're not spending the holidays alone and neither am I. We're going to stop on the way home and get a real live Christmas tree, even if we have to steal one. Then we're going to put a fire in the fireplace, turn on some holiday tunes, and decorate until we're too exhausted to know the difference between Elf on the Shelf and Buddy the Elf."

A smile played on her luscious lips, but she didn't fully give in to it. "Have you been hiding from Christmas too?" she asked.

He nodded. "This is the first one without my parents. I've been too busy to let that reality sink in. Now that it has . . ." He shrugged. "It just doesn't feel the same."

"I guess we have a lot in common."

Declan's question came roaring back.

Was he willing to take a chance?

If he didn't, what would happen?

He looked at the woman before him. She made him feel good. She made him feel wanted. She made him feel like he could do anything and succeed. He wanted to make her feel that way too. Without another thought, he stepped to the edge and jumped.

"Yeah. I think we do."

# Chapter 14

"Do you think it's leaning?"

Gabi tilted her head and looked at the seven-foot Douglas fir Parker had set up in front of his windows overlooking the Columbia River. It had taken them twenty minutes in the freezing cold to finally decide on the not quite perfectly shaped tree, and then another twenty tying it to the roof of Parker's SUV. By the time they'd gotten the darned thing inside, Gabi felt like a Popsicle.

"Nope." She squinted. "Looks perfectly straight to me."

Parker laughed. "That's because *you're* leaning."

"Then stop serving me wine if you expect my decorating views to be accurate."

"If I stop serving wine, my family goes out of business," he joked. "You're the one who chose the chilled pinot."

"Then I must have been crazy. Because, baby, it's cold outside," Gabi sang along with the stereo. "Aren't you listening to the song?"

"I'm listening to *you*."

"You need warming up?"

"Yes." He came to where she stood in the kitchen, settled his hands on her hips, and pulled her in close. "So why aren't we drinking hot toddies naked instead?"

"Because I'm standing guard over the popcorn in the microwave." For the first time she'd found a good use for the snack. They were actually going to string some and use it as a garland on the tree along with the cranberries he'd had in his freezer.

"And because we have a vineyard to support. So the more wine we drink, the better." She cocked her head then pointed with her wine glass. "That tree *is* crooked. So it looks like the naked part of the evening will have to wait until later."

"Damn it." He gave her a quick kiss then went back to tree duty.

On the kitchen counter Basil watched them from behind the safety screen of his plastic plants. The popping in the microwave stopped and Gabi opened the door. Steam rolled out and she backed up a bit. "Are we really going to string this stuff? Or can we eat it?"

"You didn't get enough to eat at Dec and Brooke's house?"

"I got plenty. And it was very nice of them to

invite us over to their new house. But I'm a snacker. If you put something that tastes good in front of me I'm going to have my mouth all over it."

"And now you're talking dirty?" He grinned wickedly as he tightened the bolts in the tree stand. "How am I ever going to get this tree right?"

"A little more to the left."

"That's not what you said last night."

"Parker Kincade, you have a one track mind."

"Guilty. Because if I'm going to be tangled up in tinsel, it's going to be with you. Even those yoga pants and Kermit the Frog colored slippers you're wearing won't deter me."

"Awww. You say the nicest things."

On the radio, as "Baby, It's Cold Outside" slipped into "Blue Christmas," Gabi poured the popcorn into a large bowl and carried it over to the sofa. The gas fireplace didn't snap and crackle, but it did add to the ambience in the room. She'd never celebrated the holiday with a man she was dating, but she was glad her first time was with Parker.

"Are you ready?" he asked.

For him? Always.

She looked up from the bowl of popcorn and found him with one hand on the string of lights and the other holding the extension cord. He looked a little like Clark Griswold and she was just a bit miffed that he didn't ask her to perform a drumroll.

"I'm ready."

A second later the entire tree lit up in the colors of

the rainbow. She hadn't been sure they'd even work after being stuck in a closet for so many years. "Oh, it's beautiful."

He stood back and admired it. Then he turned toward her. "*You're* beautiful. The tree is nice."

"You keep talking like that and this popcorn is never going to get strung."

"Is that an invitation?" He pounced and they both fell back on the sofa with him landing on top of her.

Gabi was positive she'd never giggled in her entire life until that very moment. But the laughter stopped when he pressed his mouth to hers and kissed her.

She'd spent so many holidays alone; spending this one with Parker would be nice. More than nice. Spending time with Parker could get addictive.

When they came up for air, she told him, "If we keep this up we're never going to get the tree done."

"See, there you go talking dirty again." He kissed her quick then moved off of her. "What am I going to do with you?"

"If I answer that, I *will* be talking dirty."

The sound of his laughter filled an empty space in her heart.

"Let's put on the ornaments, and then we can get to the popcorn and cranberries."

"There aren't really that many ornaments." She reached into the box and unwrapped a Santa flying in a red and green biplane. "I wasn't ever planning on having a big tree. I don't even remember what's in here."

"Discovery is the best part." He sat down beside her, pulled another ornament from the box, and unwrapped a gingerbread man in a chef's hat. "Cute."

"Have Yourself a Merry Little Christmas" played while they continued to unwrap each ornament. By the time they were done, they'd uncovered a sweater-wearing reindeer with long spaghetti legs, a girl elf holding a giant peppermint candy, a colorful glittered owl wearing earmuffs, and a snow couple sipping hot chocolate inside a teacup, just to name a few.

"You know . . ." Parker held up a miniature house made of candy. "I think I'm learning a lot about you just by looking at all these ornaments."

Uh-oh. "How so?"

"I'm discovering you have a far more whimsical side than you're willing to let out."

At one time in her life she'd had whimsy down to an art. She'd lived a life full of color. She'd believed in fairies and fairytales too. She'd had an understanding that all things were possible and that they should be explored with a great deal of laughter and fun. But like Humpty Dumpty, her world had come crashing down and the color had disappeared until she'd walked into a half-built restaurant and met Parker.

Now her life seemed to swim in the depths of his blue eyes and the brightness of his smile. Her past had taught her to be wary. That the other shoe would fall. And that anything that brought her happiness could be swept away as easily as it had fallen into her hands.

But looking at this man as he grinned and held up a silly plastic house, her life illuminated. And she dared to hope.

"Whimsical, huh?"

He nodded.

"You know what I've always wanted to do?" she asked.

"Tell me."

"I'd rather show you." She took him by the hand and helped him to his feet. Then she began to unbutton the long-sleeved flannel shirt he'd put on when they came home. When his chest was bare, she slipped her fingers down his tight rippled abdomen to the button on his jeans.

A naughty grin curved his lips. "Where are we going with this?"

"Under the tree."

"Naked?"

She nodded. "Naked."

He flashed another grin. "Naked under the tree sex?"

"Naked under the tree sex."

"What about the popcorn?"

"Mmmm." She pressed her lips to his bare chest and flicked her tongue over his pebbled nipple. "We can eat it later."

"Now you're talking."

They never did get to the popcorn, but after they made love they did manage to place all the ornaments on the tree. When they finished, they stood back to appreciate their work—naked—with their arms around each other. As all the red, blue, green, yellow, and purple lights glowed against his skin she leaned in and kissed his cheek.

"Thank you."

He smiled. "For what?"

"For putting whimsy and color back into my life."

He kissed the top of her head. "Right back atcha."

*L*ucy Diamond's house looked like something you'd find on Pinterest under *shabby chic* or *fairytale cottages*. It was picture perfect on the outside and the inside, and Gabriella couldn't imagine ever wanting to move away. But that was Lucy's plan after she and Jordan were married the following week. And then Nicole Kincade would move in. Gabi briefly wondered if Nicole might be in the market for a roommate.

Not only was the sweet little home decorated from top to bottom with a gorgeous Christmas tree and twinkling white fairy lights everywhere you looked, but it had also been decked out with an English tea party theme for Lucy's evening bridal shower.

The only thing—person—who looked a bit out of place was Aunt Pippy and her hot pink bell-bottom pants matched with a vibrant green and blue top with bell-bottom sleeves. Dangling from her ears were big circular earrings that vaguely resembled watermelons. Apparently no one had told the elderly woman that hot pink clashed with her fire orange hair. Or maybe they had and she just didn't care. At any rate, Gabi just counted it all up as adding more color to her once bland life.

Light and fluffy pumpkin spice cupcakes with champagne icing were served in pristine white laser-cut wraps. Crystal flutes of bubbly were also served. It was all so elegant. Until they got down to the gifts. Gabi was sure Lucy blushed at least ten times with each carefully wrapped present she opened. She also knew Jordan was going to be a very happy man when his new bride modeled all the pretty lace and flimsy-material pieces of lingerie for him.

The company was fun and everyone accepted Gabi as one of their own. They talked about girl things, and dreams, and Gabi realized that she wasn't the only one who thought in terms of fairytales coming true.

It was all going perfectly proper and well until toward the end Aunt Pippy stood up and said to Lili, Brooke, and Nicole, "You girls did a lovely job with the shower. Lucy, you're going to be a gorgeous bride, and Jordan is a lucky man to have you. And while all of this has been fun . . . who's ready to go hit the bar?"

Lucy's married friend Claudia was the first to jump up and head for the door. "Come on, ladies. Let's get moving. I've only got a babysitter until ten o'clock."

Everyone looked at Nicole, the only one in the

room under the age of twenty-one. Knowing she couldn't go to the bar, she crossed her arms and pouted. But when Lucy told everyone it wouldn't be right for them to go and leave Nicole after she helped plan the shower, Nicole started to laugh.

"I'll stay here and clean up," she said. "But someone better take pictures, because I want to see *everything*." She gave Lili and Brooke a wink that made Gabi think they had something up their sleeve.

Like male strippers.

Hoo boy.

"Yep." Aunt Pippy rubbed her hands together and was on the move like she knew too. "Let's get going."

The Mother Lode could never hope to be classified as a refined place of business. Plain and simple, it was a dive bar, and the red and yellow flashing sign claimed it to be the best karaoke joint in the Pacific Northwest.

Doubtful.

While the exterior resembled a garage where badass biker dudes might hang out, the interior was worse. Most of the neon beer signs had a letter or two burned out. The top of the bar was coated with a sticky substance that seriously needed to be investigated by the team from *CSI: Miami*. Bowls of beer nuts lined the top of the bar too, but Gabi would have to be close to dead of starvation to even think about sampling them. The karaoke stage—a small circle of weathered wood—was surrounded by tables and chairs with torn vinyl seats. Red and green metallic garlands had been draped across the paneled walls and a fake Christmas tree with red lights listed to one side in the corner like it had consumed too many alcoholic beverages.

This was going to be interesting.

"No body shots till later," Aunt Pippy announced as she pounded her fist on the bar to get the bartender's attention.

*Body shots?*

Gabi looked around the busy, crowded room.

*With who?*

An old guy with a grizzled beard and a missing front tooth gave Gabi a wink and a nod. She shook her head and turned away.

Yep.

Going to be *very* interesting.

How or why they'd ended up here was anyone's guess. But it seemed like the rest of them knew what they were doing so Gabi decided to go with the flow.

The bridal shower partiers had crowded together at the bar, where Aunt Pippy had Fireball shooters lined up for everyone.

Was she serious?

"Nobody pusses out," Pippy said. "Glasses up."

The group of women all looked at each other as though they were trying to figure a way out before they slammed the spicy cinnamon whiskey down their throats.

Over a boisterous and drunken karaoke version of "Pour Some Sugar on Me," Aunt Pippy started the countdown. "Ready. Set. Drink 'em down, ladies. The bridal shower is officially over. Let the bachelorette party commence!"

With a round of *woohoo*s from the girls, they counted down and simultaneously slammed the shooters.

Parker balanced his boots on the ladder as he screwed the last of the flame tip lightbulbs into a chandelier over one of the booths. The restaurant was almost done, and in Parker's mind, it was perfect. From selecting the furnishings to the lights to the serving dishes, he couldn't have managed it all without Gabriella's help and her constantly pushing him in the right direction.

In the beginning he'd thought he didn't have time for anything extra, let alone anyone else, in his life. Somehow, instead of becoming an attachment to his life, she'd merged *into* it. Like she'd always been there. Like she should always be there.

Each day she became more and more important to him, and he'd finally realized that trying to keep things casual between them was a joke. They'd moved way past casual.

For the most part, she spent more time at his

houseboat than her own apartment because Parker kept finding reasons to keep her there. Whether it was because he was sexually exhausted or not, he found he slept better with her curled up against him. He liked having her there. He liked the way she curled up in a corner of his sofa and furrowed her brow as she read a book. He liked the way she sipped a cup of tea or nibbled on a piece of cheese. He liked the way she was concerned that his brother's wedding reception be as perfect as Jordan and Lucy imagined. He liked the way she fit so well into his family. And he liked the way she gave him a soft place to land after a tough day.

At night they cooked together, and together they came up with some pretty creative meals. She'd even worked with him in the food truck a couple of times when he'd been hired for a special event and needed extra help. Hell, they'd even put up a Christmas tree together.

Keep it casual?

No strings?

No way.

Maybe it was time they talked. Maybe it was time he asked her about her feelings and where she wanted to go from here. Maybe it was time he just flat out admitted that he was pretty much in love with her and now he had to figure out a way to keep her in his life on a permanent basis.

The truth set him back on his heels and he laughed. He'd thought falling in love would be a big deal that would force him to change his life. In reality falling in love with Gabriella was like slipping into a big warm bed and sighing because it just felt so damned good.

From his jeans pocket his cell phone played "Earned It" by The Weeknd, the song he'd attached to Gabriella's name in his contacts. A sexy song for a sexy woman.

He smiled as he tapped ANSWER. "I was just thinking about you."

Instead of a reply, he heard music too loud to decipher the song and conversation too muffled to pick out any words.

"Hello? Gabriella?"

Female laughter burst through the phone.

Not just laughter; hysterical giggling.

"Gabriella?"

Still nothing but an inaudible exchange.

"Hello?"

Then . . . "Welcome to the Mother Lode!"

Deafening whoops and hollers burst through the speaker and Parker jerked the phone away from his ear.

"Damn it."

What the hell was she doing at the Mother Lode?

In a heartbeat, worry set in.

Was she calling him because she needed him? Was she in trouble? Anything could and did happen at the Mother Lode on a regular basis and it wasn't always pretty.

Only one way to find out.

He snatched up his keys off the table near the front door and locked the place up tight.

When the police came through the door at the Mother Lode, Aunt Pippy was onstage warbling a raunchy version of the Spice Girls' "Wannabe." Apparently one of the bar-goers who'd been kicked out due to the bridal shower turned bachelorette party hadn't been too happy about happy hour ending so soon.

After several sets of Fireball shooters and a heavy-handed round of Angry Balls cocktails, Lucy's proper bridal shower had exploded into a naughty *top this* version of karaoke.

Watching Parker's elderly aunt use some burlesque moves to the Spice Girls tune was a little bit like watching Minnie Mouse perform a striptease. It was comical, but the old gal was really into it and the bar crowd was cheering her on.

The cop who suddenly walked through the door and grabbed the attention of every female in sight couldn't be the real deal. He was way too handsome and his uniform fit like a glove. Although Gabi had to admit the gun, baton, and radio transmitter attached to his shoulder looked genuine. Even so, in her mildly inebriated state of mind, she just knew the man had to be a male stripper. Though why whoever hired him would choose a cop persona instead of a hockey player for Lucy was anyone's guess when the groom's previous career had been spent on the ice. Then again, Gabi figured that to Lucy, no one in a hockey uniform could ever be as smokin' hot as her fiancé.

The very tall, *very* muscular cop had short hand-combed light brown hair, a chiseled jaw, sexy masculine lips, broad shoulders, and a set of abs so rippled they could be appreciated through the fabric of his shirt.

From the moment he'd walked through the door his eyes had gone directly to Lili, who was dancing on top of the bar in a sexy LBD and wicked red stilettos.

Aware the hot cop stripper was headed in her direction, Lili—who'd clearly consumed way more than enough whiskey—got down on her knees and crooked her finger at him.

"Ma'am. Could you please come down from there?" hot cop asked.

"What if I say no? Will you frisk me . . ." Lili flashed him a man-eating grin while she checked out the name badge pinned to his shirt. *"Deputy Harley?"*

With the exception of Aunt Pippy, who was still working her bump-and-grind on the karaoke stage, all the women at the bar *oooooooh*ed.

Completely entertained, Gabi stood back and waited for hot cop to start his strip routine.

"I think I can pretty much see you're not concealing a weapon, ma'am," Deputy Harley replied with the hint of a smile in appreciation of Lili's tight black dress. "But I'd be grateful if you'd come down off that bar so you don't get hurt."

Parker's sister maneuvered around so that she was sitting on the bar when she held out her arms. "Then can you help me down?" she asked, putting Marilyn Monroe's breathy voice to shame. "So I don't hurt myself, of course."

If he was the real deal, standard police procedure would probably require the deputy to nix the whole touchy feely thing with a potential perp. He gave another indication that his uniform had most likely come from a costume shop when he wrapped his hands around Lili's small waist and helped her down off the bar.

All eyes in the room were glued to the action, sure that any second "Bad Boys" would come over the sound system and Deputy Harley would single out the bride-to-be and start stripping off that tight tan shirt.

"So where are you from?" Lili flashed him another flirtatious grin as she fingered the middle button on his shirt. "Other than dropping straight out of heaven."

He captured her finger in his large hand, held on, and chuckled. "Born and raised in Deer Lick, Montana. Took after my big brother and decided to become an officer of the law after college."

"So . . ." Lili looked all the way up into his laughing eyes. "You're a *real* deputy?"

"Last time I checked."

The crowd watching the flirty exchange groaned with disappointment. When they realized no clothes would be coming off that big muscular body, they went back to drinking and watching the fiasco on the stage.

After several more rounds of karaoke, including a trashy, horribly sung version of Miranda Lambert's "Little Red Wagon" by Brooke, it was Gabi's turn at the microphone. She didn't want to be a party pooper when these ladies had been kind enough to include her in their celebration. So she tossed down another Fireball shooter for courage. Then, surrounded by her boozed-up and blitzed-out entourage, she took her place on the stage. Not much of an exhibitionist, as the song began and the words popped up on the monitor, all she could do was throw her inhibitions to the wind and have a good time.

*B*efore he even reached the door of the Mother Lode, Parker heard a heavy drumbeat and a volley of raucous catcalls coming from inside.

When he flung open the door, the first thing he noticed was that his good friend Deputy Alex Harley had his sister Lili cornered over by the bar. Or maybe it was the other way around. One thing was for sure: Lili—teetering a little in her high heels—wasn't exactly rejecting Alex's attention. But that wouldn't stop Parker from giving his friend a little *hands off* warning.

The second thing Parker noticed was that a majority of the customers in the bar appeared to be the female friends and family from Lucy's bridal shower. Most of them were gathered in the karaoke area either dancing or bobbing to the music. And most appeared to be well on their way to a morning hangover.

The third thing that grabbed his attention—especially below the belt—was the very sexy, very breathy voice singing the Divinyls' "I Touch Myself."

After giving an I'm-watching-you nod to Deputy Alex Harley, he rounded the corner that led into the separate karaoke area. He stopped in his tracks and swallowed hard.

Onstage, Gabriella was singing the sexually suggestive song and playing the seductress like a porn goddess in a short, red dress and black high heels. When she sang the words of the song title she closed her eyes, did a sexy little move, and ran her hands down over her breasts and her curvaceous body.

Parker's heart pounded hard and wild. His mouth went dry. And his instantaneous erection pressed against his zipper. It was all he could do not to touch himself to ease the ache.

Fuck, the woman was hot.

And the hell if he was going to interrupt her.

He leaned back against a pole, crossed his arms, and watched. Each lusty little *oooh* she sang made him throb and ache to the point of pain. Toward the end of the song, she settled the fingers of one hand on the side of her face, dipped the fingers of her other hand into the apex of her thighs, and moaned like she was in the throes of an orgasm.

Parker couldn't take it anymore. He needed that. Needed *her*.

Thankful for the darkness that camouflaged his hard-on, he made his way toward the stage through the inebriated crowd who waved their alcohol filled glasses like lighters at a concert.

When she finished the song, Gabriella opened her eyes to find him standing right in front of her. She smiled like he was the best thing she'd seen all day. When she said "Parker" in the same sexy, breathy voice she'd been singing with, everything inside of him cracked and crumbled. His need to hold her, to have her, crashed down on him with the realization that not only didn't he know what to do *with* her; he didn't know what to do *without* her.

He cupped the back of her head in his hand and kissed her Fireball Whisky–flavored lips. Then without a single word, he grabbed her by the waist and tossed her over his shoulder. To the sound of whistles, whoops, catcalls, and her intoxicated giggles, he hauled her out of the bar.

Polite gentleman: 0.

Horny caveman boyfriend: 1.

"*W*hat are you doing here?" Gabriella asked through her laughter as Parker hauled her like a sack of potatoes across the parking lot.

"You butt dialed me."

"I did?"

He opened the door to the passenger side of his

SUV and set her in the seat. "I thought you were in trouble and needed me."

"Oh. As a matter of fact"—she reached up, curled her fingers into the front of his Sherpa lined denim jacket, and pulled his face down to hers—"I *do* need you."

"You're drunk." He uncurled her fingers from his coat. "Let's get you home and tucked into bed."

"I'm not *that* drunk." She grabbed the front of his coat again and grinned. "And *bed* is exactly what I have in mind. But not for sleeping."

"Your fingers are cold." He pulled off his jacket and settled it over her shoulders before he got into the driver's seat and put the SUV in DRIVE. "I'll turn the heater on so you warm up."

"I've got a better idea." She leaned across the console, cupped her hand over his hard cock, and squeezed. "How about we just go straight to *hot.*"

"Babe." With the control of a saint, he eased her hand to his thigh. "I've gotta drive."

Gabi wondered what part of *she wanted him* right *now* was he not understanding. Because that erection he sported beneath his jeans sure got the message loud and clear.

As they drove a few miles in silence, Gabi forced her semi-woozy brain to cooperate and function properly. Yes, she'd been drinking, but she was nowhere near as drunk as he probably thought.

When they seemed to be headed back to the vineyard, the needy tingle in her panties started pointing out all the delicious possibilities.

"Pull in there! Hurry!" She pointed toward a side road that she knew led down into the rows of grapevines on Sunshine Creek property.

"What's wrong?" He turned his head and studied her through the darkness. "Are you okay?"

"No." She was horny as hell. "Hurry."

The SUV bumped along the dirt road until they were completely off the main thoroughfare. Prepared to make her move, she toed off her stilettos and unhooked her seatbelt.

Parker stopped the SUV between the grapevines and turned toward her. "Do you need—"

"You, Parker Kincade. I need *you*."

Faster than she'd ever moved in her life, she crawled over the console and onto his lap. She straddled him and her short dress hiked all the way up her thighs. His erection pressed urgently against the crotch of her panties. So no matter what he said or did, Gabi knew he wanted her.

"I need you inside me right now." She teased the seam of his lips with her tongue while she reached down and unzipped his Levi's.

"Oh God." He moaned and dropped his head back as her mouth and tongue zeroed in on the smooth flesh just beneath his beard stubble. "Are you sure about this?"

"I'm sure I want you right now."

He raised his hands in surrender. "You are so fucking hot."

"I'm hot for you." She slipped her hand beneath the warm cotton of his boxer briefs and wrapped her fingers around his hot throbbing erection. She gave him a firm squeeze and smiled when he pushed into her palm.

"And I want you." She sucked the skin on his neck into her mouth then licked up the side of his throat with a purr. "Right now."

His cock got the message and jumped in her hand, so she rewarded him with another squeeze. She liked this feeling of power. To know that she completely turned him on and he was hers to do with as she pleased. Sexually anyway.

"Stop." Suddenly he captured her hands and pulled them away from his body.

Shocked, she sat back and the steering wheel pressed into her back. "What's wrong? Don't you want me?"

"Don't I want you? Baby, I want you so bad I can't think or see straight right now. What I don't want is casual."

Surprised, she peered at him through the darkness. "I hardly think fucking in the driver's seat of your SUV is casual. But I do think it's very"—she leaned in and licked up the side of his neck—"exciting."

"No." He shook his head. "I mean yes, it's exciting. But I don't mean that."

"Parker?" She readjusted her thighs so they gripped his hips harder and his erection pushed against party central. "I admit I might have had a few whiskey shooters, but I'm awfully confused right now."

"I mean . . . I don't want a casual relationship anymore." He released her hands. "I don't just want fun and no strings. I want all in. I don't want to just fuck you, Gabriella, I want to make love to you."

Her heart tripped all over itself trying to keep up with his impassioned words.

"I want a real relationship," he said, fingers gently caressing the side of her face. "I want to kiss you goodnight and kiss you when I wake up in the morning. I want this to be real and honest between us. Exclusive. No one else for me. No one else for you. I know we haven't known each other for very long, but I can't think of anyone but you. I don't want to be with anyone but you. Tonight, when I thought you might be in trouble, it killed me to think you might be hurt. I can't imagine being without you."

"Really?" Butterflies that hadn't dipped into the whiskey in her belly rose up and fluttered through her heart.

"Yes. Really. But fair warning. So far in my life, I've sucked at relationships. I've been the king of walking away because it was easier than sticking to it. I honestly don't know if I can do this. But I want to. So . . . how do you feel about that?"

The only sound in the car was heavy breathing and "Santa Baby" on the radio as they stared into each other's eyes. Gabi tried to catch her breath and still her racing heart.

A thousand thoughts tried to cram into her head, ready to have their say, prepared to find any excuse to jump up and run. She'd never been able to take a man at face value, had never been able to fully trust them with her heart. But Gabi pushed all those negative thoughts back, because Parker was different.

"I want that too."

A smile of relief burst across his handsome face. "Yeah?"

"Yeah."

He caught her face between his big hands and he kissed her with more meaning than Gabi had ever been kissed with before. She kissed him back with everything she felt in her heart.

When she lifted her head, she looked down into his gorgeous blue eyes and realized he hadn't said anything about love. Which meant he wasn't ready to go there yet, while she'd been ready to say those three little words for days. But she could tell that admitting he didn't want just fun and casual anymore was huge for him, so she didn't want to spoil the mood by pushing him into a corner.

Right now she was still in the mood to have a little fun. Talk a little dirty. And rejoice in the feeling of having him inside of her, as close as two people could ever be.

"But I still want to fuck you in the front seat of your SUV." She wiggled her bottom against his erection. "So what do you think? How do you feel about that?"

"I *think* you're sexy as hell." He threw her a wicked grin and arched his hard shaft against her now damp panties. "And *that's* how I feel about that."

"Then let's not waste any more time." She pulled her dress over her head and tossed it in the backseat. Then she reached between them to free him from his jeans.

Cupping her breast in one hand, he pushed down the edge of her bra and sucked her hardened nipple into his hot mouth.

"Damn these panties excite the hell out of me. Leave them on." He pushed the lace aside and swept his fingers between her slick folds. He followed that up with a circular rub across her clit while he inserted a finger inside of her, touching her in the exact spot he knew stimulated her the most.

"Oh." She dropped her head back. "God."

"Nope." He flicked his tongue over her nipple. "Just you and me here."

The more he stroked, the more she lost control. She needed that control back. And she needed it as fast as possible. Otherwise all the hot air would go out of the fun.

"I need you inside me." She ground against his hand. "I need you really bad. Really fast. Really hard."

"Fuck, baby. Knowing you want me that much?" He slipped his hand away with a last caress of her hot button. "I can't wait to get inside you. Ride me."

"Yes." With a long, lusty moan, she slowly sank onto him, taking him all the way inside. All her senses were amped up a notch. The sight of him focused on lathing her breast with greedy swirls of his tongue was almost more than she could bear. His echoing moans of pleasure were better than music to her ears. He smelled like musky, warm male. His skin was tight, hot, and reactive to her touch. And he tasted like all her favorite desserts rolled into one. She settled her hands on his shoulders for leverage, then moved up and down, rotating here and thrusting there. The more she moved, the harder he gripped her ass in his hands to help her along.

A short while later when the windows had fogged up and their passion crescendoed, Parker cupped his hands over the cheeks of her ass, pumped into her hard, and cried out, "I'm going to fucking love you."

It wasn't quite the *I love you* she wanted to hear, but as she held onto him with all her might as she too reached her sexual peak, she sighed with satisfaction.

At least they were on the right track.

*Chapter 15*

"*I* love the chandeliers."

Parker watched Gabriella as she stood back and admired his restaurant. Everything, with her help, had come together. Tomorrow the supplies for Jordan and Lucy's rehearsal dinner and wedding reception would be delivered and soon everyone in his family could finally see the finished product.

Pride expanded in his chest and made him feel warm all over.

None of it would have happened without the persistence and push of the woman standing before him in a killer pair of tight jeans and an old gray sweatshirt. The past few weeks had been amazing. Not to say he wasn't exhausted or stressed out, but having Gabriella by his side the entire time had changed the dynamics of everything. She was a woman who wasn't afraid to shoulder some responsibility or give him a kick in the ass when he needed it. Now, he wondered how he'd ever gotten along without her. And he wondered why he'd initially fought a relationship with her so hard.

She'd become everything to him.

He hoped she felt the same way. And he hoped they could continue to build on this foundation of trust and honesty with each other. His parents' mistakes had shown him that anything less than truth and devotion would only lead to unhappiness. Gabriella deserved more.

*He* deserved more.

"The chandeliers were your idea," he reminded her. "So you'd better love them."

When she looked at him, concern had pulled her brows together. "But I want you to love them too."

He looked at the artfully decorated booths and the black drum with crystal teardrop lights suspended from the barn rafters. "I think they're perfect."

"Thank you."

"You're perfect too," he added. "Only don't let that go to your head."

"Believe me, I won't." She gave him a sly look. "Unless you let me get on top again tonight. Then I'll show you exactly how perfect I can be."

He feigned disbelief. "You give a girl a little power and see what happens."

"Yeah. Amazing orgasms."

He laughed. "Can't say you're wrong about that."

"Glad you noticed. But back to reality." She held

up the event checklist. "The flowers will be delivered tomorrow around noon. All the perishables will arrive tomorrow morning. The waitstaff will arrive early to help set everything up. And you need to leave here by four-thirty to make sure you get to the rehearsal on time."

"I wish you could go with me. You'd do a great job keeping Groomzilla in check."

"I have a feeling Lucy will handle your brother just fine."

He crossed the room and took her in his arms just because he needed to touch her. While they continued to explore each other on a deeper level, he worked hard to be the man she needed him to be. In return, she gave him something he'd never found before with a woman—a connection to someone he could really talk to. Someone with whom he could share his thoughts and dreams. Someone with whom he could just relax and let his guard down. Someone he could trust.

"Hey." Gabriella gently touched the side of his face. "Are you okay?"

He took a breath. "Sure. Why?"

"Your eyes kind of glazed over there for a minute."

Knowing she could read his emotions so well told him something. No other woman had ever bothered to try. Not that he'd ever wanted the whole kumbaya thing before, but having someone who actually took the time to get to know him for more than just a quick dinner conversation and a fast fuck really meant something.

"Guess I'm just worried about things going well for the dinner and reception," he said.

"Are you kidding? It's going to be great." The bright smile on her face gave him no room for doubt. "We've got everything covered. All you need to focus on now is being a good groomsman and not passing out at the altar."

"Guys don't pass out."

"Are you serious?" She leaned her head back. "Don't you watch videos on Facebook or YouTube? Guys get up there, lock their knees, and bam! Down they go."

"So I guess the clue is not to lock my knees?"

"Not recommended." She kissed his cheek. "Unless you want to go viral. Then that's another story."

"Not interested in going viral. Just want to make it through the next couple of days."

She wrapped her arms around him. "What can I do to help?"

He raised an eyebrow.

"I didn't mean *that*." She chuckled.

"But we're all alone here." He lowered his hands, cupped them around her jeans-covered ass, and pressed his awakening erection into the crux of her thighs. "We could make it fast."

While he kissed the side of her neck she asked, "Will that make you forget whatever's bothering you?"

"Temporarily."

"Then unless it's permanent, it's still a no."

"Damn it." Even though he knew she enjoyed the sex as much as he did, he didn't really expect her to give in. He understood because he was taking off early tomorrow to go to his brother's wedding rehearsal, she was the one who had to make sure it all went smoothly. So at the moment she might not be focused on hot, sweaty sex. Tonight, he'd do his best to change her mind.

"You know, if you've got extra time on your hands, you might want to check your Christmas list," she said. "You only have five more shopping days left. And on that note, did you get Jordan and Lucy a wedding present?"

Presents.

Shit.

"Gotta be honest. I'm not that great at buying the perfect gift."

"Everything doesn't have to be a grand gesture, you know. Sometimes it's just the thoughtfulness behind the gift. And if it's going into the crowded stores you don't like, you can always buy online. It might cost you more for shipping at this point but—"

"I'm not shopping online. I'd rather eat worms and die."

Tiny crinkles appeared at the outer corners of her eyes as she laughed. "I hope you mean Gummy Worms, or I am *never* kissing that mouth again."

"Oh yeah?" He leaned in and kissed the hell out of her. When he raised his head she sighed.

"Okay, that was a total lie." She leaned in for one more. "I'm going to kiss that mouth every single day."

He grinned. "I have some other places you can kiss too."

"And so do I." She danced away when he reached for her again. "But right now, I've got work to do."

Tempted to follow and distract her into taking off all her clothes, he watched as she disappeared through the big swinging steel door that led to the kitchen.

She was right. Time was tight. By tomorrow she'd have everything on that checklist marked off. He trusted her to make sure the rehearsal dinner went off without a hitch, from the Popsicle drinks upon the guests' arrival to the pumpkin cheesecake dessert.

He trusted her.

And that was a damned good feeling.

While Gabriella put the final touches on the pumpkin caramel cheesecakes in the kitchen, Parker stood at the hostess station near the front door, double-checking everything on his own list. Aside from the pressure of his brother's rehearsal dinner and wedding reception in the next two days, he'd planned the restaurant grand opening for the second Friday in January. Before then everything had to be perfect for the health inspector or he'd be delayed in opening the doors.

The buzz about the restaurant had begun around

town and everywhere he went people queried him about the menu and the grand opening. Lili and Brooke already had the website up and running and had placed ads in several local magazines and papers. Before everything had started to fall into place, he'd been confused about which direction to take. Hell, he'd been confused about a lot of things before Gabriella had come into his life. He couldn't imagine it now without her.

As he worked, footsteps sounded on the stone entryway leading up to the restaurant doors. Parker looked up but could see nothing past the kraft paper he'd used to cover the windows so none of his sneaky relatives could peek inside before he opened the doors for the big reveal.

Fearing Groomzilla had been bitten in the ass with curiosity, Parker jumped to intervene by quickly stepping outside and closing the door behind him.

Utter disbelief exploded in his brain.

Not only was the man on the walkway *not* his brother, he was literally the last person on earth Parker ever expected to see.

Miraculously and confusingly, standing before him was world-renowned celebrity chef Giovanni Altobelli.

What. The. Fuck.

"Chef Altobelli." Star struck, Parker gaped at one of his culinary idols before he managed to pull himself together and offer his hand in greeting. "I'm Parker Kincade. Welcome to Sunshine & Vine."

Defying his pleasant TV personality, Altobelli looked at Parker's extended hand a long awkward moment before finally reaching out with his own. To say the man wore a pinched expression would be putting it mildly.

What the hell was he doing here?

Sure, the local marketing buzz for the restaurant had been building over the past few weeks, but how had word of his restaurant reached someone of Altobelli's caliber? And why the hell wasn't Parker just grateful instead of dissecting every possibility?

"Forgive my awkwardness," Parker said. "I'm just surprised to see you standing here."

"Are you."

Not even remotely a question, Parker realized.

Though the man was at least half a foot shorter than Parker, there was no doubt the chef was looking down his nose. It was then Parker realized the magic of television. On TV the middle-aged man looked robust with a thick head of dark brown hair and clear, intelligent eyes. In person his complexion appeared ruddy, like he'd been drinking too much for too many years. His eyes were bloodshot and guarded. His hair and upper lip were thin, so when he smiled he appeared disingenuous. And though they say TV puts ten pounds on everyone, Chef Altobelli looked at least twenty pounds over. Parker couldn't help but wonder if the chef was one of those who, on TV, wore Spanx to suck it all in.

Parker disregarded the chef's non-question response. "Absolutely. We don't plan to officially open our doors until mid-January. And while I'd love for you to sample some of our dishes, the kitchen isn't stocked."

"Hmmm."

Apparently without cue cards the man wasn't exactly a master communicator.

"But I'm honored that you're here," Parker said. "So how can I help you?"

"I've come to see my daughter, not your *café*."

The way he'd said *café* made Parker grit his teeth. Like such a place would be below him to enter. There was nothing wrong with a restaurant being a café, but that didn't describe *his* place.

Wait a minute.

"Your daughter?"

The chef gave a sharp nod. "I was told she was begging for a job at this . . . establishment."

Alarm pinched the back of Parker's neck. "And your daughter would be . . ."

"Gabriella Altobelli," the chef replied like Parker shouldn't be so dense. "Although I'm told these days she's taken to using her mother's surname, Montani."

A chill sliced up Parker's back.

"Gabriella's your daughter." Another non-question question.

"Did I not just say that?" The chef tossed Parker another how-could-you-be-so-stupid glare. "Where is she? Scrubbing dishes? I wouldn't be surprised. She's been trained for little else."

Chef Altobelli pushed past Parker and opened the restaurant door.

Speechless, Parker followed him in.

Once inside the building, the chef shouted Gabriella's name. When there was no response, he shouted it again.

Parker couldn't move. Couldn't breathe. Couldn't think.

Finally the stainless door swung open and Gabriella came into the room, squeezing a white towel in her hands like she wanted to wrap it around someone's throat.

"Father. What are you doing here?"

Parker snapped out of the fog of disbelief and stepped forward. "*This* is your father?"

Anger coiled in his gut as the woman he'd fallen in love with, the woman he'd trusted, stood there wringing her hands and staring at the floor as she nodded.

"And you what . . ." Parker curled his hands into fists. "Just happened to forget to mention that your *father* is one of the most famous chefs in the world when you came in here looking for a job?"

He knew his tone was sharp. Hell, he was practically yelling. When her head snapped up, he wanted to pull back his words. But lately he'd had enough deception in his life. The idea that she'd pulled something this monumental over on him made him a little bit wild-eyed and crazy.

She glared at him. "Would it have made a difference?"

"Hell yes. It would have at least told me where you'd been trained. Then maybe I wouldn't have fallen for that whole *audition* routine."

Obviously wounded, she sucked in a breath and narrowed her eyes.

"Well that's the problem, Mr. Kincade," Chef Altobelli piped in before Gabriella could defend herself. "Other than what she's learned in my own mother's kitchen, Gabriella has no formal culinary training whatsoever. Did she tell you otherwise?"

"Not exactly."

"So she fooled you," Chef Altobelli said. "Made you think she had experience when all she's really suited for is flipping burgers at McDonald's."

"Excuse me?" Parker looked at the chef through a veil of red. Granted, Parker was pissed off about Gabriella's dishonesty, but this was her father. The one man in her life who should be building her up, not tearing her down.

Parker got even more pissed off that Gabriella just stood there silently while her father chastised and embarrassed her.

What the hell?

"I offered her the finest education," Altobelli said. "She threw the offer back in my face."

"That's a lie." Gabriella twisted the white towel. "You never offered to pay for a culinary education even though you knew that's what I wanted. You told me I'd never make it in your world. That I wasn't good enough and never would be."

"I offered to send you to school so you could learn to be something *other* than a chef. Because I knew you'd never come close to your brother Marco's skills. And God knows you'd never have mine."

"But all I ever wanted was to be a chef." Gabriella folded her arms across her sweatshirt. "Cooking is my passion. Just like it was yours."

Parker stood back and watched the volley between father and daughter and felt like he'd been hit from both sides by oncoming trains. He didn't know what had transpired between the two of them in the past, but in Gabriella's eyes he could see the aftermath of deep emotional pain.

"Then if I'm so worthless," she said to her father, "why did you bother coming here?"

"To stop you from making a fool of yourself."

"This isn't about me. This is about *you*." Her brown eyes watered and Parker suddenly wanted to plant his fist in the famous chef's face.

"You're right," her father said. "Because I don't need any more public humiliation coming from you."

"How can I possibly do that again when I never humiliated you in the first place?" she asked. "In case you've forgotten, *you* were the one who drew blood first. You cut me out of your life."

"After you took your mother's side."

"Yes. After you had an affair that crushed her spirit and ripped our family apart." Gabriella spat the words but they barely had any effect. From what Parker could see, Chef Altobelli was one coldhearted customer.

"How did you even know where to find me?" she asked.

"Your grandmother has been bragging about how well you're doing. I had to see the impossible for myself, so I forced her to tell me."

Gabriella's shoulders fell like someone had dropped a building on top of her. Parker may be pissed off that she'd misled him, but he wasn't going to stand there any longer and let this man take her down because he was worried about his own pathetic reputation. Parker may have once respected the chef, but no more.

"That's enough."

Both Gabriella and her father looked at him as though they'd forgotten he was in the room.

"Look. I don't know what happened in your past," Parker said, "because Gabriella obviously hasn't felt comfortable enough to discuss it. But I can tell you you're wrong about her, sir. She's a talented and creative chef, and she has an impeccable work ethic."

"And you're sleeping with her," the man said.

"That's none of your business." Parker curled his hands into fists to keep from knocking the smug expression off the chef's face. "But this place *is* my business and I'm not going to stand here and listen to you disparage your own daughter any longer."

"Are you asking me to leave?" The man actually had the nerve to smirk.

"No." Parker took a step forward. "I'm telling you to get the fuck out."

Altobelli harrumphed then turned his head to

spear Gabriella with one more evil glare. "This isn't over, Gabriella. You will *not* bring down my empire because of your inept desire to humiliate me over something that happened a long time ago."

Gabriella remained silent. Her jaw quivered as though she'd either been biting her tongue so she wouldn't speak her mind or maybe because her father terrified her.

Neither was acceptable.

"Get out." Making himself perfectly clear, Parker glared at the man and pointed his finger at the door.

"I'll see you soon, *daughter*," was the chef's parting shot as he strode out.

Once the door closed, Parker turned to Gabriella. Expecting to see her in a crumpled mass of hysteria, she surprised him by maintaining a fragile composure.

His natural instinct was to take her in his arms and console her. After all, this was the woman he'd woken up next to this morning after making love to her for hours last night. But he'd trusted her, and in return she'd duped him.

*M*omentary relief filtered through Gabi's body when her father walked out the door. But that moment shattered when Parker turned and looked at her.

Something hotter—darker—than rage sparked in his eyes and flew in her direction. Without saying a single word he leveled her, wrapped her up in an emotional agony so strong, she was sure they could never repair what her father had just torn apart.

No.

*She'd* torn it apart by not telling Parker the truth in the first place.

"I'm sorry." She held his gaze, saying the two words that probably meant nothing.

The anger in his eyes dissolved, only to be replaced by sadness and pain.

"The day I showed up here, I didn't come to start anything with you," she said. "I came because I wanted a legitimate chance to make something of myself without my father's influence. I know it means nothing to you now because you feel deceived. But talking about him—claiming him as my father—is something I gave up long ago."

Without a word he let her continue.

"He shattered my life when he cheated on my mother. He abandoned me—his only daughter—because I was a teenage girl who took her mother's side after he flaunted his affair in her face. And because I took my mother's side, he told me I'd never be anything without him. I turned eighteen the month before their divorce. Since then, I've known it was all up to me. That I had to make it on my own."

She took a breath to calm her nerves. To release the regret that bound her heart in a steel vise. She knew now, had known since she became involved with Parker, that she'd wasted too many years seeking a day of reckoning with a man who cared nothing for her. Even though she was his own flesh and blood.

"Before I met you, I let my anger control me. I focused only on a need to prove him wrong about me. For years, that need to prove him wrong consumed me. I let him win," she said. The truth took another vicious stab. "Before I met you, I didn't know anything else existed in this life. I didn't know anything else mattered other than making a name for myself and proving him wrong."

Parker silently watched her with his arms folded.

"After I graduated from high school, my mother fell apart. My brother had taken my father's side and walked away from her just like my father had. And every time she looked at me, she could only see what my father had done. We stopped speaking even though we lived in the same house. When I couldn't take it anymore, I moved to Italy to live with my grandmother. The same woman who'd taught my father most everything he knew about cooking."

His silence twisted her stomach in a knot and she wondered if she was wasting her breath trying to explain. But she had to try.

"I'd always loved to help out in the kitchen. And during the summers I visited my *nonni*, I watched her cook with so much passion. I wanted to feel that too. Because after my parents' divorce, I feared all I'd ever feel again was hate. After I moved to Italy, I worked hard because I wanted to be better than my father. I guess in some twisted way, I wanted to hurt him as much as he'd hurt me."

"That's a hell of a way to live," he said.

"I didn't know any other way." She shrugged. "Not until I met you. Sometime soon after we met, the need to prove my father wrong disappeared. You've warmed a place in my heart that had been cold for so long."

Desperation rolled over her to make him understand.

"I love you, Parker. And it has nothing to do with my father or this restaurant. I love *you*. The man who's taught me to laugh and to live again."

For a heart-stopping moment, he said nothing. Gave her no reaction whatsoever. Yet, Gabi didn't regret for one moment telling him how she felt. She'd once lost the faith that love existed. Parker had not only helped her find it again, he'd made her truly believe.

"You don't have to prove yourself to anyone, Gabriella."

"I know that now."

"I trusted you," he said. "I gave you plenty of opportunities to tell me about this. To tell me who you really are."

"*This* is who I really am, Parker. I'm just a girl who wants to have a chance to make good food and be with the man she's fallen in love with. I haven't been Giovanni Altobelli's daughter in a long, long time."

His gaze flicked over her and her heart sank.

"I need some time to think," he finally said, running a hand through his hair and squeezing the back of his neck.

"Parker—"

"Gabriella. There's too much going on right now. And this?" He dropped his hands to his sides. Shook his head. "This is a lot to take in."

"So that's it?" Her heart squeezed painfully. "You won't even give me the time—a chance—to talk about this?"

He glanced away. "I'm sorry."

"I'm sorry too. Sorry I fell in love with the wrong man." She flung the towel in her hands at him and slammed through the kitchen door.

# Chapter 16

"**Y**ou let her walk?"

Parker flinched at the irritation in Jordan's tone that echoed throughout the kitchen at the main house. And yet he managed to match it with his own. "What was I supposed to do?"

"Oh I don't know." Jordan flung his hands up. "How about you realized what she'd been up against and held her in your arms so you didn't come off as douchy as her dad?"

He'd wanted to hold her. He'd wanted to take away all the pain and heartache she'd been through in her life. But his own demons had stood in the way.

His mind had been reeling when she'd told him she loved him with such genuinely raw emotion. And yet, he hadn't said it back. He hadn't said a word that might have eased her pain.

What the hell was wrong with him?

He loved her. He knew he did. But at that moment, when she'd needed him the most, he hadn't been able to say the words. He'd been so damned tangled up in the emotions of his own troubled past that he hadn't known how to soothe the pain of hers.

He was a selfish fuck.

Because as she'd stood there looking at him, practically pleading with her eyes for some comfort, for forgiveness, he'd only been able to think that maybe he didn't really know what love was all about. His parents had made everyone believe they'd loved each other, but it had been a façade. So maybe he really didn't know how love felt. Or what it looked like. Maybe all he'd been feeling was lust and infatuation.

He'd needed time to himself. A moment to push away the avalanche of uncertainty and the mountain of stress he'd been under so he could think clearly. A moment where he could pull his head out of his ass and stop comparing the way he felt about Gabriella to anything or anyone else.

Well, he'd had that moment. And he was thinking clearly. And he hated himself for pushing her away. He hated that she'd needed him and he hadn't been there for her.

"I'll call her when I get home."

Jordan speared him with a glare Parker was sure he'd once used against his opponent in the hockey arena. "Did you ever think it might be too late by then?"

Damn it. He hated when his brother was right.

"How do you not feel betrayed by what Mom and Dad did?" he asked honestly. "How does that *not* affect your life, Jordan? Because it sure as hell does mine. And how are you so sure that you're in love when everything you thought was love was bullshit?"

"So. You want to condemn Gabriella for allowing her father's behavior to control her actions and her destiny yet that's exactly what you're doing?" Jordan stepped back and shook his head. "You're a fucking hypocrite, little brother."

And . . . bam!

The truth smacked him between the eyes.

"Lucy's the most important thing in the world to me." Jordan dropped his hands onto his hips. "She's the one who makes me feel like the man I want to be. The man I need to be. She believes in me. Believes I can do anything I want if I put my mind to it. She had a shitty past with someone who treated her like she didn't matter and I'm going to spend the rest of my life making that up to her. Not because I have to. Because I want to. Because she's my future. She's the one who will bring me happiness for the rest of my days on this earth. So if you think I'm going to sit around and waste all that happiness with her on something I had nothing to do with and had no control over, you're out of your fucking mind."

"So I'm just supposed to let what happened with Mom and Dad go?"

"Absofuckinglutely. That was their problem, not yours. And it doesn't mean that whatever they did should reflect in the way you live your own life. So get your shit together before you lose everything." He punched Parker's shoulder on his way toward the door. "And you'd better not fuck up my bride's big day because you're too busy feeling sorry for yourself."

As soon as Jordan left the room, Parker rubbed his shoulder. Jordan was right. Hopefully getting Gabriella to forgive him wouldn't be quite as painful.

"*H*e stood up for me, Nonni. And then . . . he asked me to leave."

"Oh, *il miele*. I'm so sorry. I didn't mean to let your father know where you were. But he pushed and pushed."

"I'm not blaming you, Nonni. I should have dealt with him years ago instead of hiding out. It was foolish of me."

"Not foolish. You were Daddy's little girl. And then he broke your heart. I know he's my son, but he makes me so angry I could cry. He's never apologized to you for his behavior, and he continues to make mistake after mistake without caring who is in his crossfire. He's a selfish man who behaves like a selfish little boy."

"I'm sorry, Nonni." Gabriella rubbed the ache in her forehead. "I never realized how difficult all this must be for you. I never meant to put you in the middle."

"*Bambina*, I am a strong woman. I love you. And

as long as I've got breath in my body, I will always be here for you. No matter what. *Capisci?*"

"*Capisco.*" The ache in Gabi's head traveled to her heart. She wished she could feel her grandmother's arms wrapped around her right now. "I love you, Nonni. And thank you. I'll never be able to repay you for your love and kindness."

"You repay me by following your heart and being happy. So what will you do now?"

"I don't know that there's anything I can do." Gabi shrugged even though her grandmother couldn't see through the phone. "He told me he needed some time to think."

"*Stronzata!* You're just going to roll over and let the man you love walk away? I'm ashamed of you. Where's the girl who worked day and night, who worked her fingers to the bone to educate herself so she could stand tall beside her peers? Where's the little girl who used to tell me that she knew her prince was out there, and when she found him she'd never let him go?"

Gabi had forgotten those days when she'd been a little girl who believed life was like a storybook fairytale. She'd forgotten when she'd been a young woman who believed that sometimes the princess had to take the bull—aka the prince—by the horns, so their fairytale could come true. She'd forgotten the woman who believed that not every princess needed to be rescued. Sometimes she rescued herself. And sometimes she rescued the prince.

"I guess I can't grab hold of the future if I don't let go of the past, right?"

"Exactly."

"What if he won't listen to me?" Gabi took a breath. "What if he doesn't even want to talk to me?"

Her *nonni* tsked. "Then you grab him by the face and you kiss him until he does."

Gabi chuckled, even as she feared she may never have the opportunity to kiss him again.

"Do you trust him, Gabriella?"

She thought of all the opportunities he'd given her and the vulnerable way he opened himself up to her. Until the skeletons in her closet had rattled to life, he'd trusted her. She had to make him see that he could trust her again.

"I do."

"Then make it right, *la mia bambina*."

"I will, Nonni. I promise."

# Chapter 17

The Heathman Hotel was—in Gabi's opinion—the most luxurious hotel in the downtown area. It housed one of the best restaurants as well. Which was exactly why her father chose to stay there when he traveled to Portland. As the doorman dressed in an English Beefeater costume pulled open the lobby door for her, she knew she was taking a big chance. She knew for security reasons, the hotel had strict rules about revealing information about their guests. But she had to give it a shot anyway.

Her heels clicked across the marble floor as she made her way to the registration desk, where she was met with a smile by a man in a well-fitted suit.

"Good evening, ma'am. How can I help you?"

"Good evening. I'm Gabriella Altobelli." It felt strange to use her father's surname after all these years. Especially since she'd had it legally deleted from her life. Still, she smiled and pulled out all the stops as she reached across the desk to shake the man's hand. "I was supposed to meet my father, Chef Giovanni Altobelli, for a drink before dinner in your fine restaurant. But in my haste, I forgot to write down his room number. He's not answering his phone, so I assume he's discussing next week's show with his producer."

"Miss Altobelli!" The man grinned like they were old friends. "It's so nice to meet you. But I'm sorry, it wouldn't be acceptable to give out a room number. Client privacy is of the utmost importance to the Heathman."

"I completely understand." She cranked her smile up to gleaming and crossed her fingers. "And I'd never ask you to break the rules. I suppose I could sit down here and wait, but it's been a long time since he and I have seen each other. I'd hate to waste any more time."

An understatement if ever there was one.

"And I'd really love to surprise him." She pulled a bottle of Sunshine Creek Vineyard's wine, Shimmer, from her purse. A prop—or a bribe—she'd thought of before she left her apartment. "I even brought wine for the occasion."

The man behind the desk looked at her, looked at the bottle, and looked at her again. A slow smile spread across his face. "Well, maybe I can help you out. Since there's such a strong family resemblance I can tell you're legit."

Gabi really didn't know if she should take that as a compliment. In the past years her father had aged.

And not gracefully. Gabi chalked it up to living in the fast lane, being mean, and leaving so many broken hearts in his wake.

She choked out an appropriate response. "I'm told all daughters look like their fathers."

"In this case, I'd have to agree." He leaned in and quietly gave her the room number.

"Thank you so much." Gabi settled her hand atop his on the counter. "I guarantee he's really going to be surprised."

Boy was he ever.

*S*tanding in front of his door, she took a deep breath and straightened her shoulders. Before she could chicken out, she knocked.

A minute later, the door swung open and her father stood there—in a hotel robe, for Pete's sake—staring at her as though she'd ascended straight from hell.

"Hello, Father." Without waiting for an invitation, she pushed past him and strolled into the large suite like she owned the place. She refused to cower any longer.

The hotel suite looked as though he'd been there awhile. A newspaper was spread out on the sofa. Utensils and a dinner tray from room service littered the desktop. The French press was half full with coffee. And several bottles of soda from the in-room snack bar sat empty on the coffee table.

Behind her he closed the door and turned with a bitter expression. "Come to beg for forgiveness?"

"Now why would I ever need *your* forgiveness?" She swallowed past the pounding of her heart in her throat. "I've done nothing wrong."

His eyes narrowed. "Haven't you?"

"Wait." A laugh of utter disbelief burst from her lips. "Are you trying to tell me that you think *you've* been wronged? Oh. That's a good one."

"You turned against me, Gabriella."

"You broke my heart, *Father*."

For the first time in her life, Gabi had the courage to tell the man she'd once believed to be her hero, the man she'd once thought she could trust most in the world, exactly how she felt.

"You know, all I ever wanted was your love," she said. "All I ever dreamed about was making you proud of me. I never wanted to be you. I never wanted the world you created. All I wanted was for my daddy to put his arms around me and promise that he'd make everything better. That our family meant the world to him and that he'd right his wrongs."

"Gab—"

"Stop." She held up her hand. "You've had years of opportunities to talk. You chose not to. Well it's my turn now."

"Go ahead. Spew your mother's lies and influence all you want. It doesn't matter anyway."

"Oh, stop sounding like a petulant child."

His eyes widened and his face turned red. She could see he was on the verge of a temper tantrum, but that was too damn bad.

"Thanks to you, other than a few strained conversations," she said, "I haven't spoken to my mother in a long time. Thanks to *you* and the horrible way you treated her, she wants nothing to do with *me* because I'm your daughter. So thanks to your lying, cheating, and in general not giving a shit about anything but your enormous ego and the little man in your pants, I lost my entire family."

"Don't be crass, Gabriella."

"I'll be any damn thing I want to be. I'm a grown woman. And I don't need your fucking fatherly advice. Not now. You're too damn late for that."

When Gabi hoped she'd see a spark of regret in his eyes, a spark of pride or love, his lips tightened. If she'd had any love left in her heart for him, it died that very moment. He'd never change. He'd never love her the way a father should love a daughter.

"When you walked away, I lost everything except Nonni. She's been my saving grace. My champion. She's been the one person I knew I could count on when the rest of you acted like I don't exist. It's hard for me to believe that you even came from a wonderful person like her."

"Wonderful?" He scoffed. "My mother also betrayed me when she took you under her wing."

"Are you really that much of an egomaniac that you'd turn against your own mother because she chose to love your child?"

When he refused to respond, she knew the answer was yes.

"Unbelievable." Gabi turned and took a breath to regain her composure.

What was she doing here?

What did she think coming here would really accomplish?

There was no doubt in her mind that her father had fallen so deep into the narcissistic well, he'd never find his way out. He didn't care about her. He only cared that she'd embarrass him. Or that she'd attempt to bring down his empire. And she . . . didn't have time for this. She didn't need a man like him in her life. She needed a man she knew she could trust. A man she could love and who would love her back. A man she could rely on when times were tough. And a man she could stand beside when he needed her strength.

She needed Parker.

He may not be perfect, but he had a heart. And that was more than she could ever say about the man in front of her.

With a shake of her head, she walked to the door. Before she opened it she turned and searched for the man who'd once held her in his arms and called her his little princess. But that man was gone; he no longer existed.

"I want nothing from you," she said. "Not now. Not ever. Despite your abandonment. Despite your hate, I grew up okay. I found happiness. And I'll do whatever it takes to be the kind of person you never were. One who can hold her head high because she's learned how to love unconditionally and always strives to be a better, more caring person."

She grasped the door handle.

"Goodbye, Mr. Altobelli. I wish you well. But if you ever darken my door again, I promise I'll have you arrested for harassment."

Free of regret, free of his cruel, abusive words, and—finally—free of heart, she opened the door and walked out into the hallway.

When the elevator reached the lobby, Gabi strolled to the front desk. The man who'd helped her earlier looked up and smiled. "Did you have a nice visit with your father?"

"It was . . . unforgettable." She pulled the bottle of wine from her purse and handed to it him. "Thank you so much for your help."

He took the bottle and tilted his head. "I thought this was for a celebration."

"It is." She gave him a wink. "I'm just in the wrong place to start the party."

# Chapter 18

The following morning Parker felt bruised, beaten, and dirty, like he'd been run over by a herd of buffalo. Sleep had evaded him in the cold and lonely bed without Gabriella. To top things off, she'd left Basil the betta fish on his kitchen counter. All night, the fish had swum around his circular bowl, blowing bubbles against the glass and looking at Parker like he was some kind of serial killer.

Parker had tried to call Gabriella but she didn't pick up the phone. After he'd left several unanswered messages of "call me, we need to talk," he realized apparently he was the only one who needed to talk. She'd already done a perfectly fine job of explaining things.

He just hadn't been ready to listen.

Sunrise had seemed to take forever to break the horizon. By then Parker had been up for hours and was well on his way to his tenth cup of coffee. He'd finally grabbed a pair of slacks and jacket for the wedding rehearsal later tonight and headed toward the restaurant.

When he walked inside it seemed cold, and not because of the room temperature. Without Gabriella there the place seemed to have lost its heart and soul.

He felt the same.

Somehow he had to remain focused. His agenda for the day was grueling. Right now he couldn't allow himself to think about what had happened yesterday, what might possibly happen in the future, or how badly he'd totally fucked up. No matter how desperately he wanted to talk to Gabriella, tonight and tomorrow belonged to Jordan and Lucy. He had to make sure the dinner and reception went off without a hitch. That the table settings were perfect and the food sang with flavor. Once the party and his responsibilities were over, he'd find Gabriella—no matter where he had to go or how far, he'd find her. He'd wrap her in his arms and apologize. Hell, he'd beg for forgiveness on his knees if that's what it took.

Hopefully she'd give him the chance.

The day dragged by, swallowing up Gabriella and the guilt she carried for waiting until Parker left the restaurant to go in and assist with the rehearsal dinner preparations. She'd wanted to see him so badly, but the day belonged to Lucy and Jordan. She knew

Parker would be too busy to deal with anything that had happened between him and her, but she'd promised to be there for him, to help with the dinner and reception, and so help she would. Unlike her parents, when Gabi made a promise, she took it to heart.

For Parker and the Kincades, the next two days were all about family. This was their time to celebrate life, and she would do nothing to detract from their moment in the sun. She loved Parker and she cared for him more deeply than she ever thought possible. She knew he cared about her too. They just had a few wrinkles they could—hopefully—smooth out. In her mind, they had the opportunity to share a lifetime together, so what would it hurt to wait another day or two to make that happen?

Once she'd been given the green light to arrive at Parker's restaurant by her secret agent spy who had a penchant for psychedelic clothes and fire orange hair, she jumped into action.

As soon as she walked into the kitchen of Sunshine & Vine, it became painfully clear that Parker had experienced a long and difficult day trying to do meal prep and instruct the hired staff at the same time. At the last minute he'd called in his food truck staff to help him out. A wise decision on his part as they seemed to be the only ones who had a clue about what was going on.

Gabi got a surprised look from the crew as she put on her chef's coat, grabbed the checklist, and picked up where Parker had left off before he'd gone to the wedding rehearsal.

The individual dishes were simple enough; they just had to be fresh and hot when the dinner guests arrived. Lucy had worked her magic with Jordan so instead of a stuffy affair, the dinner would be casual and fun. She hoped the live entertainment and the ice cream station with personalized dessert bowls and scoops would be a nice reference to Jordan's time on the ice. And to incorporate Lucy's teaching career, Gabi also added some chalkboards with cute sayings like *Eat, Drink and Be Married*, and *You Will Forever Be My Always*.

Energized by Lucy and Jordan's upcoming happily ever after, Gabi reached for her phone to call in the troops to help with her super secret surprise. She knew the hush-hush gesture would make Jordan happy because his bride would be delighted. However, Parker's reaction to both the secret surprise and the surprise of her being there was a big unknown. And it was the only thing that made the butterflies in her stomach get up and dance.

"*I*f I ever get married," Parker said to Ethan as he settled his hand on the doorknob of his restaurant, "remind me to go to Vegas and skip the dog and pony show so I don't become like Groomzilla back there."

"I heard that." Jordan teasingly whacked the back of Parker's head.

"You'll be happy to become Groomzilla when you find the right girl," Aunt Pippy piped up from the rear of the crowd.

Parker pressed his lips together.

He'd already found her. But right now she was currently one unhappy woman and wasn't talking to him.

As the wedding rehearsal had progressed, Parker had a difficult time paying attention. All he could think about was getting through the technicalities so he could find a way to make things right with Gabriella.

Yeah, he'd had trust issues. And yeah, she might have stepped all over them by keeping secrets. But after meeting her father, he didn't blame her. What a dick. The man definitely had a God complex, and in Parker's mind, Gabriella would be better off without him. But he was her father, and Parker didn't have a say in how she felt or what she did. All he wanted to do was protect her in the future from anyone who could hurt her.

They had a hell of a lot in common, and distrust was a wall they needed to tear down. But he'd go to that battle with every weapon he had. Because he loved her.

"Are you going to open the door or not?" Jordan asked with a poke in Parker's back. "It's cold as hell out here."

As if to verify the truth, fat, fluffy snowflakes floated down and glistened in the outdoor lights.

"Brake your skates, bro." With a pull of the handle Parker opened the door and stepped aside. Then he turned to Lucy, sweeping his hand toward the opening. "Brides first."

From where he stood holding the door open, Parker heard the *oohs* and *aahs* of approval as everyone poured into the restaurant.

He wanted to rejoice. To let the sense of accomplishment flow over him. To lift a glass of champagne and enjoy every single second of the rest of the night. But he couldn't. Because Gabriella wasn't there to celebrate with him. There was no way in hell he could have done everything without her. There was no reason for him to celebrate without her either.

Once everyone in the party had entered the building, Parker followed them in and stopped just inside the door. In the center of the room stood an enormous white Christmas tree all lit up with tiny white lights and silver ornaments. There were large chalkboard signs in cast-iron easels placed about the space with sweet, clever sayings on them. The tables that had been set up for the rehearsal dinner were decorated with winter white roses, mirrored ornaments, and silver chargers beneath the new white plates. Large mirrored balls and glittery white snowflakes were suspended from the exposed beams and reflected the warm candlelight spread about the room.

It was stunning.

And a total surprise.

"Oh." Lucy kissed his cheek. "It's just beautiful."

Parker couldn't take credit; he'd had nothing to do with the spectacular staging. Only one person could have had a hand in this.

He tossed his gaze to the stainless door that led

to the kitchen and a delicious shiver of anticipation slipped up his back.

With any luck, he'd find that certain someone behind door number one.

With the knife in her hand, Gabi absently chopped more chives for the spuds' food station. The moment she'd heard the chatter and energy drift through the building, her heart raced up into her throat.

He was here.

The knowledge left her breathless, but the sting of the hurt she'd felt when he'd sent her away without giving her a chance to explain reared its ugly head.

As if her thoughts had conjured him, Parker pushed through the stainless steel door. Beneath his charcoal gray suit he wore a baby blue shirt that set off the color of his eyes. His hair had been cut and was combed back off his freshly shaven face. He looked more handsome than ever. Just the sight of him sent a jitter of nerves through her blood and brought tears to her eyes.

She didn't want to be nervous. She didn't want to argue. She didn't want him to send her away again. She'd made a promise to help and that's what she planned to do—whether he liked it or not. Judging by the muscle twitching in his jaw, he didn't like it at all.

So much for offering an olive branch.

To keep her emotions under control, she dropped her gaze back to the chopping motion of the blade.

"What are you doing here?" he asked as he strode up to her prep table.

"I may not have a formal culinary education, but it's plain to see I'm cutting chives."

"I wasn't referring to your lack of formal education and you know it."

"You're wrong. I don't know." She looked up. "So why don't you spell it out for me."

The hired kitchen staff stopped their work so they could watch the action. Apparently, keeping her personal matters private had become as impossible as walking to the moon. But if the moment and what remained of their relationship was about to explode, she'd rather rip off the bandage and get the pain over quickly than peel it away slowly and prolong the agony. She was still licking her wounds from yesterday, so if he wanted her gone—if they were truly over—she needed to know right now.

His gaze traveled around the room where everyone was all eyes and ears. "Can we talk in my office?"

"What's the matter? It was okay to air our dirty laundry yesterday when I was so embarrassed I could barely breathe, but today you want to run and hide so you don't have to deal with the same humiliation?"

The muscle in his jaw twitched again, and though Gabi knew she should back down, she couldn't. She was angry—at herself for wasting her life focusing her energy on the negative. Angry at Parker for pushing her away when she'd needed him. Angry he hadn't given her a chance. Angry he hadn't given *them* a chance. Right now she had too much emotion bottled up inside to be agreeable. So in the land of irrationality where she currently resided, she was suddenly in the mood for a good old-fashioned take-it-to-the-mat argument to get it out of her system.

"This is between you and me, Gabriella," Parker calmly said. "And *only* you and me."

"Sure. You're ready to talk now. Why couldn't you have just given me five minutes of your time yesterday to explain that the situation had nothing to do with you? It would have saved us both a lot of time."

"Truth?" He shrugged his broad shoulders. "Because I couldn't handle it yesterday."

Tears burned her eyes but she refused to let them fall. "Then maybe you're right. We should go into your office."

"Thank you."

"Believe me . . ." Gabi laid down her knife on the cutting board and headed toward the office near the back. "I'm not doing it for you."

"I wouldn't expect that you were."

She stopped and turned so fast he almost ran into her. "What's *that* supposed to mean?"

"I don't know, Gabriella." His hands came up. "My fucking head is spinning and I don't know which direction I'm supposed to go. Out there where my family's waiting for me? Or in here arguing with you when that's not what I want to be doing at all."

"That's not what I want either."

"Then let's go into my office where we can figure it out," he said. "Because this is important. And whether you want to believe me or not, *you're* important."

As he walked away, her heart ached. She'd never been in a situation like this before, and she hadn't intended for it to happen this way. She'd never wanted it to come to this. She hadn't meant to be deceitful about her father or her culinary training. She'd never expected to fall in love. And she'd certainly never dreamed of hurting the man who meant more to her than taking her next breath. All she'd ever wanted was a chance to prove herself.

Now what?

Would going into that office be the end of what really mattered? Or could they possibly find their way back into each other's arms?

Time to find out.

No matter how damn scary it might be.

*P*arker left the door open as he walked inside his office when he really wanted to slam the damn thing shut. Frustration balled up in the center of his chest.

How the hell had things gotten so fucked up?

She was pissed he hadn't given her the courtesy of hearing her out. He was pissed because she hadn't been honest at a time in his life where honesty meant everything.

He didn't expect her to follow him into the office. Any second he expected to hear the back door slam. And that would be that. She'd run like she had before, and he'd be devastated.

"I'm sorry."

Relief flowed through his body as he looked up and found her standing in the doorway. "For what?"

"For flying off the handle just now. I didn't mean to," she explained. "But at the same time, it felt really good. I'm not used to doing that. I've always kept my mouth shut. Even when someone was crushing me like a bug."

"I'm sorry that's what your life has been like." The sorrow darkening her already deep brown eyes jabbed a blade in his heart. "I mean that. And I'm sorry if I provoked you to lose your temper."

"Thank you."

"So where do we go from here?" he asked. "I don't want to argue. I don't want you to storm out the door and never see you again."

"Yesterday you asked me to leave."

"I didn't mean forever, Gabriella." He sighed. Ran a hand through his hair. "I was just taken aback. It bothered me to know you didn't feel comfortable enough with me to share something personal. It just . . . it hit me hard."

"It's not that I don't feel comfortable with you. And it's not that I wanted to keep anything from you. But now that you've met my father, maybe you can understand why I've kept him a secret."

"Yeah. He's . . ."

"An asshole?"

"Yeah." Bewildered, he leaned back on the edge of his desk and folded his arms even though what he really wanted to do was wrap them around her. He couldn't imagine growing up with a father like hers, and he was sad that she'd had to.

"So you weren't taken aback because my father is a famous chef?" she asked.

"Hell no. I was completely thrown because of the way he talked to you. I wanted to punch him in the face."

A small smile tipped the corners of her mouth. "I'd like to have seen that."

"I'd like to have felt that." He shook his head. "Look. I don't know everything that's happened in your life, but I have a sense that it's been really ugly for you for a long time."

"Because I let it be." She came further into the room and closed the door behind her. "My father was everything to my mother. She quit her own career because he wanted her to stay home and take care of the family. She took care of his every need, even when he never returned the favor. She went so far as to meet him at the door when he came home and remove his shoes. She gave up her close friends because he didn't approve of the amount of time they took her away from what *he* wanted her to do. Her entire world revolved around him. She loved him and she chose to be blind to the way he treated her."

Parker could see the story unfold, and somewhere in the mix were two hurt and confused children. One the father abandoned and belittled. The other the father coddled and praised. Parker's heart sank a little deeper.

"Two months before my father's affair was broadcast across the world, my mother discovered she had breast cancer."

Parker breathed in the news, fearing what she'd tell him next.

"The diagnosis wasn't good and she didn't have many options. She feared the treatment would make her too sick to take care of our father. She didn't worry about me. She didn't worry about my brother. Yes, I was in high school at the time and could basically take care of myself, and my brother was in college. But in all her conversations about the path she would take, she only considered my father."

When she paused, her shoulders lifted on a sigh.

"She also worried that if she had a mastectomy, she'd be disfigured and he wouldn't love her."

Parker couldn't imagine a man who wouldn't love his wife because she'd had a surgery to save her life. It didn't make sense. But lately, a lot of things didn't.

"And he didn't," Gabriella said. "He had an affair while she was going through chemo, and he divorced her. His leaving her at all, let alone after she'd had the mastectomy, completely leveled her. I never really had a very good relationship with her because she was more into being my father's wife than a mother, but what little we did have disintegrated after the divorce. And even though I worry constantly that her health will once again spiral downward, we really don't talk anymore. I've tried but . . ." She glanced away.

"I know it sounds ridiculous, but I'm so sorry," he said, trying to make sense of the whole thing. "I really am."

"It's not ridiculous. And I thank you for saying it."

"So what happened then?"

"I needed to make something of myself all on my own," she said passionately. "I never wanted my father's brand of success. I never wanted to own a chain of restaurants with my name plastered all over them. I just wanted to show him that I could cook. And that people would come to wherever I worked just so they could eat the meals that *I* prepared. That's why I came to you. I'd hoped your new restaurant could be a way to get my foot in the door so I could prove myself."

"You've proven yourself. You're an amazing chef."

She shook her head. "I can cook, but my father's right. I don't have the formal training to succeed."

"That's bullshit," he said. "You have the talent and creativity that will take you farther than any conventional method."

"It doesn't matter now." She shrugged. "Not that I don't love to cook, I just realized that I let all the need to get back at my father get twisted up in the wrong way. But in the past weeks with you, I've felt more alive than ever before. Everything became about *us*. Not about *me*. I wanted to be there with you. For you. I loved seeing and being a part of the process of your dream becoming a reality. And I honestly stopped thinking about my father. You made that happen by believing in me. Even though it's not easy, you've inspired me to be more open. And for the first time I realize there's more to life than trying to force someone to believe in you."

"I believe in you, Gabriella. You're an incredible woman who can also cook like a rock star. Your culinary skills are what you do, but they're not what make you special. That comes from your heart."

She looked away like she didn't believe him.

"That's the truth," he insisted.

Those beautiful dark eyes came back around to meet his. "The first day I came into your restaurant, I didn't expect to fall in love with you," she confessed. "But I did."

Her simple yet meaningful words warmed him from the inside. Even though there was still so much to say, for the first time in the past twenty-four hours he felt like they might be back on track.

It took everything not to just wrap her up in his arms. But if they were to ever have a chance at making it together, the air needed to be completely cleared. They needed to trust each other, and she needed to know she could count on him in any situation, at any time.

"Is it okay if we come back to that?" he asked.

"We don't have to." She glanced away. "I know you're busy and—"

"Just give me a minute. As long as it's confession time, I have something too."

"Okay."

"I'm sorry about yesterday," he said. "If I could take back the way I handled it, I would. I don't know anything about being in a relationship. I'm new at this. Right now I wish I could wave a magic wand and make everything better. But I know life doesn't work that way."

"Maybe we just met at the wrong time," she suggested. "Maybe the universe is telling us we don't fit."

"Is that the way you really feel?" He hoped not. Because if he had to watch her walk away it would kill him.

"We both have a lot of baggage," she said quietly. "Maybe it's too much. Maybe I want more than I should. Maybe I expect more. Maybe I'm not any more ready for this than you are. I love you but . . . I don't know."

When she shrugged, Parker feared everything was slipping away.

Unable to wait a moment longer, he crossed the room and wrapped her in his arms. After a moment of resistance, she settled her cheek against his chest and her hands on his back.

It felt so damn good to hold her again.

"I can stand here all night trying to convince you that everything will always be perfect—that *I'll* always be perfect," he said. "But it would be a lie. Life isn't perfect and I'm as far from perfect as you can get. We might have a lot of things to work on, but as long as we're honest and we trust each other, I think we deserve a chance."

She didn't say anything and that made him worry even more.

"But that's what *I* think," he said. "What about you, Gabriella? What's right for you?"

He wanted to shout that *he* was right for her. There wasn't a doubt in his mind. But right now they had to tear down this damn wall between them before they could go any further. She had to believe in him, and right now, he was pretty damn sure she didn't.

Judging from the way things went down yesterday, who could blame her?

The clang of a cooking pot startled them apart.

Without an answer, she backed up and glanced away. "I . . . have to go."

Before he could stop her, she reached for the door. "Gabriella?"

Without a word or a backward glance, she walked out. In her wake the ache in his chest nearly exploded.

What the hell just happened?

Dragging a hand through his hair, he replayed the conversation in his mind.

Fuck.

How could he be so stupid?

He hadn't thanked her for making the restaurant so beautiful for Jordan and Lucy's party.

But as bad as that was, he knew it wasn't the reason she'd left.

She'd been waiting for him to tell her how he felt about her. She'd been looking for reassurance that her feelings weren't one-sided. She'd been looking for some kind of life preserver in the flood of emotional upheaval she'd been drowning in.

After all she'd been through, she'd been brave enough, amazing enough, to tell him she'd fallen in love with him.

Twice.

And he hadn't said a goddamn word.

He needed someone to bash him over the head. Because when a woman gave you her heart, you did *not* just tell her "let's come back to that" without fucking coming back to that.

$B$y the time Parker opened his office door to find Gabriella and right that wrong, the staff was scurrying about making things happen, and Gabriella was gone. He started to go after her, and it took him a moment to recover before he realized he had obligations. He couldn't disappear to find her, even though he wanted to. His entire family was waiting for him. He felt absolutely torn as he pulled himself together, tossed a few instructions to the crew, and headed toward the stainless door to go back out and rejoin the party.

Even if it was the last thing he felt like doing.

When he gave the door a push, it met with resistance. He pushed harder and it flew open. On the other side, people scrambled to get back to their seats and act like they hadn't just had their ears pressed to the door listening to what was going on on the other side. If Parker didn't feel like dying right now he'd laugh. Instead he disregarded the curious stares his family shot in his direction as he walked over to the bride-to-be.

"I have a favor to ask you," he whispered close to her ear.

Lucy looked up and smiled as though she already knew what he was about to say.

"After you've given us such a beautiful dinner in such a beautiful venue, how can I refuse? What do you need, Parker?"

"I need you to make sure Gabriella is at your wedding tomorrow."

He'd give the woman he loved tonight, but there was no way in hell he'd let her walk out of his life forever.

# Chapter 19

When Gabriella entered the little white country church the next day, she felt like a fifth wheel. She hadn't known Jordan and Lucy long enough to have been on their wedding invitation list, but when Lucy called late last night gushing about the amazing touches Gabi had put on the rehearsal dinner and begging her to come to the wedding, Gabi had been unable to refuse.

She'd spent the rest of the night thinking about what Parker had said, but mostly what he hadn't said.

She'd been a fool for telling him she'd fallen in love with him when he clearly didn't feel the same way. Even after his pep talk about trusting each other and that they deserved a chance, he'd given her no response to her declaration. And he'd let her walk away.

The hours between midnight and morning had

been sleepless, and it had taken half a bottle of eye drops to get the red out. But this was a special day for the Kincade family. For Gabi's new friends. It was no place for personal issues. This was a day for celebration. For love and hope. For the marriage of two incredibly nice people.

Even if her own heart was breaking.

She waited in her car until the last possible minute to slip into the church. The sign at the back of the church welcomed the guests and asked them to choose a seat, not a side. Gabi found a place at the end of a pew near the back where two elderly couples seemed more interested in what flavor of cake would be served than the actual wedding. She could have let them know the cake would be a delicious triple layer red velvet, but her goal was to remain as inconspicuous as possible.

Soft violin music played while guests awaited the arrival of the wedding party and Gabi took the moment to enjoy the atmosphere. The little church displayed a variety of pine boughs, poinsettias, white roses, lace, and sparkles. As beautiful and elegant as everything looked, it was understated in a way the bride preferred.

When the pianist on the side of the altar began to play "A Dream Is a Wish Your Heart Makes" from *Cinderella*, Gabi smiled. Jordan had managed to find a way to honor his very own princess without going overboard.

From a side door on the right, Jordan came into

the church followed by his brothers. Though Gabi tried not to look at Parker, she couldn't stop herself. In his black tux and bow tie, he stole her breath. Gabi commanded her heart to slow down, but just looking at him made it take up a mind all its own. When his gaze started to wander across the guest-filled pews, she looked away. She couldn't make eye contact and expect to remain composed.

She just couldn't.

Knowing she was a complete crybaby at weddings, she removed a tissue from her purse and clutched it in her hand. A moment later the bridesmaids began their walk up the aisle. Nicole came first in a long dove gray simply cut dress. Since Lucy wasn't the fancy over-the-top kind, Gabi was interested to see what kind of gown she'd chosen. In anticipation, Gabi kept her eyes glued to the center aisle, just in case they tried to wander back to the altar and the devastatingly handsome groomsman second from the end.

When the first strains of the bridal chorus began everyone stood, and Gabi was thankful that the subdued blue dress she'd chosen to wear blended in with the crowd.

In the doorway, Lucy appeared on the arm of Ryan, the oldest Kincade brother, and everyone else might as well have been invisible. The moment Jordan saw his bride with the winter sun glowing at her back, he grinned. And then he teared up. As he looked at Lucy he seemed gentle as a kitten and so in love that Gabi could practically hear his heart pounding.

In a surprisingly sexy fitted gown of Chantilly lace with a slit up the front and a bare back, Lucy was stunning. Her brown hair had been pulled back in a low messy bun with a few white roses tucked here and there. Her bouquet was a magnificent surprise. The white flowers were actually feathers made to appear like ruffled peonies. But no matter how breathtaking the bride looked, nothing could come close to the beauty of the smile she wore for her groom as she slowly made her way up the aisle.

Gabi's heart skipped.

Oh, to have a love like theirs.

She chanced a peek at Parker and he was looking right back. Somehow he'd found her in the crowd. She tried to smile, but the quiver of her lips probably made her look like some kind of lopsided jack-o'-lantern.

When the minister asked everyone to be seated, Jordan took Lucy's hand and kissed the backs of her fingers. The vows they'd personally written were sweet, tender, and often funny. Before long they were pronounced husband and wife and Jordan was told he could kiss his bride. The kiss started out sweet, but Jordan quickly leaned Lucy back over his arm and gave her a taste of what the honeymoon would be all about. The guests chuckled at his exuberance. They were still chuckling when "The Wedding March" began and the bride and groom headed back up the aisle.

At the moment the rest of the bridal party started

up the aisle, Gabi realized she was trapped. Any second Parker would walk by. Would he be waiting for her outside the church? Or would he ignore she was even there? Panic set in, but it was too late for a quick getaway. She'd have to wait for the bridal party to pass before she found another way out.

Parker, with Lili on his arm, came up the aisle with his eyes locked on Gabi. She crumpled the damp tissue in her hand and scanned the room again for an escape route.

"Don't even think about it." Parker reached out, grabbed her by the hand, pulled her to his side, and held her tight so she had no choice but to walk out of the church with him and Lili.

Once they reached the steps outside, and Gabi saw that the crowd had begun to gather around the new Mr. and Mrs. Jordan Kincade, she thought she'd found her diversion. She attempted to slip her hand from Parker's grip but he held on tight and looked her right in the eye.

"Not a chance, Houdini."

Before she could argue he was pulling her away from the front of the church. Her heels wobbled in the snow-covered grass but he didn't stop until they were at the rear of the building. Alone.

He pressed her back against the white clapboard wall and leaned in close. Her heart pounded so hard beneath the long-sleeved dress she was sure he could feel it against his tuxedo-covered chest.

"Parker—"

"I love you, Gabriella."

"What?"

"I love you," he repeated. "I'm crazy about you. I can't live without you. And I want a new start. An honest start."

"But . . ." He'd totally caught her off guard. She'd expected nothing from him today.

"I want to show you that I'm a man you can trust. A man who will be there for you, loving you whether you're young and beautiful, ill, or old and taking your last breath. I want to be the man you know you can come to for anything at any time. I will never, ever stop loving you for any reason. And by the way, I think we met at the perfect time."

"Parker, I . . ."

"Don't say no, Gabriella. Give us a chance. Please." He framed her face with his hands and kissed her so sweetly it nearly shattered her heart.

When he raised his head, his thumb gently swept her bottom lip. "You can trust me, baby. I promise you that everything I said is true."

"I was going to say . . . I love you, Parker Kincade." She curled her arms around his neck and he lowered his forehead to hers. A sigh lifted his chest. And for the first time in her life, Gabi felt truly loved by a man she knew she could trust. She felt safe. And she felt hopeful. "And I will never tell you no."

He kissed her again and she could taste the promise on his lips.

"Will you come to the reception with me?"

"Yes."

"Will you dance with me?"

She chuckled. "Yes."

"And will you wake up in my bed on Christmas morning?"

"Oh yes I will."

*A* gentle snow fell over the Columbia River on Christmas morning and the dock in front of Parker's houseboat was covered in white. In the corner of the living room the tree glowed with brightly colored lights and the fireplace roared. From the oven, the warm aroma of pumpkin spice muffins wafted through the air. In his bowl, Basil blew bubbles from behind his plastic foliage. And on the floor in front of the fire, Parker held out the silver foil and pink ribbon wrapped present he'd gotten for Gabriella.

"For me?" She blushed as she took the box, held it to her ear, and shook it. "Is it an elephant?"

"Smaller."

"Is it a puppy?"

"Smaller."

"Is it a—"

Parker laughed and kissed her hard. "Just open the present and find out."

"Okay. But first . . ." She reached beneath the tree and pulled out a blue foil wrapped package with a red ribbon. "The color matches your eyes."

"This is for me?"

She nodded. "Basil didn't like it so I figured I'd just give it to you."

"Thank you, Basil." Parker hadn't felt this happy

on Christmas morning since he was a kid. Everything was perfect. Jordan and Lucy's wedding reception had gone off without a hitch. Parker had managed to talk Gabriella into helping him do some Christmas shopping for his family. And ever since the wedding, she'd spent the night in his bed, wrapped around him like she'd never let go.

They'd spent hours talking. He learned she'd visited her father and finally had her say. She seemed resigned that he'd never come around and be the father she'd always dreamed he would be, but Parker was going to hold out hope. He believed that as long as a person had breath in their body, they could still make changes in their life.

God knows he had.

"How about we both open our presents at the same time?"

Her childlike exuberance tickled his heart. Parker kissed her again. "How can I ever say no to you?"

"You can't." She pulled her present closer. Her hands hovered over the ribbon. "Ready?"

"Set. Go."

They each ripped off the ribbon and tore into the paper. The box lids flew and the tissue was pushed aside. They both held up a cooking apron. His was green and said "Hot Stuff Coming Through." Hers was white with ruffles and a blue checkered border like *Alice in Wonderland* and said "Eat Me."

"Great minds think alike?" he asked, hoping she found the gift funny.

"You know what I'm thinking, right?"

He shook his head.

"I'm thinking whenever I cook in your kitchen, I'll be wearing this. And *only* this."

"I do love the way your mind works." Relieved that she liked the gift, he leaned in and kissed her.

"This is our first Christmas together." She sighed. "And I'm having so much fun."

"So you're not disappointed with the apron?"

"No." She hugged it to her chest. "I love it."

"There's something in the pocket."

"It has a pocket?" She held up the material. "I love pockets."

Parker watched her reach inside and pull out the small white box.

Her eyes widened. "What is it?"

"Open it and find out."

Her hands trembled as she lifted the lid and pulled out the silver bracelet. The charms jingled as it came out of the box.

"Oh, Parker."

"I love it when you say my name all sexy like that." She leaned in and kissed him. "It's beautiful."

She laid the bracelet out in her palm.

"Each one of those charms makes me think of you."

"You designed this?"

"Of course."

"But I didn't think you liked to shop."

"I don't. But everything is different with you." He took the bracelet and held it up, pointing out the charms. "A fish for Basil. A heart for how much you care about the women and children's shelter. And me. A lion for the courage you showed standing up to your father. A frog prince because you changed me from a toad."

She chuckled.

"A castle where you can build your dreams. An angel because you rescued me from becoming a grumpy old man. A chili pepper because you're hot stuff. A spoon because you're always stirring up something good."

He received another laugh for that.

"And a star because wherever you are in the universe is where I want to be. I want this life to be ours. I think of the restaurant as ours. When I look into the future I want us to be together, blissfully married, with children, and a dog. And I promise that every day I will do everything I can to make you happy. How does that sound to you?"

When he looked up her bottom lip was caught between her teeth and she had tears in her eyes.

"Are you okay?"

She nodded. "That sounds wonderful. I love you, Parker."

"I love you more." He wrapped her in his arms and pressed his lips to hers. "And you can completely trust me on that. Merry Christmas."

# Nonni's Ricotta Cheese Cookies with Lemon Icing

## Cookies

**INGREDIENTS:**

2 cups sugar
1 cup butter, softened
1 container (15 ounces) ricotta cheese
2 teaspoons almond extract
2 large eggs
4 cups all-purpose flour
2 teaspoons baking powder
1 teaspoon salt

**DIRECTIONS:**

1. Preheat oven to 350 degrees.
2. With mixer on low speed, in large bowl, beat sugar and butter until well blended.
3. Increase mixer speed to high, then beat mix until light and fluffy.
4. With mixer on medium speed, beat in ricotta, almond extract, and eggs until well blended.
5. Reduce mixer speed to low. Add flour, baking powder, and salt, then beat until dough forms.

6. Drop dough by level tablespoons, about 2 inches apart, onto large ungreased cookie sheet. Bake about 15 minutes or until cookies are very lightly golden (cookies will be soft). With spatula, remove cookies to wire rack to cool.
7. When cookies are cool, prepare lemon icing.

# Lemon Icing

**INGREDIENTS:**
1 teaspoon fresh grated lemon rind
3 tablespoons butter
3 cups sifted powdered sugar
2 tablespoons lemon juice
1 tablespoon water
Dash salt

**DIRECTIONS:**
1. Add lemon rind to butter; cream together well.
2. Add part of sugar gradually, blending after each addition.
3. Combine lemon juice and water; add to creamed mixture, alternating with remaining sugar, until right consistency to spread.
4. Beat after each addition until smooth.
5. Add salt.
6. With small metal spatula or knife, spread icing on cookies. Set cookies aside to allow icing to dry completely, about 1 hour.

# Sweet Onion Carbonara

**INGREDIENTS:**

2 teaspoons olive oil

4 ounces thinly sliced pancetta, chopped

1 large sweet yellow onion (Maui, Vidalia, Walla Walla, etc.), halved and thinly sliced

2 cloves garlic, minced

$3/4$ teaspoon kosher salt, divided

$2/3$ cup whipping cream

$1/2$ cup freshly grated parmesan cheese

$3/4$ cup shredded gruyère

$1/2$ teaspoon grated lemon zest

4 large eggs

1 pound rigatoni

Coarsely ground black pepper

2 tablespoons chopped chives

**INSTRUCTIONS:**

1. Heat olive oil in large frying pan over medium heat.
2. Add pancetta and sauté until brown and crisp.
3. Remove pancetta from pan and let cool.
4. Add sweet onions to pan and cook for about 10 minutes or until golden brown and lightly

caramelized. Add garlic and $\frac{1}{2}$ teaspoon salt.
Cook 2 minutes more. Set aside to cool slightly.

5. In large bowl, whisk whipping cream, remaining
   salt, parmesan, gruyère, lemon zest, and eggs.
   Blend well.

6. Bring large pot of salted water to a boil over
   high heat. Add pasta and cook until tender but
   still firm to the bite, stirring occasionally, about
   8 to 10 minutes. Drain, reserving 1 cup of pasta
   water.

7. Add pasta into the pan along with the onions,
   cream mixture, $\frac{1}{4}$ cup pasta water, and pancetta.

8. Toss over low heat until sauce evenly coats
   pasta. Add pasta water as needed. Heat all about
   2 minutes (do not boil).

9. Season pasta to taste with pepper.

10. Transfer pasta to a large serving bowl. Sprinkle
    with chives and serve.

# "Sure Thing" Mascarpone Sorbetto with Rosemary Honey

**INGREDIENTS:**

## For Mascarpone Sorbetto:

¾ cup sugar
1¼ cups water
1 teaspoon grated lemon zest
2 tablespoons lemon juice
⅛ teaspoon kosher salt
1½ cups mascarpone cheese, room temperature

## For Rosemary Honey:

¾ cup orange-blossom honey
3 sprigs rosemary
2 tablespoons water

**INSTRUCTIONS:**

1. Combine sugar and 1¼ cups water in small
   saucepan. Place over medium-low heat. Bring to

a simmer, stirring occasionally to dissolve sugar. Simmer for 1 minute.

2. Remove from heat and add lemon zest, lemon juice, and salt to make lemon syrup. Set aside to cool.

3. In medium bowl, whisk mascarpone to soften.

4. Add lemon syrup; whisk till smooth. Allow to completely cool, about 30 minutes.

5. Prepare ice cream maker.

6. Whisk mascarpone mix one more time to incorporate, then use ice cream maker according to manufacturer's instructions.

7. Transfer sorbetto to freezer to completely freeze.

8. While sorbetto freezes, place honey, rosemary, and 2 tablespoons water in small skillet. Bring to a simmer over low heat and simmer gently for about 5 minutes. Strain through a fine-mesh strainer and cool to room temperature.

9. To serve, scoop frozen sorbetto into dessert glasses, drizzle with rosemary honey.

# Gabriella's Ultimate Mac and Cheese

**INGREDIENTS:**

6 slices of semi-crisp bacon, chopped (use more if you'd like)

Salt to season pasta water

1/2 pound dried cavatappi or corkscrew macaroni pasta

3 tablespoons butter

3 tablespoons all-purpose flour

3 cups half & half

1 teaspoon fresh rosemary, chopped

1 teaspoon fresh thyme

Kosher salt and freshly ground black pepper to taste

1/8 teaspoon cayenne pepper

1/8 teaspoon nutmeg

4 cloves fresh garlic, minced

1/2 cup fresh parmesan, finely grated

2 cups sharp cheddar, shredded

2 tablespoons fresh basil, chopped

1 1/2 to 2 tablespoons green onion, chopped

1 cup whole milk mozzarella, shredded

2 to 3 tablespoons seasoned panko breadcrumbs

**INSTRUCTIONS:**

1. Preheat oven to 400 degrees.
2. Line large baking sheet with foil. Lay each slice of bacon down with at least an inch of space between each slice. Place baking sheet full of bacon on the lowest rack of your oven and let cook for 8 to 10 minutes or until crisp but still pliable. Don't crisp too much. Drain on paper towels. Chop into bite sized pieces. Set aside.
3. In large pot, boil water for pasta. Once it starts to boil, season with about a tablespoon of salt and stir to dissolve. Add pasta and boil for 5 minutes. Reserve one cup of the pasta water. Drain pasta and rinse with cold water to stop the cooking process.
4. Don't toss the pasta around, just let it sit while you rinse it. This helps keep some of the starch in place. Drain the cold water and set cooled pasta aside while you make cheese sauce.
5. Rinse the pot you boiled the pasta in with cold water to cool it off completely, then place back on top of your stove over medium heat.
6. Add butter to melt. Once it starts to foam/sizzle, it's ready for the flour.
7. Add flour and whisk vigorously until smooth and free of lumps. Let this cook for about 1 minute.
8. Add 1 cup of half & half. Continue to whisk vigorously till smooth, about 20 to 30 seconds.
9. Add remaining 2 cups of half & half and continue whisking.

10. Add rosemary, thyme, kosher salt, freshly ground black pepper, cayenne pepper, nutmeg, and minced garlic. Mix well, then taste. Adjust seasoning to your preference.

11. Increase heat to medium-high. Allow mixture to come up to a simmer—whisking the entire time. The mixture will thicken quickly. Once the mixture is thick enough to coat the back of a spoon, completely remove it from heat.

12. Add parmesan and cheddar cheese. Stir gently until melted and smooth.

13. In same pot combine the cooked and cooled pasta with cheese sauce. Gently fold together until it's completely coated. Mixture should be slightly loose but very creamy and easy to work with. If it's too thick, thin out with a little of the starchy pasta water.

14. Fold in basil and green onion.

15. Transfer half of pasta and cheese mixture to a lightly greased baking dish.

16. Sprinkle $1/2$ cup of mozzarella cheese over the first half of the pasta/cheese mixture, then pour the remaining pasta/cheese mixture on top as a second layer—add remaining mozzarella cheese on top.

17. Gently swirl a spoon or butter knife through the mac and cheese mixture to ensure the mozzarella cheese is evenly combined throughout the dish. Sprinkle top with bacon and breadcrumbs.

18. Bake in 400 degree oven on middle oven rack for 25–35 minutes or until golden brown on top and bubbly all over.

19. Allow to sit and cool for about 10 minutes before serving.

*Explore the rest of Candis Terry's Sunshine Creek Vineyard novels!*

# a better man

*Available Now!*

Hockey star Jordan Kincade wasted no time ditching Sunshine Valley and everyone who mattered for a career in the NHL—a truth Jordan confronts when his parents' deaths bring him home. Now he's back to make amends, which begins with keeping his younger sister from flunking out of school. It's just his luck that the one person who can help is the girl whose heart he broke years ago.

Lucy Diamond has racked up a number of monumental mistakes in her life, the first involving a certain blue-eyed charmer. She has no intention of falling for Jordan Kincade again, but when he shows up asking her to help one of her students, Lucy just can't say no. Worse, the longer he's back the more she sees how much he's changed. And so when a blistering kiss turns to more, she can't help but wonder if her heart will be crushed again . . . or if she'll discover true love with a better man.

# perfect for you

*Available Now!*

Declan Kincade has spent so much time chasing success he's almost forgotten how to just live. Lately though, his all-business routine has been thrown into disarray. Brooke Hastings is the best employee Dec's ever had: polished, capable, and intelligent. After four years, he's just realized that she's also smoking hot. But their working relationship is too valuable to stake on a fling, no matter how mind-bendingly pleasurable it promises to be . . .

What's worse than never meeting the right man? Finding him, and then working side by side every day while he remains absolutely blind to your existence. That is, until one temptation-packed road trip changes everything. Teaching her gorgeous, driven boss how to cut loose and have fun is the toughest challenge Brooke's ever faced. But it's one that could give both of them exactly what they need, if Dec will take a chance on a perfect—and perfectly unexpected—love . . .